WITCH OF TALERA

BEING

THE THIRD BOOK OF THE TALERA CYCLE

by

Charles Allen Gramlich

The Borgo Press
An Imprint of Wildside Press

MMVII

CONTENTS

To Ahrethane

Who is as real as they come

WHAT HAS GONE BEFORE

Talera is a world of warriors and heroes, not all of whom are human. It is a world where sailing ships ply the skies as well as the waters, and where beasts are as likely to hunt men as be hunted by them. On Talera, beauty and steel are equally dangerous weapons, and sorcery is the deadliest talent of all.

In 1914, a twenty-six year old American named Ruenn Maclang found his way to Talera. He and his younger brother, Bryce, along with their cousin, Eric Ryall, were on a sea voyage to Japan when a storm forced their ship to anchor at an uncharted island. Eric and some of the crewmen were kidnapped by interplanetary slavers, and in pursuing them Ruenn and Bryce stumbled upon the world gate that the slavers had used and were themselves drawn through to Talera.

The tale of Ruenn and Bryce's disappearance from Earth was told in the book *Swords of Talera*. The two brothers were separated as they passed through the world gate, and *Swords of Talera* told of Ruenn's search for his brother on a planet as lethal as it was lovely. In that search, Ruenn failed. But he did find a place for himself, and he found a woman to love. His place was as a warrior and a leader of warriors; his love was Rannon Jystral, a princess of the empire of Nyshphal. Still, he hoped one day to see his brother again.

It was in *Wings Over Talera* that Ruenn finally located his brother, only to discover that Bryce wanted him dead. *Wings* began with Ruenn's adopted homeland of Nyshphal under attack by mysterious raiders. Suspicion even fell on Ruenn after it was discovered that Bryce was involved with the raids. Ruenn was forced to flee both Nyshphal *and* Rannon, who he believed had betrayed him.

Ruenn cracked the secret of the raids, discovering that a powerful sorceress named Vohanna was behind the plan to bring down Nyshphal as a first step toward world conquest. It was Vohanna, worshipped as a goddess by her followers, who had corrupted Bryce. And though Ruenn defeated Vohanna and rescued his brother, it was clear at the end of the book that Bryce was a different man than he once had been. So, too, was Ruenn, even though he had found his way back to the arms of Rannon Jystral.

And now—*Witch of Talera.*

CAST OF CHARACTERS

Major Continuing Characters

Ruenn Maclang: an earthman. An American born in 1888. Tall. Lean. A swordsman.

Bryce Maclang: Ruenn's younger brother.

Rannon Jystral: Princess of the island empire of Nyshphal. Ruenn's lady.

Eric Ryall: Ruenn and Bryce's cousin. Also from Earth.

Vohanna: a member of the Asadhie, the race that created Talera. She has been locked in a world-wide struggle with other Asadhie to control the planet. She is evil. But at the end of *Wings Over Talera* Ruenn killed her. Perhaps.

Supporting Continuing Characters

Ahrethane: a beautiful forest Druid who helped Ruenn against Vohanna.

Diken Graye: a human mercenary.

Hurnan Jystral: father of Rannon.

Kuurus Jystral: younger brother of Rannon. He does not like Ruenn.

Kreeg: once a fighting slave, now Ruenn's self-appointed bodyguard.

Rhandh: Rannon's personal bodyguard. Of a race called the Vlih. The Vlih look much like humans but have prehensile tails and tentacles growing beneath each arm.

Heril Rolvfshern: a Koro warrior. One of Ruenn's first and closest friends on Talera. The Koro are human, though dwarfish in stature. Heril is an exception.

Valyan Tiersal: a Llurn. A human being with emerald skin and yellow eyes. Also a close friend of Ruenn's.

New Characters in *Witch of Talera*

Taskin Bhent: short, stout, blunt-featured. A soldier who commands the Nyshphalian army.

Chalathar: a mysterious warrior who appears on the novel's stage at a critical moment. But he *has* appeared before, hidden in each of the previous books.

Rajan Critus: dark-complected with dark black eyes and a rather sinister face. He has been called "deadly handsome." Commander of the Imperial guard, which also serves as the Nyshphalian police force.

Arca Heskern: a woman. tall, gray-haired and gray-eyed. Head of the scientists (alchemists).

Horlis Kazhian: whipcord lean and sharp-featured. Head of the Nyshphalian navy, which includes both ships of the air and the sea, as well as the saddle bird cavalry corps.

INTRODUCTION

By One Who Knows Ruenn Maclang

Twice before, in cold October, I had met with Ruenn Maclang. Twice he left me manuscripts detailing his adventures on the world of Talera. (Perhaps you have read one or both of these manuscripts—*Swords of Talera* and *Wings Over Talera*). I regret that I did not get to see Ruenn the third time he came to visit.

One evening this past fall I was called from my home by an emergency at work, and when I returned just after midnight I found, lying on the porch before my door, the manuscript you now hold in your hands. It is the third installment in Ruenn Maclang's strange story. I hope you enjoy it. And I hope, wherever Ruenn is now, that he is still staying a sword-point ahead of the danger that forever seems to dog him.

—Charles Allen Gramlich

ABOUT THE AUTHOR

CHARLES ALLEN GRAMLICH grew up on a farm in Arkansas, near the foothills of the Ozark Mountains, then moved to the New Orleans area in 1986. He's since sold several novels and numerous short stories. His tales, while mostly in the genres of horror, science fiction, and fantasy, have also included westerns, children's stories, mainstream fiction, slipstream works, and experimental pieces. He has also published poetry and nonfiction, the latter ranging from reference works to articles on writing. He refuses to comment, however, on rumors that most of his work is actually written by Ruenn Maclang.

Charles is a member of REHupa (the Robert E. Howard United Press Association), HWA (the Horror Writers Association), and SFPA (the Science Fiction Poetry Association). He produces a regular column on writing for *The Illuminata*, an online magazine, and is the horror moderator at United Sci Fi Forums. His blog can be found at:

http://charlesgramlich.blogspot.com

CHAPTER ONE

FIRST MOVEMENT

It is a custom on Talera for those about to be married to spend the last hour before the ceremony meditating alone. Thus, I was in my apartment within the great pile of Jystral Castle when the assassin came for me.

I was gazing out over my balcony at the clear red sky of the Taleran autumn, and out over the sprawling city of Timmuzz, the rose-stuccoed capital of the island kingdom of Nyshphal. Throngs of wedding revelers filled the broad streets, decked in festival-bright colors and loud with shouts and song.

But the lushness of my adopted world and the noise of my adopted people did not turn my mind from Rannon Jystral, the daughter of Nyshphal's emperor and my soon-to-be bride. Rannon, of the raven-dark hair and the pale beauty like morning mist on the silent ocean, filled my thoughts. Then those thoughts shattered as the door slammed opened behind me and a grating voice called out:

"Ruenn Maclang!"

I turned. A lean and narrow-hipped Kaldi with dirty white fur stood there. Kaldi are not human, though they resemble us in having two each of arms and legs and eyes and ears, and only one of mouths and noses. This one wore a grease-stained brown sash around his waist that marked him as a cook's aid in the palace, though I doubted he'd been much help around the kitchen with the heavy stabbing sword that he held in his left fist.

Something else was in the Kaldi's right fist, a white towel or shirt wrapped around something small and sleek. But I didn't wait to identify it. The smell of kahurra coppered the air, the stench of that drug used by gladiators to fuel their rage for battle, and by certain assassins when they are about to kill.

I was already dressed for my marriage, in cream colored breeks and a long sleeved shirt of white silk. A scabbarded sword hung at my belt, a bejeweled piece of weapon maker's art made especially for my wedding. But its edge was sharp and I filled my hand with its hilt as I leaped across the room toward the one who knew my name and had come to murder me.

Smoke puffed from beneath the towel in the being's hand and a hornet stung my side as a sharp clap of sound crashed in the room. *Gunfire!* But my sudden attack had startled the assassin's aim and I took no time to wonder at the presence of a gun here on Talera where gunpowder had so recently been unknown.

My booted foot lashed out, kicking the weapon from the Kaldi's grasp before he could fire again. I followed with a quick sword thrust toward the being's chest, but somehow he got his blade shifted from his left hand to his right in time to parry my stroke. Steel rang. We fenced.

Afternoon sunlight pouring in over the balcony spattered red off the bright weave of our swords. And for long moments the only sounds were our panting breaths and the click-clack of sharp edge on sharp edge. The warrior before me stood taller than I, his face darkly suffused with blood where it was bare of fur. I had no idea why he wanted my life. Or of who might have hired him to take it.

"Lart," the Kaldi snarled at me then. And despite the fact that he'd just called me a filthy rodent I did not respond. With words, at least. Instead, I drove in close in attack and while our swords were engaged I slapped him open-palmed across the face with my left hand before stepping back and away.

Enraged, he hacked down savagely at me with the short, heavy gladius that filled his fist. I blocked with my longer weapon, driving his strike to one side, but at the point where metal met metal my blade shivered and broke. I cursed. I

14

should have insisted on carrying the rapier of fine Tyzinn steel that I'd found in the ruins of the Witch-Queen Vohanna's black pyramid some seven months gone. That blade hung above my bed, across the room and a lifetime away.

My would-be assassin screeched in triumph as my weapon snapped. His sword came slashing in to rip me open. I stepped into him, caught his wrist, held him. His muscles strained as he tried to push his blade into me; his face filled with surprise when he could not. He was bigger than I, and he must have thought himself stronger surely than any human. His surprise evaporated as I dropped the useless ruin of my sword and slapped him again with the back of my free hand, whipping his head to one side. His lower lip split, spackling the polished white walls of my room with blood.

The Kaldi growled, swung a fist at me. I blocked with an elbow, slapped him yet again, then jerked him forward by the wrist, twisting his arm down to smash it across my knee. His gladius went flying.

He punched me in the side and I shoved him away. He straightened, a dagger flashing in his hand, drawn from the grimy sash at his waist. That knife was leaf-shaped, tapered at the tip and flat and wide along the blade, like a spearhead on a hilt. It was a type I'd not seen before, but it was sharp enough to draw a tithe of blood as the edge whicked through my shirt sleeve to score my arm. I was already leaping away, and as I landed I spun and snapped a kick to the Kaldi's rough-whiskered chin.

He staggered, slumped to his knees, the tip of his dagger ringing on the stone flaggings. I leaped upon him, roped an arm around his corded neck. He gave a strangled bellow and dropped his knife to grab at my forearm, his black fingernails digging. I punched him on top of his head, the only part of him I could reach, but he rolled sideways into a massive table of bansul wood, breaking my hold and leaving me sprawled awkwardly on my back.

Surging to his feet, the Kaldi lashed his own kick—at my head. His foot seemed to come from nowhere, but my mind didn't have to register it for my hands to catch it. With the toe of his scarred boot an inch from my face, I twisted savagely at his leg. He was off balance and toppled backward; the base of his skull slammed into the stone flooring as he hit. I heard the bone in his leg snap.

He grabbed for the broken limb and writhed, a moaning bubble bursting from his throat. I rose, picked up his sword where it lay a few feet from me, then turned back toward him. My jaws hurt from being clenched around tension. I forced them apart, smiled cruelly as the Kaldi looked up at me with fear in his onyx-black eyes.

"Now we're going to have a little chat," I snarled at him.

I should have realized what would happen next.

Fear turned to resignation in the being's gaze; his smashed and swollen lips curved in what might have been a smile. He let go of his leg and shook his head slightly. Then I saw his mouth work and leaped forward. My hands came down, my thumbs stabbing into the corners of his jaws to try to pry them open. But I was too late. He gave a harsh shudder and his whole body jolted and stiffened.

I backed away as his mouth fell open, not sure what poison he might have used and knowing that some toxins are deadly even at a distance in open air. A pale green vapor purled from the corner of his lips to dribble onto the polished floor. I smelled the acrid tang of laith venom and felt my throat burn with disgust.

Disgust obviously wasn't what the now dead Kaldi had felt. His face had taken on the beatific expression that is supposedly reserved only to saints and angels. Perhaps in his last thoughts that was exactly what he'd become.

Cursing thoroughly in a mixture of English and Nyshphalian, I took a step toward the door to call for my friends, and a sharp, slicing fear snicked its way up my spine.

If there had been one assassin, why not two?

And Rannon was as alone as I had been!

Darting toward the hallway I suddenly paused, hesitating for an agonizing instant. Rannon's apartment was on the same floor of the palace as mine, but two corridors removed to the south, to the right of my rooms. And there was no linking door directly through from my hall to hers because the intermediate area was one large room that was used for storage. I'd have to go down the stairs to where they branched and then back up the steps on the other side.

16

Too far! Too long!
The balcony, my thoughts shrieked.

Still carrying the assassin's blade, I turned and rushed through my apartment and out onto the balcony. That structure extended the length of my room, about thirty heka, or fifteen paces, and was girded by a low railing of dressed gray stone worked with bas-relief figures of vines and grapes. A gap of some ten heka separated my balcony from the next, and beyond that was another gap and a third balcony—Rannon's.

I was not now in the same apartment where I'd been when I'd first come to live in Jystral Castle. We were five stories up, with a steep drop below onto the paving stones of a courtyard. I didn't care. Backing up, I took a running start and leaped the gap between my room and the next, pushing off from the railing with my right foot, my legs and arms churning for distance while below me flashed a blur of greenery and the colored dots of people staring up with mouths wide.

I cleared the railing on the far side balcony and landed hard, stumbling, nearly twisting my ankle, but recovered my stride in a few steps and kept going, leaping next to Rannon's balcony, my boots scraping the top of the last railing so that I lost my balance and sprawled onto all fours. To my right, the glass doors that opened into Rannon's room were closed, the fern-lace curtains drawn. But inside I could see quickly moving shadows and hear a thud as of something falling. Then there came a shout from Rannon.

Insane with terror for my love, I lurched to my feet and smashed a kick through the glass to leap in under a chinkling rain of shards. Rannon had her back to the wall, her dark hair having come partially unbound from the curled glory of her wedding day coiffure. Her gown of ivory satin and spring-green silk was brilliantly splotched with scarlet at the right shoulder. And Bryce stood looming before her, sword to hand.

Bryce! My brother!

For an instant my mind flashed to a memory of a snarling Bryce lunging with a shimmering blade to impale me in Vohanna's arena, his eyes refulgent with the crimson light

17

that marked his possession by the Witch-Queen. I'd thought that with Vohanna's death and the removal of the mind amplifying toir'in-or power stones from his body that he'd been cured of the evil that owned him.

Or had I only hoped?

"No!" I screamed out.

An echoing "no" came from Rannon's throat, but I was already charging. Bryce half turned to meet me, his white hair streaming and his mouth opening, the lines of faded tattoos flushing again in his face. I nailed him with a shoulder into his chest, my elbow pulping his dark lips to blood. His sword crashed away. We went down in a tangle, me punching, punching.

Bryce grabbed desperately at my wrist, at the hand that held my sword. But I tore free, hit him with the weapon's pommel of dark iron, then spun the blade up as I straddled him. I saw his pale face, his eyes as grey now as they had ever been. The sword quivered in my fist.

"No!" Rannon shouted again. And suddenly my arm was grabbed from behind and hauled down.

I struggled, cursing. Bryce shoved me from his chest with a thrust from his artificial hand, and I saw that it was Rannon who had caught my arm before I could stab my brother through the heart with an assassin's blade. Her face was a mask of fear, but it was fear *of* me rather than for me. I slumped, my thoughts roiling in confusion.

Bryce pushed to a sitting position, wiping blood from mangled lips with the back of his human hand. Then I saw, lying on the floor beside Rannon's bed, a dead Kaldi wearing a brown sash around his waist.

"Bryce saved me from that one," Rannon said.

I glanced from the body to Rannon, and then to Bryce.

"I— I—"

Bryce's lips curled as he rose to his feet. He flicked his hand toward my feet, scattering his blood—shed by me—on the golden carpet before turning and stalking out.

"I...didn't...," I said.

But Bryce was gone.

CHAPTER TWO

SHATTERED FAITH

With Bryce gone out the door, my teeth clicked shut over an apology that could never have been enough for what I'd done to him. To so easily assume that it was *he* who threatened my wife-to-be showed how little I trusted him, my own blood. Even, it seemed, I'd been ready to kill him.

Rannon dropped to her knees beside me, enfolded me with a rustle of silk. I turned toward her, squeezing her tight as the fallen curls of her soft hair brushed my face, as her bright scent swept my nostrils clear of violence's musk.

"It's all right," Rannon said.

We helped each other to stand and I kissed her lush mouth. Her lips parted for mine. After a moment, I drew back. The body of the dead assassin lay, still bleeding, on her floor.

"I thought...," I started. Then: "I was so afraid I was about to lose you again. For good this time."

"I know," she replied, touching my cheek. "You can't believe how happy I was to see you come bursting into my room in a shower of glass." She grinned. "Not because I was in danger, you understand, but just because it meant that *you* were alive."

I almost laughed, though what came out sounded more like the shadow of a chuckle.

"I...uh...made quite an entrance, didn't I?"

"Yes. But I love the reasons *why* you did. As I love you."

I started to say something else, no doubt something gallant and entirely silly, but through the doorway at that moment burst a dozen and more soldiers. At their head came Rhandh, the huge Vlih warrior who served Rannon as her personal bodyguard. Someone, it seemed, had witnessed my balcony gymnastics.

Rannon's father, Hurnan Jystral, followed only moments behind the guards, and I stepped back as he grabbed his daughter with big hands and hugged her tight, smearing blood from her dress over his maroon and gray tabard. It was the assassin's blood, not hers.

Valyan and Kreeg arrived, the Green Llurn and the former fighting slave who had made himself *my* personal bodyguard. With them came Heril Rolvshern, the Koro, my first friend ever on Talera and the one who had been set to stand beside me this day as my best man—a custom of my new world as well as my old, though it wasn't always a *human* male who acted in the role.[1] These, my friends, gathered around as I explained what I knew of the assassination attempts. It wasn't much.

"You're hurt!" Rannon exclaimed, coming up to me then.

I glanced down in surprise, saw that my shirt was torn at the right side and that blood had run down to rust the cream-white of my breeks. I'd almost forgotten the gunshot in my room and the tug of the bullet as it grazed me. The shallow groove across my ribs had bled like a much worse injury than it truly was. The dagger scratch on my arm had scarcely

---

[1]Talera is populated by many intelligent races, some of whom evolved naturally on alien worlds, and others who were bred or even "built" by the Asadhie, the advanced race who created the planet and brought its inhabitants here. I've already mentioned the Kaldi, who might be said, vaguely, to resemble bears.

Rannon and her father, and Kreeg among my other friends, are full humans. But Rannon's bodyguard, Rhandh, is of a warrior race called the Vlih, who are humanoid but with a tail and a pair of tentacles to compliment their arms and legs. Valyan and Heril are from races that the Asadhie bred from humans. Valyan is a Llurn, who look much like typical humans except for exotic skin and hair colors. (Valyan has green skin.) Heril is a Koro, another "bred" race. The Koro resemble nothing so much as the dwarfs of ancient Earth legends, though some of them, including Heril, are close to the human average in size.—Ruenn Maclang.

bled at all.

"Moth bites," I said, but Rannon was already wetting a cloth in her bedside basin to clean the wounds.

Hurnan Jystral placed a hand on my shoulder. The touch startled me, even though the man had thawed a bit toward me since learning of my part in crushing the Witch-Queen Vohanna's recent scheme to conquer Nyshphal. I do not say that he loved the idea of having me as a son-in-law, but he had resigned himself to it, and, it seemed, had even begun to accord me a grudging respect.

It was unfortunate that Rannon's brother, Kuurus, had not experienced a similar warming. From our first meeting there had been tension between us. And this past spring, after he'd tried to arrest me and I'd locked him in his own dungeon while I went to free Bryce from Vohanna, that tension had grown into hatred. He'd not been happy to find that I'd somehow wormed my way back into Rannon's favor and was even, apparently, accepted by his father. A week ago he'd left the city rather than stay to see me marry his sister.

"Once again," Hurnan Jystral was saying, "you've risked yourself to protect my daughter. It won't be forgotten."

"'Twas my brother who saved her," I said. "I would have been too late."

He shook his head, turning to smile fondly upon Rannon. "Perhaps not. My daughter would have fought. You might have been in time anyway."

"Yes, she would have fought," I said in agreement, smiling as I remembered her in battle-leathers on the deck of her dying airship, a blooded sword in her hand as she faced Vohanna for my life some half a year ago. "She might well have needed no one."

Rannon blushed at our words as she finished with my cuts and straightened up. Her father, meanwhile, was looking at the crowd of guards, most of who were standing around.

"Well?" he said to them. "What are all of you lazing about for? Get this...," he toed the assassin's corpse, "thing out of here. And get someone to clean this place up."

"There's another dead one in my room," I added. "But be careful of them both. Mine had a capsule of laith venom in his jaw. This one probably does too.

"And." I looked around. "Mine had a gun."

Except for my friends and the Jystrals, who had heard me talk of such weapons, everyone in the room looked blank at my mention of a "gun."

"A hand held cannon," I explained. By now everyone in the city of Timmuzz had heard of "cannon"—thunderpults they'd been dubbed—and everyone knew how Vohanna's small air fleet had used such weapons to nearly destroy the great sky navy of Nyshphal.

"Is this the...cannon?" one guard asked.

Walking over to where the man stood, I saw the barrel of a pistol peeking out from under the edge of Rannon's bed.

"Yes," I said. "A gun."

I picked it up, tried to turn a startled gasp into a cough. I'd barely glimpsed the weapon the killer in my apartment had carried, but if it was like this one then we were dealing with something far worse than simple assassination attempts. Though the gunpowder genie was loose on Talera now, and attempts were already being made to construct guns of various types, *this* was no crudely manufactured local weapon. On the blued steel barrel were incised the words, "Smith & Wesson!" It had to have been brought here from Earth!

But by whom?

Rannon came to rest her hand on my elbow. I glanced at her and she knew something was wrong. So, too, did Valyan and Heril as they saw the dismayed look that I was not quite able to hide. But none of them said anything. They knew I'd explain when there weren't so many ears to overhear.

Kreeg, a loyal warrior who, for good or ill, had joined his fate to mine soon after I'd arrived on Talera, showed only anger at himself for not having been in position to protect me. Once a gladiator, Kreeg was tougher than whalebone but not overly gifted in his ability to read the subtleties of emotional expression. There were times I was grateful for that. As he griped and complained, I slapped the former fighting slave on the shoulder.

"I'm not sure you're built for jumping balconies, old friend," I told him, grinning. He was nearly as wide as he was tall, strong as a stugah—that Taleran ox—but not light on his feet.

Rannon chuckled with the rest, but then leaned to whisper. "Love, you should go to Bryce now. Before he does something foolish."

Again I felt myself lost in dismay. "How can I?" I asked.

"He's your brother," Rannon replied. "Seek him as such."

"And I," Hurnan Jystral said, "have the unenviable task of telling thousands of people that a wedding they were so eager to celebrate has to be postponed."

Rannon and I looked at him suddenly, both our faces stricken.

"Temporarily," he said, almost chuckling. Then his face darkened. "We have to get to the root of these assassination attempts before I risk you two in a crowd. Besides," he eyed our bloody and torn clothing, "it would appear that neither of you is quite adequately dressed for the ceremony."

I glanced from my tattered shirt to Rannon's scarlet-stained dress and laughed spontaneously, though Jystral had not intended to be funny.

"I see your point," I said, as Rannon joined me in the humor of the moment.

Hurnan stared for a long few seconds, then shook his head at our levity and turned to go, to postpone the wedding for which the people of Nyshphal and Timmuzz had been preparing for weeks. I'm glad it was he who had to bear that message.

I kissed Rannon and parted from her reluctantly, taking the revolver with me as I returned first to my room to change into battle-leathers and buckle on my Tyzinn sword. The dead Kaldi had been removed but guards stood around his gun. It was an exact duplicate of the one I carried, which struck me as curious. After dismissing the guards, I hid both .38s in an old arrow quiver and then went in search of Bryce.

I found my brother in his room, where incense burned a sweet odor into the air. He was not packing his belongings as I'd half feared, but was standing before his wash basin, hands pressed to the wall as he stared at himself in the mirror. He'd not heard me come through the door he'd left open, or at least did not choose to acknowledge me, and I took the opportunity to study him.

The old Bryce, from Earth, had been a brown-haired youth of about five feet, eleven inches. He might have weighed 170, carrying as he did a lean physique earned from years of swimming and riding. His eyes had been grey, his face and arms tanned by the outdoor sun.

This new Bryce was the same height as the old, but thinner, built all out of tight flesh and sinew stretched over prominent bones. His hair was much longer than before, hanging halfway down his back, and was dead white. The tanned skin of his former life was now nearly as pale as his hair and was marked by the fading Nazca lines of what had once been a brilliant web of tattoos.

Though I couldn't see my brother's grey eyes, I knew they sometimes now sparked with a disconcerting flash of crimson. And worst of all to me in that moment was one of the hands that Bryce pressed against the wall of his room. It wasn't human, but a thing built out of rage, a monster's hand of strung black wire and meshing metal parts covered with a translucent latex flesh.

For another few minutes, a dhorrin in Taleran time, I stood there, and then, sure that Bryce knew of my presence, spoke:

"Thank you for saving Rannon's life."

My brother's gaze met mine in the mirror, and then he looked down into his wash basin. He said nothing, but slipped his hands into the basin to rinse them, drying them after on a fluffy towel.

"You saw...," I continued, "how much she means to me. It was out of fear for her that I attacked you. I'm sorry that I didn't realize you were there to help. But I'm not sorry for trying to protect Rannon. I love her."

Bryce turned slightly, putting his left side toward me, hiding his right side and the artificial hand that hung from his wrist there. He looked at me obliquely over his shoulder, a smirk curving his lips, which shone dark against his pale face from where they had been tattooed black for Vohanna. His lower lip was swollen, and there was a knot on his cheek that would soon turn to bruise. Both were my marks.

"And for that love of Rannon you would have killed me,

brother," Bryce said.

I shook my head. "I've been thinking about that. I could never have put that sword in your heart." Allowing myself a small smile, I added: "Might have been able to hurt you some more, perhaps."

He shrugged. "A few months ago it was I who was trying to kill you. And I *could* have done it."

That his words were neither snide nor angry surprised me, and I did not speak. Nor did Bryce at first.

An oaken table stood near the bed and Bryce moved toward it, dropped into a chair of sanded ahmbr wood. He looked down at his hands, curled his normal one over his artificial one as if to hide it again. I wondered if he were conscious of such acts.

"You're lucky, Ruenn. To have someone like Rannon love you."

"Yes. I know how lucky. I know how close I've come to losing her in the past. And today."

"Ironic isn't it," he said. "We arrive on Talera in separate places but we each find a woman to love. You found Rannon. Beautiful. Resilient. A princess even. But with a strong right arm. A woman who would go through hell for you. And I? I found Vohanna. Beautiful also. And a queen. But vile as the muck at the bottom of a sewer. Someone who would put a man. Or a world. *Through* hell."

There was little I could say against Bryce's despairing words. Oh, I might have told him the Taleran equivalent of "there are more fish in the sea," but such would never cure his melancholy. Only time and another love would do that.

I joined him at his table, sat across from him.

"I'm sorry I doubted you," I said.

Bryce looked up, and though his eyes were grey like old times, there was something else within them that I would wish never to see in *any* man's eyes. My brother carried a haunted place inside of him.

"You were right to doubt," he said suddenly.

I was taken aback.

"But I— But you—"

He lifted his artificial hand and placed it on the table. In the faded crimson light of evening that hand...pulsed—with a

25

scarlet light of its own that mocked the dying sun. And in my brother's eyes now lived a mute pleading, and the sting of tears.

"Vohanna is alive," Bryce said.

It took me a moment to realize what my brother was saying, and when I did I leaped to my feet.

"No! I saw her dead. I killed—"

"*Alive, Ruenn!*" Bryce shouted, his gaze burning up into mine. He clenched his false hand into a fist. Then his voice dropped almost to a whisper. "Do you not think I can feel her? How do you imagine I knew the assassins were here? They were hers. I felt *them* too. Like a...," he looked down, "...a crawling."

I started to grab Bryce by the shoulders, to do...what I did not know, just something to make him recant what he'd said. But his words froze me as he went on.

"I awoke from meditation, knowing. And I rushed. To Rannon's apartment first. Because she was closer and because I knew that you loved her."

And still a denial burst from my lips. "Some other explanation perhaps. Maybe—"

"Don't!" he broke in. Then his shoulders slumped and he hid his face in his hands. "Don't you understand, Ruenn?" His voice murmured with ache. "She's still in me. Inside of me."

He began to sob. "Help me, Ruenn. Help me. Don't let her take me again."

CHAPTER THREE

GUNS AGAINST TALERA

Just before the sixteenth dhorr, the Taleran dusk, I left my brother's apartment to join Hurnan Jystral for a meeting that had been called in his war room, stopping, as I'd been asked, to pick up the revolvers the assassins had carried. Behind me I left Bryce, calmer but with no real help for his pain, no true balm for his fears. It was a failing for which I cursed myself.

The hall outside Jystral's inner sanctum was thick with guards when I arrived, but Rannon was there to usher me past into the quiet, sealed place near the heart of Jystral Castle where the emperor and his military advisors met to decide on issues of war. Besides Rannon's father, four other men and another woman occupied the room. All were human. Though non-humans were welcome in Nyshphal, this was primarily a human country.

The woman was Arca Heskern, tall, with hair and eyes of steel-wool gray. She led Nyshphal's scientists, which, given the level of culture on Talera, were akin in interests and knowledge to the alchemists of old Earth. She was also the closest thing Nyshphal had to a wizard. Hurnan Jystral despised sorcery, but Arca was said to, at times, be able to foresee events. I had no direct evidence of this myself.

The first of the four men was Taskin Bhent, a short, stout, blunt-featured soldier who commanded the Nyshphalian army. He always smelled of terval steak and onions to me. There was also Horlis Kazhian, whipcord lean and with a sharp-planed face, who was in charge of the navy. In

Nyshphal this included ships of both sea and air, as well as the saddle bird corps.

The third man was Rajan Critus, a dark complected swordsman with acid-black eyes. Once I'd overheard a woman of the court refer to Rajan as "deadly handsome." Such a description seemed accurate. His dueling scars and the intent burn of his gaze lent the fellow a dangerous air, but I'd always found him friendly and remarkably cultured. He was captain of the Imperial Guard, the emperor's own legion, which doubled as the police force within the city of Timmuzz.

The presence of the last man surprised me. I knew he'd been out of the city only hours earlier and wondered how he'd heard so quickly of the assassination attempts and the postponed wedding. But I suppose the powerful have their ways. Kuurus Jystral, Rannon's brother, favored me with a smirk as I strode to the table in the center of the room and laid the revolvers on the polished oval surface.

"So. Those are the...guns," Kuurus said. He lounged in a chair that he'd tipped back against a wall.

Kuurus's father, seated at the head of the table, glanced at Kazhian and Bhent, who stood conversing together in low, anxious tones. They quickly sat, leaving only myself standing. It was *me* they all wanted to hear now, and I let my gaze brush the room, judging. Despite Kuurus's studied nonchalance, I thought the one person truly relaxed here was Rajan Critus. I wondered why.

"Yes," I said finally in response to Kuurus's comment. "This type is called a revolver."

"They are smaller versions of the cannon that the Witch-Queen used against us at the battle of Vohan?" Hurnan Jystral asked.

I shook my head. "Not really. Though more powerful because of their larger size, those cannon were primitive in comparison. One of these," I stroked a finger along a cool, blue barrel, "built to the scale of a cannon could penetrate any wall of this castle with a single shot."

Kuurus snorted and his father silenced him with a look.

"How could such have been constructed?" Horlis Kazhian asked. "After Vohan we confiscated all the remaining

28

thunderpults...uhm, cannon that the Witch had caused to be built. Along with her supply of exploding dust. Those materials were handed over to the Saaress Heskern and her scientists."

Arca Heskern, who was studying one of the revolvers as closely as she could without touching it, looked up at the unexpected mention of her name. "These were not made by us. We have not such skill."

"They weren't made by anyone on Talera," I added.

Even the unflappable Rajan looked surprised, and a babble of voices erupted until silenced by a slash of Hurnan Jystral's hand.

"Explain," he commanded.

I took up one of the revolvers, the smell of gunpowder lingering upon it, and pointed out the words "Smith & Wesson" engraved on the darkly gleaming barrel.

"These symbols are written in my native tongue. My *Earth* tongue. English."

"But it was your men, from your captured Earth crew, who helped Vohanna build her cannons," Jystral said. "Could not they have made—"

"No," I said bluntly, interrupting him. "For three reasons. One, the molds and machines needed to produce such as these do not exist on Talera. Unless they've been brought from elsewhere. Two, our searches indicated that none of my crew survived Vohanna's slavery so they *couldn't* have built more guns. And, three, this model of gun did not even exist on *Earth* when my crew was taken by Vohanna. I only know of such weapons because I've been *back* to Earth, and because of the destruction of the sphere gate that brought me here I went back into my home world's future."

"Then *you* could have made them," Kuurus stated flatly. "Or returned with them."

I was taken aback. The statement seemed preposterous to me. But I noted the calculating looks on the faces of many of those present, and only Rannon did not lean away from me as if I'd suddenly developed Quivers Disease.[2]

---

[2]Quivers Disease results in uncontrollable tremors of the face and limbs and gets progressively worse over time until it results in death. Since it is generally believed that the disease is contagious, the sufferers have been

"I don't have the tools to make them," I finally managed. "Nor knowledge of the steps involved. And though I suppose I could have brought them back from Earth, I didn't."

A retort was forming on Kuurus's lips when Hurnan Jystral again slashed his hand through the air for silence.

"Speculations are useless when we need facts," he said.

I wondered if it meant anything that Jystral had not prefaced the term "speculations" with "wild." Only hours before I'd been convinced that Hurnan had thawed in his feelings toward me. Was he freezing again?

"Someone tasks us," Jystral continued. "But who? And why was it important to them to stop my daughter's wedding?"

"Ubai ships have been pushing further and further into our waters of late," Kazhian said. "Testing our resolve, I think. Or seeing how much we were weakened by the war with Vohanna."

"And," Kuurus added, "the new peace between Ubai and Revenor means that the Ubains will soon have access to Revenor's airship works. A *marriage* created that peace."

I remembered months ago when Kreeg had suggested that Ubai was behind what turned out to be Vohanna's attacks on Nyshphal. We had all laughed then.

Things change.

Ubai was a young empire on the nearby continent of Pangala, and half a year ago had been at war on three fronts. In the ensuing period the Ubains had crushed the Thorn Nomads to their east in a huge battle that scattered the remnants of those tribes, and now they'd allied themselves with the small but highly advanced country of Revenor to their north.

Though I didn't think Ubai was behind the attacks on Rannon and myself, it was true that a marriage—between

---

ostracized much as lepers used to be on Earth. They have their own colonies and often appear decrepit and wasted, though whether it's the disease or the social consequences (such as poverty) that result in that wasting is unclear.—Ruenn Maclang.

[Note: Quiver's Disease sounds like a particularly virulent strain of Huntington's chorea to me.—CAG]

Sadek, the tyrant of Ubai, and Eskirina, the sister to Revenor's king—had sealed the alliance between the two countries. The possibility had to be considered that Sadek was moving against Nyshphal, whose naval power in the air and on the sea had long served as a brake on his ambitions.

"I don't see what Ubai would get out of killing me," I said. "I bring no airship factories or anything else of military value to Nyshphal through my marriage to Rannon."

Kuurus snorted again, and I rushed on, feeling my face flush.

"Another thing to remember," I said. "Where these guns came from," I jerked my chin toward the twin revolvers, "there are likely to be more. Possibly far more powerful ones."

Hurnan Jystral nodded as worried murmurs filled the room. I caught the emperor's eye, tried to indicate that I had more to say—to him alone. At first it did not seem as if he'd noticed.

"I want to know exactly what those Ubain krutt-lovers are up to," he said. "More scouts. Spies. Whatever it takes. And I want," he looked pointedly at Rajan Critus, "anyone who knows anything about our Kaldi assassins and their guns to bleed their guts out. Literally, if need be. I especially want to know how those two wastes-of-tissue got into the palace as cook's aides."

He rose from his chair in a gesture of dismissal, but said: "I'd like Ruenn Maclang to stay for a moment." Apparently he *had* noticed my look.

I squeezed Rannon's shoulder as she turned to kiss me on the cheek. She went out then, knowing I'd tell her everything later. Kuurus was the last to go, giving me an angry glare as he passed. He muttered a single word under his breath, a word that he knew his father wouldn't catch.

"Mucker," he said in English.

I was startled for a moment, until I remembered that I'd been steadily teaching Rannon my native tongue and that Kuurus had overheard us often enough. He was gone before I had a chance to reply in kind.

When the door closed behind the prince, the Emperor Hurnan Jystral walked around the table to me. He picked up one of the pistols, a look of distaste on his face, and held it for a long moment before speaking.

"These...things. I know they are not sorcerous but still they stink as if they are. I don't know how to fight such weapons. Give me a sword or an axe. Even an arrow that kills at a distance makes more sense than these."

"I agree," I said. "I like them no more than you."

He looked at me, as if to judge whether to believe me or not. But when he spoke it was of other matters.

"What did you wish to talk to me about?"

"Something bad."

His eyes narrowed, but still I hesitated, trying to decide how best to tell the emperor of Nyshphal a thing he would not want to hear.

"After the assassination attempts," I finally said, "I spoke to Bryce. He knew. Sensed. That the assassins were here. That's how he was able to get to Rannon in time."

Jystral's frown deepened. "Sensed?"

"Yes, sensed. Because he can still sense Vohanna and Vohanna sent them."

My words staggered him, and in that moment he looked haggard and old. The scent of sweat was upon him.

"She's...."

"Not dead," I said. "We knew that she owned different bodies to move between. And that temporarily she could take over the bodies of other intelligent—"

"Yes. I remember," he interrupted impatiently. "We checked for those black eyes that always gave her away."

"We should have checked the animals," I said.

"Sevarian!" He breathed the name of Nyshphal's god. "I did not think of that."

"Nor I."

Jystral sighed, laid the revolver back on the table and slid heavily into a chair.

"The Witch. Back." He did not look at me. "With one airship and its cannon she destroyed a third of our fleet. And many good warriors. We've still not recovered. Which is why Ubai feels safe in pushing us now."

I nodded. "I know."

I also knew what he didn't say, that Nyshphal could

hardly sustain another such war as we'd just been through.

"It was well that you did not tell this in front of the others," Jystral said. "No need to panic our people. But we must prepare."

I said nothing at first. I was remembering what my cousin, Eric Ryall, had told me just before the moment when Vohanna possessed him and bade him murder himself on a sword. When I had thought that I'd removed the milkstones by which she controlled him, he'd laughed mirthlessly and told me that there were other stones—inside of him.

Though the physicians at court had removed milkstones from Bryce's tattoos after we'd brought him in, I wondered if he, too, had more inside. Would he, like Eric, be forced to kill himself? Or me? Or Rannon?

"Ruenn!" Jystral's words were sharp and I realized it was not the first time he'd called my name.

"I'm sorry," I said, glancing down at him. "I was thinking of Rannon."

He nodded. "I, too. And yet, to protect Rannon we must protect Nyshphal."

I thought: *Protect Nyshphal*? Against a sorceress who could look like anybody? *Be* anybody? Against the same Vohanna with better guns?

"Agreed," I said.

CHAPTER FOUR

VISITORS FROM THE NIGHT

"A woman waits for you in Moonrose Garden," Heril said.

I frowned. "A woman?"

Heril shrugged the wide shoulders that over the years had borne many burdens because of his friendship for me. His short, golden beard jumped as he spoke:

"She wouldn't give a name."

It seemed that while Heril and Valyan and Kreeg had been haunting my quarters for my return, someone had come to see me who none of them recognized.

"And did this woman give a reason for her visit?"

Again Heril shrugged, though I thought there was a grin peaking out of his dark eyes.

"She said that you would know her."

"Let *me* have words with her," Kreeg growled.

I smiled. "I don't think that'll be necessary. I'll find out what our mysterious guest wants."

"It could be another attempt on your life," Valyan said, his luminous yellow eyes a contrast against the emerald of his skin.

"An unusual way to go about it, if so," I replied. "But if it'll make you gentlemen feel better you can stay within shouting range."

Heril nodded as he came up beside me. "Be assured of that," he said. "You get into too much trouble when left alone."

I chuckled and slapped him on the shoulder. It was good

to have such friends. In that, as in so many other ways, I had been lucky since coming to Talera.

* * * * * * *

Moonrose Garden is one of many such gardens that lie within the sprawl of Hurnan Jystral's palace. Others are named after colors, Blue and Green, or after animals, Aestor and Vull. One is even called Kyrel, after the Taleran version of chess. I knew where they all were, having walked them many times with Rannon.

The garden that I sought now was named after a rose the like of which I'd seen only on Talera, a rose that combined in its petals the pastel versions of the four moon colors— rouge red, delicate gold, turquoise, and palest blue. A set of oaken doors, hung on hinges of butter-brass, opened directly into the garden from off a small auditorium within the castle proper where plays and the like were performed. I stepped through those doors onto a walking path of rust-red brick, leaving Heril, Valyan, and Kreeg waiting behind.

Beds of crimson hysis, silver nyxe, and moonroses broke the small courtyard into squares and rectangles of color separated by branching brick paths. Here and there the garden was dotted with trees under which benches of snow-wood sat waiting patiently for passengers. I found my visitor sitting on one such bench, beneath an ahmbr tree on which had been hung vellum lanterns that spilled a saffron light.

As I approached, the figure climbed to its feet, cloaked and cowled against the autumn coolness. Overhead arced two of Talera's four moons, Sieona and Tisiminna, with a third, Rath, peeking in crimson splendor over the horizon. The first moon to rise, tiny Nimeru, had already set.

"You were looking for me?" I asked the figure, trying to keep my voice neutral as I stopped a few paces away along the path.

A slender-fingered hand, unadorned with jewelry, lifted and brushed back the cowl of the cloak to free a wild mane of hair that even in the fluttering light of the moons and the lanterns gleamed a brilliant copper.

"Ahrethane!" I said, with a gasp of surprise.

"Ruenn," Ahrethane replied, smiling and walking toward me. She offered her hand and I took it with both of mine, squeezing it tight.

Only months ago, in the jungle surrounding the ruined city of Vohan, this woman had saved my life and guided me on the way to rescuing Bryce and stopping Vohanna. I owed her much. Nyshphal owed her much.

"It's good to see you," I said, smiling hugely. "But how on Talera did you get into the palace? Guards are everywhere."

Her heart-shaped lips curved in a crooked smile. "You forget that I am efrinore," she said.

I chuckled. "Yes. A druidess. A woman of many talents. Can you stay for a while? I'd love for you to meet Rannon."

"Your wife to be?" Ahrethane asked.

I nodded. "Unfortunately our wedding has been postponed. I'm sorry I didn't invite you. I didn't know how to get word to you."

"Don't worry on that. I heard of the attempt on your life, though. I'm glad it did not succeed. It is well," her mouth slid again into a smile, "that you are very hard to kill."

"I'm just stubborn," I said.

She laughed then, and I realized I had not heard her laugh before. I had assumed that the inner sadness she felt because of the loss of her family to Vohanna would not let her laugh. But I had spent scarcely an hour with her in the jungle. How foolish to think I knew her so well in such a short time.

"After I heard of the assassination attempts," she said, "I almost left the city before talking to you. Surely you must have much on your mind."

"I'm glad you didn't go." I looked at her closely then, trying to catch the jade gaze from her eyes. "I suspect that you have something on your mind. Will you tell me?"

She sighed; her smile fell away. She found her bench again and sat. I sat as well.

"The forest," she said after a bit. "For a while after the destruction of Vohanna's black pyramid things were better. New growth. New life. But all that has changed."

"How?"

"A few months back. Always at night. I began to find the savaged bodies of small animals. You remember the red-eyed howlers—the vashok?"

I shuddered, recalling a wild chase through the trees with myself as prey for a band of creatures who looked like a cross between baboons and demons.

"I didn't know their name," I said. "But I *remember* them."

"Well, they disappeared right after Vohanna's death. I don't know where. But they came back. It was they who were killing in the forest. At first. Later there were...other things."

"Tell me."

Restless, she rose once again to her feet. She stood barely five feet in height but looked taller there in the shadows. "Let's walk," she said.

I joined her as she moved along down the brick path toward the far end of the garden, her fingers touching here and there against leaves or blooms that seemed to enjoy the caress.

"Just in the last month," she continued, "things have begun to appear in the forest that should not be there. Animals and plants of unknown origin. Creatures from outside. Not Taleran. Horned, savage, bloody. Killers. Even the plants."

I felt my brow furrow into a frown. "If not from Talera, then where?" I asked.

She shrugged. "More than one place, perhaps. There is, I think, a wild gate in the jungle."

My heart thumped a little quicker. After the Asadhie created Talera they had populated it by bringing plants and animals, and beings, through "sphere gates," which are doorways between worlds that are opened by means of the milkstones, the toir'in-or power stones. It was through such a gate that Bryce and I had come here.

In the present age, since the Asadhie are gone or dead— or so it is generally believed—the gates are seldom used. In fact, the locations of most have probably been lost, along with the knowledge of how to open them with a milkstone. I knew of only one operable gate and had used it twice to return to Earth and then come back to Talera.

Vohanna had used a second gate to kidnap men for the armies she had hoped to raise to conquer Nyshphal. Though I hadn't seen that gate, I'd assumed it had been destroyed during the war, along with Vohan, the Witch's ancient city.

Sphere gates are fixed in physical location and open only if the milkstones are activated in a specific pattern. Few on the Talera of today know those patterns. And, each gate opens to only a limited number of worlds. A "wild gate" is one that opens on its own, from no fixed site, and no one can predict what worlds it might link to.

"I've heard of wild gates," I said. "But I thought them a myth. Could it not be Vohanna's gate still operating somehow?"

She shook her head. "I always knew Vohanna had a gate in her pyramid, but this is not the same. It moves. Only wild gates act thusly."

Troubled, I nodded.

We stopped our stroll then, having reached the garden wall.

"Have you sensed any agency behind the gate's activity?" I asked.

"Only that the choices of what gets brought here are not random. Uniformly, the transfers are malevolent."

"All?"

"All."

I told her what I knew. "Vohanna is still alive."

She gasped. "But I thought...." She trailed off.

I offered her a wry grin. "Everyone says that. Too bad that thinking it doesn't make it true."

"How do you know? I mean. I haven't felt her."

"I doubt she's in your forest anymore. Though the wild gate sounds like her work. I know she's alive because of Bryce. My brother. He was possessed by her for many months. They're still connected at some level."

She shuddered. And I knew she was afraid. But there was strength in her that few possessed.

"Perhaps if I could see your brother...," she started, then paused as a frown flitted over her face.

A moving shadow occluded the moons' light and I looked up. Almost directly overhead, its prow clearing the garden's trees by only a few feet, there drifted an airship. *A patrol craft*, I thought. But why was it so low?

Then my eyes widened and my heart clenched before pounding. The broad, flat bottom of the ship! The almost square prow! It wasn't Nyshphalian.

I had time to wonder how such an alien ship could have gotten through Timmuzz's air defenses before someone aboard dropped an egg-shaped package over the side to tumble toward us. And I was moving, on instinct, grabbing Ahrethane, throwing her and myself over a thick hedge of hanris bushes and rolling, rolling.

In the next instant an explosion bludgeoned the ground where we'd been, painting the night with streaming light, filling the world with a hammering roll of noise that sent dirt and wrecked plants and shards of brick geysering.

I covered Ahrethane with my body, the both of us stunned as bits of earth and stone and greenery rained around us. But even through the belling of sound that filled my ears I thought I heard other explosions, all across the city.

I rolled onto my back. The ship was drifting. Past us now. Toward the castle. I shoved to my feet, shouting for Heril and my friends even as more egg-shaped packets of explosive arched from the deck of the ship toward the palace auditorium.

Screaming at Ahrethane to stay down, I took off, racing toward the castle through a mist of dust that choked the air. More explosions rocked the ground, throwing me from my feet. But I got up again, raced on—and saw where gaping holes had been torn in the roof and walls of the auditorium. There was no sign of my friends.

Rage took me. I cursed the ship that had attacked us. I cursed the Nyshphalian air patrols that should have been here to protect us. Scarcely did I think of Ahrethane, or even of Rannon. The enemy craft was past the garden's low, outer wall now and I swarmed over that wall in pursuit.

More bombs punched holes in the castle, and then the ship started to come slowly around to starboard to avoid an ironwood tree that stood tall and straight in its path. I ran to the tree, jumped to grab the first of the broad limbs that were spaced almost evenly up the thick, clean truck. Faster than

I'd ever climbed before, I climbed that tree, in an adrenaline-fueled rush.

The ship was turning, its railing almost brushing the topmost leaves of the tree. I ran out along a limb that should have been too narrow to hold me and leaped upward, my fingers clawing, catching at the railing, hanging on. The ship rocked under my weight, but I was pulling myself up and over the rail, drawing my Tyzinn blade so that it smoked with light.

Two men stood there, both human. One held a bomb, its fuse already sparking. The other came at me, his own blade to hand, reaching for my life. I cut him down in a shower of black blood, jumped past him toward the other. In desperation, that one threw his bomb. At me. I dodged, sworded him through the throat. But the explosive hit the railing at the back of the ship and went off, churning six feet of the stern into confetti.

The rear of the ship dropped like stone. Men screamed. My boots were torn from under me and I fell, slamming chest first into the deck, losing my wind. Somehow my free hand caught at a piece of torn railing and clutched. Bags, and barrels, and bundles, and men tumbled past me, the men grabbing at anything as the ship started to slide from the sky toward the earth.

The piece of railing that I held snapped like a stick and I was falling, spinning. I hit, knocking every ounce of energy and thought from me. But we'd been scarcely twenty feet in the air and I'd landed on grass. I lived.

The enemy ship went down, pile-driving into a shed where wagons were parked. Most of its remaining bombs went off all at once, crescendoing the night.

I got up, feeling blood running at my nose. Across the city, more explosions thundered. And I saw other enemy ships. But the alarm tocsins had finally begun to clang, and saddle birds were rising from the defense towers, moonlight limning the dark shapes of their riders. The attacking ships turned, began to accelerate away, the birds and their warriors in pursuit. There was still no sign of our own flyers, our airship patrols.

Voices shouted toward me and I turned, lips curving in a

snarl as I brought my sword up. But it was only members of the imperial guard rushing about, checking to see if any of the enemy flyers who'd been thrown from their crashed ship lived. Those who did were quickly bound.

Then, I saw Ahrethane through the smoke and dust. She was near where the auditorium of the castle had stood, that structure now a sagging wreck, her hands scrabbling at broken rock as she dug frantically. I rushed to her, fear running like a fever through my body.

Where she worked was where Heril and Kreeg and Valyan had been awaiting me. An arm stuck up through the rubble there. Even in the dim light cast by the remaining garden lanterns I could see that arm clearly. On it, the skin was emerald green. It was Valyan's arm, Valyan's skin.

CHAPTER FIVE

GRAY AS HEARTH'S ASHES

Valyan's arm! Sticking up from the rubble.

My heart seized but I dropped to my knees beside Ahre-thane, began frantically to pull away broken chunks of rock and masonry, tossing them behind me to crush the few gold-enswords and moonroses left standing in the garden. Other men and women joined us. Rannon came from somewhere and fell to work beside me. Torches were brought, throwing a harsher light over the terrible scene.

We uncovered Valyan, broken-jawed and bloody about the face. His left shoulder was crushed; he barely breathed. A half dozen of us tugged him free of his almost-tomb and carried him out to lie upon clean grass that was wet with dew. Ahrethane plunged to work on him, her lips muttering spells, her hands moving with the words to hide his spirit, his khi, away from the death that hunted him.

I returned quickly to the pile of rubble we were excavating, and despite my fear for my remaining friends I forced everyone to move slowly. All around, the walls and parts of walls that were left standing were groaning and teetering, still spilling pieces of themselves to the ground. A further collapse might bury us all. But in a few more dhorrin we uncovered Kreeg, curled up in a fetal position but fully conscious despite bruises and what were, apparently, cracked ribs.

"Heril," Kreeg said, gasping in pain. "He shoved me from under the door when it came down." Lifting an arm, a gesture that must have cost him much in the coin of agony, the former fighting slave pointed to a jumble of large stone slabs to one side. "There," he said.

As others lifted the ex-gladiator up from the dust, I turned to where he had pointed and began to dig, for my first and best friend on Talera. Elsewhere in the city, some in places where fires burned, other men and women dug for their loved ones. I could spare no thought for them. I moved aside rocks with hands that trembled.

One huge stone slab rested in my way. I crouched to wrap arms across it, let my anger and fear spill their strength to my muscles as I straightened my legs and stood. I threw the stone aside. Heril lay beneath, ruddy of cheek, his blond hair dyed gray with dust. His eyes were closed, and though his face looked as if he were sleeping I knew he was dead. Where his chest had been there was nothing but a red ruin.

I cried out, "No!" staggered back, went to my knees. Rannon grabbed my shoulders, giving her own despairing cry as I fell forward onto my hands and vomited bile.

But our despair did not matter. Heril was still dead.

I got slowly to my feet. Kreeg and Valyan were being attended to. I knew they would live. Rannon slid her arms around me, tried to offer comfort. I clung for a moment, then pulled back. I did not want to hurt her but I had to get away. I shook my head when she protested.

"I have to...have to walk," I said. I turned, strode away, not looking back.

* * * * * * *

I was not accustomed to loss. Throughout my childhood on Earth I had been lucky. Unlike so many in those days, I had lost no brother, no sister, no parent. And though my sisters and parents were gone now, I had not even been on Earth when they died. I had not seen their bodies or attended their funerals. Their deaths, in a way, were not real to me. My last memories of them were living ones.

Since coming to Talera I *had* seen loss, my cousin—Eric Ryall—and a friend named Jedik, a swordsman who had taught me much of the skill with a blade that I had needed to survive on this world. But time and time again my best friends had escaped death. They'd been hurt. We'd all been hurt. But we'd held onto our lives while all around us others were losing theirs.

And now? If Heril could die, who was safe? Not Bryce, nor Kreeg, nor Valyan. Not even Rannon.

I walked, through streets where crowds eddied, past buildings where fires still burned. The air patrols had finally shown up and the moonlit sky swarmed with ships and saddle birds. I was too empty to feel those scenes. At last I found a place beneath a bridge over a canal and sat, my sword stabbed into the moist, crumbly soil beside me, my soul as gray as hearth's ashes.

Hours had passed and the sun was on its way. In the growing light, a small beast, a lart, came from hiding to make a last meal of the night on a dead fish beside the water. The lart is much like a tailless rat, though with webbed toes and fur that grows in thick clumps between patches of bare, scaly skin. This one did not notice me where I sat still, and I watched it feed, my mind like quicksand through which the thoughts slipped quickly.

How could one live knowing that death was ever close? How could one love when that love might be torn away in an instant? How could one build amid the wreckage of what others had built and failed to keep?

There were no answers to such questions. No cure, I thought, for such despair. And so I watched the lart with a void behind my eyes. And after a bit I saw the fur under the beast's belly stir, and saw tiny pink eyes and tiny snouts of black peek out. The creature had babies, and even as I thought it a small one let go of its mother's fur and dropped with a plop to the mushy earth. It waddled toward me, its nose seeking, its burgeoning whiskers testing at the air. It did not yet know that I existed in its world.

The mother finished with her banquet of half-rotted fish and turned away, moving back toward the hole through which she had come up from the sewers. Her other young still clung to her belly fur and she did not miss the lost one that was working its way closer and closer to me.

I made a sound in my throat, a tst, tst, tst that spun the mother lart in her tracks as her sharp ears locked in on my location. She crouched, her neck fur feathering as her beady eyes looked me over. Larts and humans don't get along. This one was surely old enough to have had boys shy rocks at her, if not more deadly weapons. To her I must have loomed as a pale giant, a dangerous beast big enough to tear her apart in one bite.

Then her baby, the one lost and wandering scant inches now from my boot, gave a little cry. The mother froze, crouching further, then sniffed rapidly along her belly. She looked up, her eyes and nose searching. The baby cried again, realizing now that it *was* lost, that it wanted its mother. And she came for it. She came slowly, inch by inch, her eyes on me, every muscle tensed in her small, lithe body. She came; she took the baby in her mouth; she carried it away.

I thought, perhaps, that I would never use the name lart as an insult again.

And at dawn I went home to Rannon.

CHAPTER SIX

CLOUDS OF WAR

War!

The word ran wild through the streets and alleys of Timmuzz, through the stalls of the merchants and the rooms of the inns, through the homes of the rich and the poor alike.

War with Revenor. For it had been airships from that country which had bombed our city. The vessel we'd brought down proved that.

And war, perhaps, with Ubai, allied to Revenor and, many assumed, the main enemy that we faced. That last was incorrect. I knew who our main enemy was. Vohanna! But I feared we'd have to go through both Revenor and Ubai to get her.

When I returned from my crisis of faith, I found Rannon practicing her own faith in the streets where she helped to put out fires and dig men and women and children from the rubble. Shamed, I joined her. And later I visited Kreeg and Valyan, both of whom lived, though Valyan remained without awareness. Ahrethane sat beside the Green Llurn's bed and I thanked her with the squeeze of a hand on her shoulder.

The last visit I made was to Heril's body, which had been laid to temporary rest with dozens of other victims in a cold chamber within the catacombs of the palace where many of them would soon be interred. For a long time I stood there beside the slab on which Heril lay, but in the end I could find nothing of importance within the emptied husk that I gazed upon.

"Heril," I murmured to the chill air. "I've called you

friend and that will not change. I will remember."

I turned then and carried my memories of a living friend up the stairs into the castle proper. Afternoon had come and the fires had finally lost their war on Timmuzz. A sharp breeze had risen to shred the clouds of smoke and let spill the rose light of the autumn sun.

I sought Rannon, found her in her apartment sitting streaked with soot and sweat and exhaustion. But when I kissed her it seemed to me that her tiredness was more than just physical. I had told her, of course, about Vohanna being alive, but I thought something else was troubling her now. My eyes questioned. She answered with a sigh.

"Horlis Kazhian has been arrested."

"Kazhian! Why?"

"*Someone* ordered our patrol flyers to investigate a disturbance upriver. There was no such disturbance. But it got the airships out of the city. No one seems able to say exactly *who* gave the order, which is strange in itself. But...."

"Kazhian commands the fleet so the ultimate responsibility is his," I finished for her.

"Exactly."

"Do *you* think Kazhian could have given that order? You've known him a lot longer than I have."

Rannon shrugged. "I can't believe *anyone* in our government could be involved. Yet, someone is. So I find that I must suspect everyone. As does my father. We have a traitor in our midst. Perhaps more than one. They *will* be rooted out."

I gazed at Rannon in startlement. She sounded so much like her father, and I could not remember her ever speaking so harshly before. But then she stepped forward to stroke my cheek.

"Of course that suspicion does not extend to you, my love," she said. "*You* I shall never doubt again."

I kissed her. "Thank you," I said.

She smiled, moved closer into my arms with her head tilted up for more kisses, but at that moment the bells of the city pealed out in brassy song and we both jumped.

I frowned. "It can't be tolling the fourteenth dhorr yet."

Rannon drew back from me, her face twisted with sudden concern.

"It's not. That's a call signal. There's going to be an announcement. I have to find my father."

"Of course," I said, moving to join her even as a knock bammed on the door.

Soldiers awaited us in the corridor. They had no idea either what announcement was to be made but had been sent to fetch us by Hurnan Jystral.

The emperor was pacing within his day-room in the palace when we arrived. In his hand he held a fold of paper that I suspected of being responsible for the bright red anger in his face. He turned to us, started to speak, but at that moment Kuurus, who was already present, interrupted.

"The crowds assemble, father."

Hurnan's mouth snapped shut over the words he'd been about to utter. He reached to grasp Rannon's shoulder and I saw her wince at the strength in that grip.

She grabbed his arm. "Father? What?"

"Listen," he said, his voice torn.

He pulled away from her, turned and strode from the room onto the balcony. We followed. Kuurus, and then Rannon, and then I. There were others present—Rajan Critus, Taskin Bhent—but I watched only Hurnan Jystral.

Jystral castle was shaped like a wheel, and the emperor's quarters lay along the first spoke of that wheel. Just below where we stood was a small courtyard and the outer wall of the palace complex over which could be seen a great cathedral square where thousands could gather. And had.

I heard the throngs shout as they saw their emperor, saw them quieten as he raised a palm. His other hand grasped the balcony's copper-lined rail, the fingers clenched to bloodlessness. From everywhere within the city the people had gathered. They were a sea with tributaries feeding in from the wide avenues beyond the square.

"Friends!" Jystral shouted.

His voice carried well and firmly, echoing off the public buildings that cornered the square and parted the waters of humanity. And in all that mass of frozen color there came no sound. Even the remnants of the smoke seemed stilled within the reddish-bronze sky.

"Friends!" the emperor called again. "You know that I have seen war. I had hoped never to see it again. But that hope is not to be. This morning, our people, our city, our land, came under attack without provocation by cowards who deliberately targeted the innocent."

And now there *was* a sound from the throng, a restless murmuring that began to bubble and roil. Jystral quelled it by lowering his upraised hand and grasping the hilt of the great silver sword that hung at his belt.

"There can be no peace," he continued, "with those who would gleefully cut our sleeping throats. Whether we will it or not, war has come. And yet...I *will it*!"

The crowd surged forward at these words. The murmur became a roar that lifted, crested, and then broke as Jystral stood before them in stillness.

"I will it because there must be justice for blood!" the emperor shouted. "I will it because our enemies think we are weak when I know we are strong!"

And now there were individually recognizable shouts among the people, questions that asked: "Who...? When...?"

Jystral drew his sword, that great flaming brand of shining steel that he'd carried ever since I'd first met him aboard an airship above the island of the Klar slavers. He rested the blade's point on the stone of the balcony railing, wrapped both fists around the hilt, and leaned forward.

"I will tell you the who and the when," he said. "Give listen. It was Revenor airships that attacked us in the night. This you all know. But there is more. A message was delivered to me moments ago. A note from the city of Teleur, our port on the coast. My birthplace. At dawn, a Ubain fleet, with Revenor air support, overwhelmed our harbor defenses and stormed the city. Troops were landed. Resistance still rages. But Teleur is burning."

While Jystral had spoken a well-deep silence had built within the crowd. But now the square erupted in cries of grief, outrage, and terror. Beside me, Rannon had tears in her eyes, her hands pressed to her mouth. I squeezed her shoulders, my own eyes hot.

Hurnan let the sound from below build, let it grow and swell until it seemed to shiver the very air. Then he lifted one

49

hand for quiet. He got it.

His voice when it came seemed scarcely above a whisper. Yet it carried and the people of Timmuzz hung upon every syllable.

"Before evening I and my son leave for the coast. A counterattack will follow. But you must know that there will be no quick end to this conflict. You must gird yourself for battle. Merchants. Farmers. Craftsmen. All of us. We must all become soldiers. We in Nyshphal have won wars before. More wars than we might like to remember."

Jystral held up his sword, let the dying sunlight strike it and flash like rose-colored flame along it. Then he sheathed the blade at his hip, and he shouted, his voice whipping like a martial flag in the breeze:

"We will win again!"

He turned then, and stalked from his balcony back into his room. The rest of us followed. While outside in the streets of Timmuzz, a slumbering dragon awoke with a many-throated growl and spread its talons for war.

CHAPTER SEVEN

ARROW THE MAD SKY

On the evening of the first day after war came to Tim-muzz, the sky navy of Nyshphal left for the coast with banners flying and battle shields proudly displayed. It made a brave sight against the scarlet flush of fading day, the great sails bellied blue with wind, the smaller flyers circling like gnats around the huge galleons.

Only someone who had seen the fleet before the war with Vohanna would know how diminished it was. I was such a person, and it hurt me now to know the losses we had suffered. But still, Hurnan Jystral's flagship was there, gray hulled with the image of the trenkil, the Taleran eagle, emblazoned in dark maroon beneath its prow. And, loaded with soldiers, there were many other ships, their martial histories written in symbols of blood and glory on their shields and flags. If a war could be won, then it seemed to me that such a fleet would win it.

I, too, left Timmuzz after the city was raided, but I did not sail with the navy. On the morning after the fleet departed, a single ship flew north under brightening skies, headed away from the coast and toward the jungle of Vohan where once a lost city had hidden and where now there were rumors of a wild gate that might be tied to our enemy.

The ship was called the *Aestor II*, and it was Rannon's ship, as slim and white as its mistress, and powered by crystalline wands charged from the toir'in-or stones rather than by the sails that drove the much bigger warships of the Nyshphalian navy. I well remembered the first ship to bear the name *Aestor*. It had been shot down amid the opening salvos of the recent war with Vohanna.

This new ship was better armed and armored. Its builders had even applied what they'd learned from studying the wrecks of the steam-powered airships that Vohanna had once hoped to use against us. From that knowledge had come propeller systems that gave us both greater control and greater speed.

Though all Nyshphalian flyers are provided with lift through the use of the toir'in-or power stones by a carefully trained caste of pilots, small vessels like the *Aestor* have traditionally gotten both lift *and* drive from a pilot's mental manipulations of a stone's matrix. In a craft like this one, a pilot would have to concentrate intensely to keep the flow of power smooth at the transition point between the wands and the propeller. The new drive systems had eased the pilot's burden, allowing changes in speed and direction to be managed strictly by mechanical means.

Rannon accompanied me aboard her ship, of course. Her father had originally planned for her to command in Timmuzz while he and Kuurus went to the coast. She'd convinced him otherwise and he'd left Rajan Critus in charge in the city instead. There was little Hurnan Jystral had ever been able to deny his daughter.

Besides Rannon and myself, there were twenty-four others aboard the *Aestor*. One was the pilot. Twenty were Rannon's Gray-Cloaks, her elite bodyguards. These were commanded by Rhandh, the tall Vlih warrior who even now bore the kossett, the five blade array that his race wears when battle is nigh. Two blades were fitted to the tentacles that grow midway between a Vlih's hips and arms. The hilts of two others stabbed up from his boots. The last was a dagger lashed to a prehensile tail. Only Rhandh's hands were empty, though swords for those hung at his belt.

The remaining two members of our party were Bryce and Ahrethane. I had not wanted Bryce to come. In truth, I feared what might happen to him as we got closer to a possible link with Vohanna. I did not want to see him possessed again; I did not want to have to kill him.

Ahrethane was a different matter. I was glad she was

with us, glad to see her slender, elfin frame at the *Aestor*'s prow as half a day of flying brought us to the rich green sea of the Vohan jungle.

The presence of a jungle here had always intrigued me. Nyshphal lies mostly in a temperate clime. Its forests are filled with hardwoods and evergreens, with vast prairies between that roll on for verlang after verlang of tall grasses and wild flowers. A jungle was as out of place here as a rose garden in a dune-field.

It had occurred to me once that Vohanna's sorcery was what kept this jungle growing. But now, gazing from the corner of an eye at the fire-tressed Ahrethane, I thought, perhaps, that it was she who gave life to this tangled wood. The rainbow plumaged birds. The gorgeous blooms that caressed the air with scent. The shy creatures who peered furtively from within the canopy. All these, I felt in that moment, were part of Ahrethane, connected to her by skeins of love and magic.

The pilot slowed our craft as we arrived above the site in the jungle where six months ago Vohanna's great sky pyramid had crashed to earth. None of us were exactly sure what we were looking for, but I'd figured the best place to start was with a dead past that didn't seem to want to stay dead.

Huge chunks of black stone lay strewn among the shattered trees below us, and here and there were raw gouges where the red earth had been slashed open to show the clay body beneath. But the jungle was already reclaiming its own. New growth lifted riotous fingers toward the sun, the general green patched here and there by brilliant explosions of flowers. Vines wove themselves everywhere.

More than the jungle, I watched Bryce. He and I were at the prow, with Ahrethane and Rannon and Rhandh. I wondered how the crash site would affect my brother? *If* it did. Did Vohanna's influence linger here? Would I see it in Bryce's eyes? Perhaps with a red gleam swirling in their depths?

But Bryce stood quietly, his artificial hand gripping the *Aestor*'s rail, his human one resting on the basket hilt of a rapier. I relaxed, a little.

From somewhere near the stern came a scream that

seemed to tear the throat from the air. I spun around.

"By Sevarian!" Rannon shouted beside me.

I heard Rhandh grunt, heard Ahrethane gasp. I heard a vast thrumming sound. Above the aft deck of the ship, holding a man before it in praying mantis talons, a monster hovered on blurring wings, an insect nearly as big as the biggest of the Taleran saddle birds.

The captive guard screamed again, writhing, and the creature, some chimera of mantis and wasp and dragonfly, punched him in the back with its abdomen. In a froth of bright blood, a stinger as big as a rhino's horn erupted through the man's chest. The man gurgled, his eyes wide, his head falling forward then on a neck from which all strength had fled.

Rannon cried out, "No!"

I leaped forward, shouting for archers, shouting in hopes someone would break through their shock and react. The mantis-wasp was hornet-striped in blacks and reds. Its wings flickered as it backed away from the ship's rail, dragging its human prey with it. There had been other guards around the one who'd been struck. They drew their weapons now, rushed forward. The chimera backed farther away, out of range of their blades.

I reached the port side ballista, a war-machine that could hurl five steel-tipped bolts upward of four hundred yards. The original *Aestor* had carried only two such weapons. There were six aboard this ship.

I grabbed the ballista's handles, spun it toward the monster and jerked the lanyard back to fire it. The mechanism released with a sound like a bellow's breath. Three of the bolts, each weighing nearly four pounds, impacted the creature just above the limbs that held the dead guard. They nearly tore the thing in half. It dropped away; men cheered.

The cheers failed an instant later as the very air seemed to come alive and a dozen and more of the chimeras lifted on whirring wings over the rails of the ship. Our pilot had started to take the *Aestor* higher but now we were hemmed in with nowhere to turn. We'd have to fight. I cranked the handle to reload the ballista, but the things pounced upon the guards before I could fire, talons grasping, stingers thrusting.

Men went down, stabbing, stabbing, but sword-steel did little against the moist, heavy bodies of the monsters. The talons and stingers of the insects did much, crunching through muscle and bone with equal ease, birthing raw screams from dying throats.

I loosed the ballista again. Razor-edged bolts obliterated one mantis-wasp's head, tore off the wing of another. The wounded beast crashed to the deck, thrashing madly, its mandibles clacking, snapping closed on the leg of a guard and shearing through in a splatter of blood that came with shrieks of pain.

Suddenly, Rannon was beside me, a short horn-bow in her slender hands. She drew and released, punching a tlatel-wood shaft into the compound eye of the wounded chimera. The thing shuddered to stillness, and now more arrows were slashing into the mantis-wasps, spackling the decks with black ichor from where three foot shafts pierced swollen bodies.

Rhandh reached a second ballista, Bryce a third. They fired together into a cluster of monsters tearing at a make-shift fort of barrels that some of Rannon's Gray-Cloaks had thrown up for defense. Bolts tipped with heavy steel sleeted into the crush of insect forms, cutting away limbs and heads and wings, sending wounded beasts tumbling to deck. Immediately the Gray-Cloaks rose from their positions, heavy bows to hand, firing, firing, pinning squirming chimeras to the oaken planks.

A huge mantis-wasp with the white slash of an old wound across its nearly black head leaped toward me, wings beating at the air. With no time to reload the ballista, I dropped the handles and grabbed for my sword. Rannon fired her bow at point-blank range. The arrow disappeared into the creature's thorax but didn't even slow it as it swarmed over me.

The creature dipped its head, mandibles clacking, barbed claws hooking. I brought my sword slashing up, hacking off the business end of one deadly talon. My free hand caught the thing's other mantis-like limb, held it for the moment, the feel of it more like cool wood than warm flesh. At the same time I punched the thing in the mouth with the sword's hilt.

Its jaws clashed shut an inch from my face, spattering droplets of dead man's gore all over me.

I heard Rannon screaming my name, heard the shnnkk of another arrow plunging into the wasp-thing's body. My feet kicked out desperately to keep away the stinger on the thing's abdomen as it stabbed and stabbed at my legs, its vicious tip clattering off the plankings of the deck.

The insectile mouth worked, the feelers wriggling like worms over my hand as they tried to gain purchase around the sword's hilt. But the curved sickles of the mandibles couldn't close tightly enough around the bar of the steel blade to cut off my arm. That couldn't last. The thing was too strong.

Again and again the monster lunged against me, battering me against the deck. I couldn't get it off, couldn't get it off. The lashing stinger sprayed yellow venom as it tore off my left boot-heel; a talon-barb scored a comet's tail of fire down my cheek. I began to panic as the clacking mandibles drew closer and closer, the rotted stench from the gnashing mouth purling over me, making me gag.

Then an explosion of stinking black fluid bucketed me and the lower part of the insect's body fell away from the head to writhe madly on the planks. I saw Rannon standing above me, panting in her stained leathers, a sword in her hand that dribbled a dark rheum.

She'd hacked through the creature's thorax, but still the mandibles clashed, still the feelers worked. I shoved madly from below, and Bryce arrived at just that moment to grasp the beast's antennae and drag the detached head away. With a grunt of revulsion he hurled it across the deck.

I sat up, gasping, tasting a bitter ichor in my mouth. Rannon and Bryce each took one of my shoulders and helped me to stand.

"It's over," my brother said. "We've run them off."

I glanced around. Insect bodies and parts of bodies were strewn across the deck of the ship like flotsam after a storm. But the black blood of the monsters was mixed with the crimson of human gore, and there were dead ones on our side as well.

"I hope you're right, Bryce," I said. "Yet—"

I had no time to finish before the ship suddenly rocked beneath us and a huge screech rent the air. We spun together, to see at the prow, what had to be the insect queen.

CHAPTER EIGHT

JUNGLE QUEEN

Just above the *Aestor*'s prow, the insect queen hovered on six sets of blurring wings. She was better than half the size of the ship, painted like some alien goddess in burnished strips of gold and silver. Her mandibles were big enough to scythe an ox in two; she shrieked with a sound like ice floes grating together.

Our pilot tried to reverse the propellers, to back us away. Front talons the size of saplings grasped the ship's rail, jerked us to a halt, rocking the deck back and forth so that all of us staggered.

Rannon grabbed me; we fell to our knees. Men screamed as they were knocked off their feet or tossed over the side of the ship into the trees below. I saw Bryce hanging on desperately to the ballista to keep from being thrown down. Beside him swayed Ahrethane, still standing somehow. She was gesturing, her fingers scoring runes of color into the crisp autumn air. Those runes sizzled, like bacon fat frying.

The queen whapped the bottom of the ship with her swollen abdomen—once, twice, a third time. Planks crunched; the whole vessel jarred savagely. Another of Rannon's Gray-Cloaks lost his grip and was flung over the rail with a scream. I hoped he would live. We were only thirty feet in the air but hitting the trees or the ground from that height could still snap a man's bones. Or his neck.

"The ballista," I shouted at Bryce.

My brother tried, grasping the handles of the weapon,

pulling it around. But a sudden wild lurch of the deck as the queen tore loose part of the front railing broke Bryce's grip and sent him sliding away.

I started to let go of Rannon, to make a dive for the ballista myself, and just then Ahrethane shouted, her voice like a whip. How she was still standing I did not know, but with a quick thrust she shoved her hands out in front of her, palms open. A wave of air went rushing past, nearly dragging me along behind it. Rannon saved me with a grab to my belt.

The insect queen shrieked again as the efrinore-called wind struck her. And she released the *Aestor* abruptly, backing up. The ship righted itself so suddenly that I was nearly thrown over the side. For a second time Rannon's death lock on my leathers saved me.

Ahrethane's hands were moving again, fingers weaving with light. For a moment I thought I saw a hammer forming in the air. Then I threw myself away from Rannon toward the ballista. I reached that weapon at the same moment as Rhandh did. I didn't know where he had come from, but we worked together to crank the elevation down and fire.

The four heavy arrows whickered free of their oaken beds, but it was as if the queen sensed them coming. She seemed almost to leap higher into the air over the slashing bolts. For a moment she hovered. The ship started again into reverse but we were far too slow. The monstrous insect dove in attack.

Rannon was upright now, legs braced wide against the movement of the ship, her bow snapping out shaft after shaft. Each of those arrows struck the queen but they were naught but pinpricks to a whale. The creature's dive forced Rannon to the deck, but Ahrethane was the true target. I grabbed the efrinore woman and dragged her down an instant before razor-clawed talons slashed open the space where she'd been.

More men were running forward with bows now. The insect queen lashed at them with her abdomen, sending them rolling. Ahrethane was fighting me, struggling to pull free, shouting at me to let her go. I released her and, from still flat on her back, her hands came up and...pushed against the air as the queen dropped toward us on sonic wings. A wave of heat blistered the breath from my mouth and the queen stopped as if she'd hit a glass wall.

Instantly, Ahrethane began to chant again, her words brittle, snapped off short and hard. Her fingers seined the air. Colors leaped up and I swore I saw the shape of a net form within those hues. The queen fought as the net engulfed her, hissing, talons lashing. But more and more tethers of light whipped around and around the bloated body, seizing her tight.

Rhandh had grabbed up a bow that some guard had dropped, was pouring arrows rapid fire into the beast at close range. Bryce joined him. I rolled toward the ballista, determined to finish the creature off while Ahrethane held it in sorcerous bonds. But by accident or design, a stray swipe of the queen's abdomen struck the weapon, smashing it from its moorings on the deck and spilling steel tipped bolts like toothpicks across the planks.

For a moment, while the monster twisted and writhed above me in its attempts to free itself, I glimpsed something strange beneath and behind its jaws. There, at the base of its mouth, was an oval surface, dark and polished like a blackened window. And through that window I saw motion, a seething of weird tendrils and shapes.

Only for an instant did I glimpse those shapes. Then talons lashed down at me and I rolled from beneath the queen's belly to comparative safety, my hand clutching a ballista bolt that I dragged along for a weapon. It was barely three feet long but I could use it as a spear.

Ahrethane had made it to her knees but a glance told me she was tiring. I stabbed my makeshift lance into the outside of the monster's jaw, leaped back as the massive head lashed from side to side. Rannon and the others pressed in, firing with their bows; I stabbed again with my spear. But nothing seemed to hurt it except magic.

The queen began pulling back, and back, stretching the tendrils of light that bound her. Ahrethane cried out with strain. She was losing her hold on the creature.

Then once more I glimpsed the strange, moving shapes and tendrils that I'd seen beneath the giant insect's head. This time they were located between and behind the thing's black on gold compound eyes. There was some kind of liquid there. And some...thing squirmed within the liquid.

"Shoot *between* the eyes!" I shouted to Rannon. "Behind them! Something there!"

Rannon heard, drew and released as fast as my words could register. The eyes of the beast were already pincushioned with darts, but this time the arrow slashed between and just above those alien orbs, cutting deep into a soft dome of globular flesh that we'd previously ignored. A spurt of some pinkish elixir sprayed from the point of impact, and the monster queen shuddered all over.

"Again!" I shouted. But Rannon was already drawing, and loosing. Bryce and Rhandh added their fire to hers, the arrows sleeting into the creature, hacking open a gap in the dome of its head through which strawberry fluid began to gush.

The queen seemed caught by a sudden epileptic tremor. A mad writhing filled the dome behind her eyes. With a growl, I leaped forward, bringing the ballista bolt up like a spear and hurling it toward where the squirmings were thickest. Through the gap slashed open by arrows that lance flew. And struck.

An inhuman shriek split our ears, and the queen's massive bulk spasmed, spasmed again, then came crashing to the deck. I had an instant to grab Ahrethane and drag her clear before the monster hit, its abdomen lashing the *Aestor*'s cabin to splinters, crushing the pilot who worked from within a glass enclosure inside that cabin. The whirr of the propellers ceased. The ship dropped beneath us.

There was no time even for a shout before we smashed to earth in an explosion of dirt and splintering wood. I lay stunned, the breath driven from my lungs. Motes of dust swirled redly in the autumn sunlight. The world seemed silent in wake of the crash; all I could hear was the rasping of my throat as it worked for air.

Eventually, I caught a breath. Then two. And the natural sounds of Talera began filtering back into my ears, the rustle of leaves and grass, the raucous cries of birds griping at us from the jungle canopy all around.

Groaning, I rolled over, pushed up to my hands and knees. We'd come down between several huge blocks of black stone left over from the wreck of Vohanna's pyramid half a year ago. Vines already nearly covered them.

"Ruenn?"

My gaze found the source of the voice. It was Rannon. Her eyes were open and I smiled when she sat up. She still held her bow, though now it was broken into two halves. I crawled over to her and we helped each other to stand.

We were still on the *Aestor*'s deck, though the impact had buckled and warped it until it resembled a wrinkled carpet. I couldn't see Ahrethane or any of the others and was about to move off in search of them when Rannon grasped my arm hard.

"Look," she said, pointing to the insect queen where she lay only a few feet from us.

I turned. A chill ridged my flesh with goose bumps. The head of the monster had split completely open and I could see now what the strange writhing shape inside that head had been. It was a human female. Or a nearly human one. She had no arms or legs, only masses of snaky cables, gray and coiled like intestines, that linked her to the inner workings of the giant insect body.

The skull of the woman, too, was not quite human. It was domed at the back and pierced with hundreds of small silver sockets from which black wires grew that connected her to the monster around her. But the breasts between which my thrown lance had struck seemed human enough, and the blood that ran from that awful wound was red.

The union of the strange with the familiar was repulsive and I gagged. Beside me, Rannon wiped her own mouth again and again as if to keep from throwing up herself.

"What is it?" she asked finally. "What in Sevarian's name is it?"

"Something like a machine," I said. "A living machine. She...." I shook my head and spat. "That...thing was somehow controlling the queen insect's body."

"It's an abomination," Rannon said, her voice thick with disgust.

"Yes," I agreed.

Almost without thought, I reached down and picked up another of the heavy ballista bolts that were scattered on the broken deck. My hands twisted around the three-foot haft; the steel head glittered.

"Yes," I said again, as I half lifted my stubby spear.

"It is a Kurshan," someone said from behind us.

I turned to see Ahrethane. She looked paler than usual and leaned exhaustedly on Bryce. Rhandh and a few of the other Gray-Cloaks were behind them, one holding a broken arm, another limping on a twisted ankle. I was glad to see my brother and the rest alive. There were few enough of us left, it seemed.

"And what are Kurshan?" I asked.

Ahrethane's gaze slipped past me to linger on the monster at my feet. Her thoughts seemed distant and I wondered if she were thinking of *her* brother, the one she'd once told me about, the brother she'd been unable to save from the Witch Vohanna.

"Experiments," she finally said in answer to my question. "Vohanna's experiments. The melding of beast and human and machine. Of intelligence with savagery. Either grown in her vats or spliced together through surgery. You were her prisoner for a time in the black pyramid. Surely you saw such beings there?"

I thought then of what I'd called "hybrids," the unholy combinations of animal, insect, and intelligent beings that Vohanna had used for her personal guard when I'd confronted her in her lair. I had not known to name them "Kurshan."

"Aye," I spat. "I saw more than I wanted to see of the grotesque obscenities that Vohanna cobbled together from spare parts in her laboratories."

My words came without thinking, with Bryce standing right there beside Ahrethane. And instantly I wished for those words back as I saw the stricken look that crossed my brother's face, as I saw him clench the false right hand that was also a legacy and an experiment of Vohanna's.

I opened my mouth to apologize but Bryce turned away and strode to the rail. And Ahrethane put up a hand to stop me when I would have followed. Her eyes seemed to accuse me, but her voice was soft when she said:

"What ails him now cannot be fixed with a brother's

love. I'll...speak to him." She turned to follow Bryce, and I sighed, feeling sick and angry with myself.

Rannon came up beside me and squeezed my hand. It didn't help. I'd been doing too many things of late that I'd needed to apologize to Bryce for. It was time I *stopped* doing them.

Rhandh joined us, his broad, dark hand resting on the pommel of his sword. "Your brother will be all—" he began. Then: "Dahh!" he cried out, his hand dragging free his blade as he gave an involuntary leap backward.

I spun. The half woman, the Kurshan, had opened her eyes, and those orbs were a limpid and crystalline scarlet with golden viper slits for pupils. In revulsion I lifted my ballista-bolt spear, my hands bloodlessly tight around the shaft.

But I could not strike.

The woman/thing gazed up at me, her hell-kite eyes filled with promises and decay. She arched her upper body toward me, pushing her full and very human breasts against the lance that pinned her.

Bile burst into my mouth and I stepped back, dropping the ballista bolt to the deck. Rannon had drawn her sword. But neither could she strike. I took her arm.

Out of nowhere came Bryce, leaping past me, his voice raised in an inarticulate shout. He grabbed up the bolt I'd dropped and lunged forward to drive it straight through the naked throat of the Kurshan. For a long moment he seemed to hang there, then drew back, the lance quivering, its head buried through flesh and six inches into the decking beneath.

The woman/thing smiled, blood the color and consistency of cooked raspberries foaming from her mouth. Bryce stood above her, fists clenched, his breathing harsh, irregular. I stepped forward but there was nothing I could do.

Ahrethane called from somewhere behind us. "Get back!"

I scarcely heard her. I reached for Bryce's shoulder. He pulled away, moaning.

"Get back now!" Ahrethane shouted.

This time I heard clearly and looked up. The remaining Gray-Cloaks were milling about, looking confused, but

Ahrethane had grabbed one of Rannon's arms and Rhandh had taken the other. They were pulling her with them as they backed away down the deck.

My love's eyes were on mine. "Run!" she shouted, even as she struggled to free herself from the hands that held her.

I turned toward Bryce, unable to understand what was going on. Beyond my brother lay the Kurshan, its body writhing in the final throes of death, and even as I watched, the creature gave a last shudder and fell limp.

At the same moment there came a blooming, tearing sound that rattled in the trees. And along with the sound came the sight of the insect queen's abdomen splitting open to spill a wriggling mass of white forms down onto the deck. Those forms looked like scorpions but were much larger. Much, much larger.

At least as big as wolves.

"The larva!" Ahrethane shouted. "Run!"

I grabbed my brother's shoulders, my heart lurching. He slung me off, drew his sword. I heard him scream the name "Vohanna" as his steel flashed, catching the autumn sun and bursting into gleaming fire.

Again I grabbed him, as the roiling mass of the larva swarmed toward us over the broken husk of their mother's body. He fought but I got my arms hooked under his and practically threw him over the rail of the ship. Then I froze.

It was only a few feet from the *Aestor*'s ruined deck to the soft loam of the forest soil. But Bryce's feet never reached that soil. In that heartbeat of time, while my brother hung like a flag in the air, a snarling white void opened...and took him.

I gaped. *The wild gate!* The gate we'd come to this jungle seeking had instead found us. Or found Bryce. And for just another moment it swirled below me, filled with an opalescent mist that arced with sparks of blue.

From all around came the skittering, hissing, rush of the insect queen's larva closing in. And at the raw edge of the jungle I could see Rannon and the others. Rhandh held my love, held her tight even though she screamed at him to let her go and struggled violently to break free. I knew he would keep her safe.

Below me, the wild gate swirled like a maelstrom. In another second it would close.

I threw myself after my brother into the abyss.

CHAPTER NINE

THE WILD GATE

I had been through sphere gates before. I remembered the glacial cold and the feeling as if I'd been turned inside out. I remembered the blackness and pain.

This was different. It was bright instead of dark, and stifling with heat. And here the sound of the void did not roar. It beat, beat, beat. Like some mammoth heart.

Only the pain was familiar, wrenching at me from all sides as if I were a ship buffeted madly by warring currents. I think I screamed. Then brightness dimmed.

And movement became stasis.

The world paused. Always before, the transition through a sphere gate had been nearly instantaneous, a matter of fractions of seconds. But now we seemed to hang...between. I say "we" because Bryce was standing there with me, caught in a void of white mist that had frozen to perfect stillness. Only directly in front of me was there anything to break the monotony of the pale. It was like an oval window without glass, about man-sized, and through it I saw—

My heart thumped. I grabbed Bryce's elbow hard enough to hurt, but he didn't wince or try to jerk free. He seemed dazed. But was that a leftover from his insane rage of moments before or did it mean that he was seeing now what I saw?

Looking out through the "window" was like looking out through the door of some temple pyramid. Stairs of ivory led down and down, each step fitted together from human skulls with the eye sockets staring upward to heaven. From the foot of the stairs ran a straight black road, with slender, stone columns of gold marching along beside the road toward the horizon. On each of the columns there hung the crucified body of a winged human.

But, horrific as the skulls and bodies were, what truly sowed my mind with fear was the sight of what was lifting over the near horizon into the blood red sky. It was Talera. The *planet* of Talera.

My universe slid drunkenly. My stomach fluttered like a loose sail in the wind. I wanted to punch something and keep on punching until everything was hammered back into some semblance of normalcy. But the only thing here I could even touch was my brother.

"Bryce!" I said. "Bryce! Do you see?"

My brother's voice was distant when it came. Flat and hollow. And when I looked at him his eyes seemed to have cleared of anger and filled instead with something I could not name.

"I see it, Ruenn," he said. "We're no longer on Talera."

"But where? One of the moons maybe?" I could hear my words racing, feel the tension crackling in my voice.

Bryce shrugged.

"But the gate didn't open completely at this end," I rushed on. "What the hell are we supposed to do now?"

I started to reach toward that oval of clear space before me. And as if movement were a trigger, the "window" irised closed and the gate took us fully again, whirling us away into pain and acid white mist, into the booming sound of a vast heart beating.

I tried to reach for Bryce in the wildness but almost instantly the gate froze again with us still trapped inside. Only the view through our window had changed. This time it showed huge, churning banks of purple clouds torn with the ruddy fire of streaking meteors. Lightning bolts the size of rivers sizzled the ozone, and I gaped in awe as between the lightning and the meteors came riders on steeds that resembled nothing so much as animate zeppelins.

The riders were clad entirely in armor of glowing blue and stood upon the backs of their huge mounts, reins in one hand and in the other long whips that dripped with sparks of pearl flame. I did not like those whips, or the speed with which the riders approached, but before they could reach us the gate closed again...and opened on a world where black and crimson ships clashed in smoke and blood on a great sea of ice.

Barely had I time to register this new scene before the gate whirled us away once more. In quick succession I caught glimpses of a dozen worlds, of watery wastes and of lands that bubbled with sulphureous mud, of worlds where oceans of mercury burned and brazen skies flowed like liquid. And always there was war and warriors, men...and far stranger beings, fighting, dying, shrieking in madness and fear.

The gate was not going to stop. Faster and faster the windows opened and closed, pinning us in our cosmic cage. I could think of only one way to free ourselves. One very dangerous way. At the precise moment when our window opened its narrow face we would have to throw ourselves through it. There'd be no time to look and see whether the world was suitable, whether it was even livable for humans. By the time our minds registered the answers to those questions the chance would be gone.

I groped in the blinding whiteness for Bryce's hand. I found it, and tried to explain in shouts what we had to do. I think he understood. Or perhaps he did not care if he lived or died, if he leaped from this prison into paradise or suicide. I *did* care, but I didn't intend for us to spend the rest of our lives trapped like wasps in amber.

Counting, I marked the quicksilver intervals between the openings of our window, and an instant before it was to open again I shouted "now" to Bryce and hurled myself forward with my brother's hand in mine.

CHAPTER TEN

THE VAST AND THE BLACK

To break free of the wild gate was like being born. From out of a womb we were thrown into a world. From out of warmth we were cast into cold. The window opened as we expected, just as Bryce and I hurled ourselves forward. We struck some sort of membrane that clung, then tore through into a burst of light that daggered my eyes.

I cried out, lost my grip on Bryce's wrist. An instant later I slammed into the ground with numbing force. Clouds of frozen crystals whirled up and settled again, and when I staggered to my feet I saw that it was snow—blue snow that stretched out around me on a flat and nearly featureless plain.

There was no war here, though I had expected it after what I'd seen through the window of the wild gate. Alone of the places we'd visited, this one seemed at peace.

I shaded my eyes against a brutal luminosity, a luminosity that blazed down from a distant sun of furnace white and reflected blindingly from the vast frozen fields. And across those fields a hard and ceaseless wind hurried, stabbing me with razor sharp spicules of ice torn up from the crusted snow.

Maybe it was too cold to fight.

Of a sudden, I realized that there was no sign of my brother next to me.

"Bryce!" I called, my heart beating frantically now.

It was achingly cold.

I shouted for Bryce again, turning this way and that in

search. There was no opalescent doorway to mark the opening of the sphere gate. It must have moved on. And for a moment of stark terror I feared that Bryce had moved on with it, that he had been caught once more in the void.

I gritted my teeth. *No!* He'd been with me as we jumped. He had to be here, buried in the snow that drifted above my waist. I dropped to my hands and knees, began feeling around urgently. My left hand struck something bulky, something warm. It was Bryce. He moaned as I rolled him over.

I could see little of my brother through the piled up snow that cascaded steadily around us as I dug him free. I got my hands under his shoulders, tugged, trying to pull him to his feet.

At first he was dead weight, but in a moment he vented a louder moan and opened his eyes, then began pushing with his legs to help me lift him. Blood trickled from a cut to the left side of his forehead. I had no idea what he could have hit his head on in this wasteland of blue.

"Where the hell are we?" Bryce croaked, hooding his eyes against the glare and wind as he got his feet fully under him and looked around. He shook with cold.

"I don't know," I said, feeling my own body shivering. "Not Talera. Our weight. We're lighter here." I had to half shout to be heard over the rushing, terrible wind.

He nodded, hugging himself for warmth. We'd been dressed for Talera's autumn, in leather breeks of stugah hide and long-sleeved shirts woven from Nyshphalian grown cotton. They weren't made to fight the arctic winter that we now faced.

"We've got to find shelter," I shouted. "We'll freeze here. And it won't be slowly."

Again Bryce nodded, then pointed. "There's a dark line over there. Might be trees of some sort."

I looked where Bryce's finger led, saw the black blot of which he spoke, though it didn't look like any trees I'd ever seen. Still, there was nothing else in any direction except the rippled fields of snow across which the freezing wind howled.

I started off toward the "trees," forging my way through

the drifts with the cruel wind in my face. Bryce followed. Within moments I was gasping, black stars exploding through my vision as I struggled for breath. I stopped. Bryce came up beside me, face frowning with concern.

"The...air," I panted. "Not...right. It's...."

"Weak," he finished, nodding. "Not enough oxygen." He was breathing hard himself; the pulse of a fast heartbeat throbbed in the arteries of his neck.

"Let me," he added, pushing past me and striking out through the drifts. I followed, but in moments we had to switch places again as the toll of breaking through the crusted snow in this world's thin atmosphere exhausted Bryce as quickly as it had me.

At last we reached our goal, and I suppose it is right to use the name trees for what we found there. At least they were as tall as trees, though whip thin and with trunks that resembled leather more than wood.

Small polyps about the size and shape of a baby's fist bulged from the trees in place of limbs or leaves. But the trunks grew close together and for the first time we found ourselves out of the wind.

We could not escape the cold so easily. Already it had bitten deep within us. Bryce was shivering violently and both of us had chattering teeth.

"F...f...fire," Bryce managed.

I nodded. We had to try, though I was not at all sure these alien trees would burn. As a test, I plucked a half dozen of the polyps from one tree—they squished between my fingers like stewed mushroom caps—and made a small pile of them on the snow.

The Talerans have invented a little thing called a "striker." Or, some say they got it from the gods. It's a simple device really, just a small metal tube filled with rundal oil into which a wick is inserted. There's a cap over the device that contains an attached flint and a tiny metal spike. When you pop the lid open it drags the spike over the flint and sends sparks onto the wick. And you have fire, an important commodity on any world and one that might just save our lives now.

I flicked the striker open, held the flame to the small pile of crushed polyps. Oily, black smoke puffed up as an emerald flame raced across the pile. Bryce whooped in joy. I grinned.

Then the grin was ripped from my face and I threw myself backwards away from the smoke. A visage had formed within the swirling black, a visage with eyes gleaming darker than the smoke and with a mouth twisted in sadistic glee. A mocking, funereal laughter rang in the frigid air as the mouth opened to show Hell's flames scorching within.

I scrambled from the snow to my feet, drawing my sword. Bryce had already drawn his. We backed further away as the smoke twisted and corkscrewed, birthing arms and legs and long, sinuous hair. A human shape rose to stand there, sketched in a roiling blackness. It was a woman.

"Vohanna!" Bryce shouted.

"Witch!" I growled.

"How delicious to be remembered," Vohanna said, inclining her head in acknowledgement. "Especially by those of whom I am so fond."

Bryce shouted again, some wordless threat, and leaped forward to swing his sword down at Vohanna's neck. The steel slashed through the smoky shape, cutting the shadow head from the shadow body, sending tendrils of vapor swirling madly in the air.

More laughter boomed as the smoke-Vohanna instantly reformed and went spinning away over the snow like a dust devil. I grabbed Bryce, who would have run after her. His eyes bulged in his head; his throat was swollen, pulsing intensely with blood.

"No! Bryce! No! You can't hurt her. She's not really here."

Bryce struggled against me for a moment, went still, then slumped in on himself.

"It's only some kind of projection," I added, giving my words to Bryce while my gaze followed the Witch.

Vohanna paused in her spinning and laughing. From a dozen feet away her jet eyes stormed at us. Her shadowy lips seemed to pout.

"Unfortunately true," she said, sighing dramatically. "Though I *do* wish I could be here to share your misery. Or...

taste it at least."

I spat on the snow. "And I wish you were as dead as I thought you to be."

Again the Witch pouted, her lower lip protruding like that of a spoiled little girl who wasn't getting her way.

"How cruel, Ruenn," she said. "Do you speak so rough-ly to your sweet? To your...." She frowned as if in concentra-tion. "Your Rannon, isn't it? Or perhaps she likes it when you are mean to her. Do tell."

I snarled, my mouth twitching, my fist tightening on the hilt of my rapier. But from beside me at that instant came a tortured moan and I glanced in startlement at Bryce. He was not looking at me, not looking—I thought—at anything in this world. His eyes had gone a wintry grey and were marred with something akin to madness. I wondered what horrors he was reliving from his days with Vohanna.

Not wanting to lose my brother to his inner devils, I grabbed his shoulders and shook him. And he came back to awareness of this *time* and *this* place. His pupils focused on mine, his body jerking, then calming. He turned to look at Vohanna. He smiled, the lips curving back, cutting lines in his overly pale cheeks. For a moment the faint, faint coils of his facial tattoos glittered.

"I remember what you like, Vohanna," he whispered.

She chuckled, with the sound of chimes tinkling. "Oh, I imagine you do, Bryce," she answered. "I imagine you do."

Not liking the interchange between the two any better than I'd liked Bryce's lost look of moments before, I stepped forward, drawing the Witch's blackened gaze back to me.

"Someday, Vohanna. You'll find a death you won't be able to weasel out of. I'll make sure of it."

The smoky form of the Witch's projection swirled a lit-tle closer, leaving no disturbance in the snow over which she passed.

"That may be a little difficult, my dear Ruenn. It's rather a long way from here," she waved her hand around at our icy prison," to here," she drew a finger like a knife across her throat and smiled.

I found a smile to put on my own lips. "A distance I shall endeavor with great fervor to cross," I said.

Vohanna shook her head, the smoke hair whipping across her shoulders as if those coiling tresses were real.

"It shall never come to pass, Ruenn. The gate you fell into was mine. And when you leaped from it to this world you sealed your exile. For there are no toir'in-or, no milkstones in *this* land. No way to open a door from here to Talera. You will remain here until you die. Which...." She licked a shadow finger and held it up as if judging the wind and the cold, "is not likely to take long." She gave a mock shiver that stirred her misty form.

I tried not to let my smile falter at her words, but it was hard. My heart seemed already frozen, beating only weakly amid the cracking of ice that had formed suddenly in my chest.

"Well," I finally managed. "We all know what a liar you are, Vohanna. I don't believe you! We'll find a way."

She shrugged, a rather ridiculous motion for a being of smoke. "Waste your time searching then," she said. "In the meantime I'll be enjoying myself over a meal of your precious Nyshphal. Even now her armies splinter beneath mine."

Bryce snorted but said nothing. I didn't do so well at holding my tongue.

"I've already told people that you're behind the attacks from Revenor and Ubai," I said. "They're warned and ready."

"Ready? Really?" She chuckled. "I'm almost sorry you won't be there in Timmuzz at the end when I reveal myself. I think you would be...surprised."

I frowned, but she went on, leaving me no time to question her meaning.

"However, I must take my leave of you gentlemen now. There is much that requires my attention back on Talera. For one, I must set the wild gate to seeking for the others of your jungle party. Rannon, of course. And this...Ahrethane. I think it is time I dealt with her. But when the gate finishes dragging them off to some equally forlorn landscape as this, then I shall dance, dance, dance."

My fists clenched helplessly, the knuckles creaking with tension. Already this woman had taken my friend Heril from me. Now I tried to keep my fear for Rannon from reaching my face. But something came through that the Witch could detect. She chuckled again, then snapped her fingers, though the action made no sound.

"I must tell you about my gate, by the way. It's rather interesting, I think."

I said nothing, but she needed no word from us to trigger her gloating.

"Ruenn. You remember Diken Graye?"

I started. Indeed, I did recall that name. Graye had been one of a group of mercenaries hired by Vohanna to carry out raids on Nyshphal during the last war. But that was before he learned what she was like and joined us instead. As punishment he had been possessed by Vohanna and forced to serve her as a kind of zombie. I had counted him my friend but had assumed him dead in the crash of the great black pyramid that had ended the war. I remembered, though, that his body had never been found.

"What of him?" I demanded.

Vohanna lifted her open hand in front of her face, closed it into a fist as if crushing something. "I found an interesting use for him," she said. "Once I'd implanted a milkstone or two and set him some appropriate limits, I let him free to wander in the jungle. *He* is my gate. I fear, though, that the opening of it is *quite* painful. And worse, it is his frustration and anger that draw the killing breeds through to Talera. Whatever evil comes through is *his* evil. An appropriate end for a betrayer, don't you think?"

She was looking at Bryce as she said her last words, and I lost control, throwing myself toward her with a shriek of rage. She recoiled, though there was no need. I tore through her form in nothing more than a swirl of vapor and crashed face forward into the snow beyond.

I rolled over instantly, surged to my feet, but she was already spinning away across the snow with a wave of a dark-mist hand.

"Farewell, farewell," she called. "I've enjoyed you both so much."

I ran after her, not caring that it meant nothing, that I could *do* nothing. And in another instant her form dispersed like a poisonous dust on the constant wind.

Collapsing to my knees, I gasped for oxygen that my lungs could not find. My eyes swam with brightly colored floaters. But I fought against passing out, fought and was winning when I heard the crunch of Bryce's feet through the snow.

My brother reached a hand to aid me. I took it; he pulled me to my feet. He was grinning. I wanted to snap at him, call him crazy, but was afraid I'd be right and that he'd do something to prove it.

"Vohanna is a fool," Bryce said, his twisted grin mutating into an even more demented smirk.

I could not help but say: "A fool who seems to have beaten us at every turn."

He shook his head. "She just told us how to escape this place."

"How to escape!" I sputtered. "She just told us we were exiled here forever!"

Again my brother shook his head, more vigorously, his pale hair whispering about his face. "She said there were no milkstones on this world. She was wrong."

I jerked as if slapped, beginning of a sudden to catch on. My heart started to pound because I was sure that I knew what Bryce was about to say. I prayed I was wrong.

His words seemed almost gleeful when they came. "If Diken Graye can be a doorway because of the milkstones inside of him, then so too can I."

I hadn't been wrong. And it made me afraid.

CHAPTER ELEVEN

SHADOWS FROM THE SNOW

We sat, Bryce and I, around a tiny fire within a small, crude shelter of snow blocks that we'd hacked out with our swords. I'd cut a hole in the roof for our chimney, but the fire was virtually smokeless. It turned out that the bark of our alien "trees" burned much more slowly and cleanly than the mushroomy polyps that covered them.

Even though our flame was weak in the thin oxygen atmosphere, it was sufficient to heat our little hut of snow. At least for now we weren't in danger of freezing to death. Bryce had even rolled up his sleeves, and it disturbed me to see the grid map of tattoos on his arms. Faded as those lines were, I knew that they marked every part of his body, their outlines broken only by the puckered scars that also dotted his frame.

I wondered upon those scars. Bryce had gotten them on Talera. Along with the tattoos they were a kind of brand to mark his time with Vohanna. What horrors had my brother seen in those dark days? What torments had he suffered...did he continue to suffer?

And yet, as my brother sat across from me, his eyes mirroring the fire, a smile played across his lips as if he were thinking of pleasure rather than pain.

Finally I spoke, unable to stand what I imagined might be Bryce's thoughts.

"Even if you do have milkstones inside you, we don't know how to use them to open a sphere gate. Much less a gate to Talera."

Bryce looked up at me. "Oh, I know the stones are there," he said. "I'm just not quite sure where. And it may be that I *do* know how to use them. I spent better than a year with Vohanna. Do you think I didn't pay attention? That I didn't study her every move?"

"But you're no sorcerer," I protested. "It's not like some witch story that grandmother might have told us. There's more to it than a boiling cauldron and some arcane spells. The power of the milkstones is real, but it's alien. I've read the histories. No human has *ever* learned how to truly manipulate the toir'in-or. Parlor tricks maybe, but not sorcery. Our minds aren't built that way."

Bryce shook his head, looked back into the fire. "You don't understand, Ruenn. After all my days—and nights—with Vohanna, I'm not completely human anymore. She changed me, brother. At all levels. I'm not the Bryce you knew. Not your little brother from Earth."

He paused for a long while as I groped for something to say and could not find it. Then he added: "I rather think you resent the changes that have developed in me."

My eyes narrowed. "What the hell is that supposed to mean?"

He leaned forward. His lips seemed to drip shadows as he smirked; his pupils glittered.

"It means that you can no longer control my thoughts and actions and you don't like that. You don't like how I've grown beyond you."

A muscle spasmed in my cheek; my jaws clenched. I felt my fingers curl inward toward the palms. In a low voice, I replied. "I don't think I like your tone...brother."

Bryce chuckled, and the sound was so alike in character to the laughter of Vohanna that I jerked with a sudden chill and my anger evaporated to be replaced by worry. Did I sit across the fire now from a Bryce who was once again possessed? Was Vohanna speaking through Bryce now? Or had my brother indeed changed into something that wasn't completely human?

"I'm not concerned with your likes or dislikes right now, Ruenn," Bryce said finally. "I'm concerned with getting us home to Talera so we can put a stop to Vohanna."

I stared at him. "And how do you know that opening a sphere gate is not exactly what the Witch *wants* you to do?" I asked. "You think she just *forgot* that you had milkstones inside you? What if she told us about Diken Graye being used as a gate for a reason other than just to torment us?"

He shrugged. "You'd rather stay here?" He gestured about our tiny hut of snow. "To starve? Or maybe you'd rather us go out into the snow and freeze to death. I hear it's not a hard way to die."

"My concern is for you, Bryce," I said. "What if it kills you to open the gate? Or even if you survive, how will *you* pass through it? You haven't thought this out."

He smirked again. "Your concern is touching, brother. But, as usual, you disparage both my intelligence and my abilities."

My anger erupted. "Belay that," I snapped. "It's Vohanna who's tainted your thoughts with such. On Earth we were friends as well as brothers."

"I don't remember it that way," he replied, growling. "I remember when you...." He frowned. "I...remember...." He glanced from my face to the fire and back, his expression suddenly stricken. "I...."

I leaned forward. "No, Bryce. You *don't* remember. Not what Vohanna wants you to remember.

Bryce's upper body jerked at my words. His eyes flickered with what might have been a reflection of the flames. At least that's what I hoped it was.

"You can't let Vohanna rule you!" I said fiercely. "Not by her presence. Or by her absence. You are Bryce Maclang. No more, no less. Your father is Kendall Maclang. Your mother is Cathlin. You have two sisters. Andrea and Elizabeth. And I...I *am* your brother. Your only brother. And I love you."

Bryce had looked away as I spoke, his body twitching. Now a faint keening suddenly filled the snow hut and it took me a moment to realize where it came from.

I frowned. "Bryce?"

My brother seemed to curl in on himself and I started to rise from my place at the campfire. With an abrupt moan and a lurch, Bryce turned and threw himself toward the low door to our shelter, scrambling on all fours as if to escape some terror in the hut with him. But the only thing with him was me.

"Bryce!" I cried out, hurling myself toward the hut's doorway after him, my hands and knees sliding in half-melted slush as I exited. Then I was free into the world, screaming again my brother's name.

It was black night now, a night made brutal by the total lack of stars or moons, and a knife of bitter wind slashed me, stealing in moments all the warmth my body had hoarded over the past few hours.

There was no answer to my calls, and no sense of movement anywhere around except for the swaying of the leathery whip-trees under which we'd built our snow hut.

"Bryce?" I called again, more softly now, knowing that he could not have gone far in such a short time.

I began to shiver with growing cold. "Bryce. Come back to the fire before we both freeze. Please! Bryce!"

Twisting this way and that, shivering more violently with each passing second, I strained my eyes against the darkness for any sign of my brother.

He must have gone into the trees, I thought. I stomped in that direction.

A sudden rushing sound filled the world behind me. I turned, thinking it was the wind. Then torches flared to my left, their light a cold, acidic blue. By reflex I drew my sword, dropped into a crouch.

Riders came charging across the snow toward me. No! Not riders. Something else. I couldn't quite make them out amid the wild melee of shadows and flickering light.

A stone-headed lance rammed into the snow-pack at my feet. Another blasted up powder to my right. I lunged toward our tiny hut, hoping to put it at my back. My enemies came crashing after, racing hard. Big they were, nearly as big as horses.

I reached the hut, turned at bay. Three of my attackers loomed, with more behind. One of the closest reared, smashing aside blocks of cut snow with hooves the size of plates. The others pressed in.

I slashed an overhand strike toward one foe, felt the jar

as my sword banged on some shield of thickly latticed wood. A roar came. A lance stabbed down at me and I leaped aside, chopping the haft of the weapon in twain with a backhand stroke. The head of another spear ribboned the sleeve of my shirt. I hacked at the lancer and he fell away; the black fluid of his blood, stinking of sulphur, sprayed over me.

For a bare moment I stood free of foes. But my enemies could replace their wounded, and already in the thin air I was gasping for breath. I thought of the trees then, but the next attack came too quickly out of the darkness for me to make a dash for that haven.

I dodged a charge that scattered snow like dust, ducked beneath the lashing hooves of another attacker. More of the shadowy beings closed in. Bobbing and weaving like a boxer on the ropes, my sword cutting left and right, I kept them back. But now dark floaters serrated my vision and my lungs burned as they labored for oxygen.

From the distance a cold horn sounded, its voice brazen. I stumbled. Something struck me across the back. The butt of a lance slammed into my gut. I went down to my knees in the crusted snow, lunged to my feet again, my throat roaring for air.

They were all around me. My enemies. Tall over me. I swung wildly with the sword and they backed away. No longer were they attacking. My head reeled; my vision blurred and pulsed. My heart drummed a savage rhythm that left my body shuddering. I sank back to my knees, defeated by the thin air, by something I couldn't even see. And though they could have killed me then, they did not.

Through the crowd there pushed a single figure, holding high a torch of blue-white. For the first time I saw one of my foes clearly. In childhood my mother had read to me of ancient lives and ancient myths. Here stood a being drawn from one of those myths. My attackers were centaurs. Or nearly so.

Four footed they were, but built more on the lines of bighorn sheep than horses, and not quite as big as horses. Their bodies were long and covered with curly white fur, with tails like those of cattle and a torso broader and thicker than that of a man. Upon that torso they had shoulders and arms, and on the arms were six-fingered hands that looked human. They held weapons in those hands, heavy lances with stone blades, and clubs spiked with shards of bone and granite.

Above the wide shoulders, on bull necks, sat heads that—even more than the bodies—resembled those of big-horn sheep, complete to the massive, curling horns. The faces were brutal, flat nosed and thick lipped, with both the noses and the lips pierced with rings of jade and ruby and garnet.

The one who had pushed through the crowd, he who held the torch, reached over one thick shoulder and drew forth a crude crossbow of wood and leather. He pointed it at my chest but did not immediately loose the bolt. Yet, his threat was clear, and from such a distance it would be hard to miss. I knelt panting in exhaustion before him, then slowly climbed to my feet and sheathed my blade with a shrug.

"What is it you want of me?" I asked, even though I knew they would not comprehend my words. I hoped, at least, that Bryce was safely hidden in the trees.

The one who held the torch over me, the leader perhaps, lowered his crossbow. "The Bringer commanded us to take you," he said, and I understood him. For his language was of Talera.

Surprised that he knew a Taleran tongue, I gaped at him."What Bringer?" I demanded.

He and all the others bowed their heads.

"The Bringer of Pain and Beauty," the leader said. "She who is known to you as Vohanna."

CHAPTER TWELVE

BLIND MAGIC

They led me in bindings of leather through the snow, the beast-men, the servants of Vohanna. I had considered renewing my fight when I'd heard them call out the Witch's name, but that would have been sure death against so many enemies in the thin, thin air. Better for now to be bound than dead. And there was Bryce to consider, as well. He had to be out there somewhere, hiding. I could not think only of myself.

At least my captors did not want me to freeze to death. They had taken my sword but given me in place of it a cloak of feathers and fur, and boots of dark hide that were too big for me but which kept my feet from the cold. They wore no such garments themselves, though the cut of the cloak suggested to me that they did so on occasion. I wondered. Did it get still colder here? Would there come a time when even beings like these needed the protection of clothing? I prayed that I would be long gone before ever I saw such a winter as that.

Of course, I might well be gone into death before many more hours passed. I did not think it was concern for my health that had prompted Vohanna's minions to invite me home with them. The Witch surely had plans for me that did not include pampering.

The hooves of the Centaurs—for so I thought of the beings then—were flat as small dinner plates on the bottom to distribute their weight on the snow so that they did not break through the crust. I floundered more than they, though the boots they had given me helped some as we went down-valley from the site where Bryce and I had exited the wild gate. Torches of blue fire lit our way.

Soon, we came upon more leathery groves of what I'd began to call the whip-trees, and then upon trees of a different kind that stood gray and huge as dolmens of stone. At first I thought they *were* actual stones. They had no limbs but grew what appeared to be crystalline spicules all over them that glittered in the torchlight like fool's gold. But when we came among them I touched one and it was warm as a living thing, the texture so different from that of unfeeling rock.

"Guard-trees," one of my captors grunted when I looked at him questioningly. He did not explain how these things served as guards, nor what they might guard against. I wasn't sure I wanted to know.

The field of guard-trees stretched for several verlang (one verlang is about a mile and a half), and dawn found us before we found the end of them. The torches were extinguished. Our pace increased.

We reached a cliff of slick reddish rock that was capped with drifts of snow. I half expected to see the dwellings of the Centaurs built into that cliff, but there was only a passage through the stone that was wide enough for two wagons to roll abreast. We took that road, and though it curved back and forth enough to show that it was a natural path, I could see tool marks on the walls where the Centaurs—or some other race—had widened the way.

At the far end of the twisty road we found a sheltered valley where the snow was all gone from the ground and the temperature was at least thirty degrees warmer than it had been outside the cliffs. The earth bubbled with hot springs that explained both the warmth and a mist that coiled in the morning air. Ahead of us through that mist I saw the Centaur city, a compact place of jagged, multi-tiered houses that looked almost like natural rock.

In the center of the city, rising higher than any of the other buildings, stood a black pyramid chased with gold. Though smaller, this pyramid was a virtual twin to the one wherein Vohanna had dwelt on Talera—before the war in which we'd thought she'd been slain.

It was toward the pyramid that my captors forced me, through streets curiously empty. I saw no other beings than the ones who accompanied me, though behind slatted windows in some of the houses I thought I glimpsed movement.

The steps of the pyramid were of black marble veined with gold, and were much wider and deeper than a human would have needed. I was led up them and into the nave of a temple built just below the apex of the structure. Above me, the very top of the pyramid was open to the sky, and through that opening curled the ever-present mist. The temperature here was warmer still, from the burning of huge, nearly smokeless fires in pits in the floor.

Upon a raised chancel at the end of the temple there stood a life-sized statue of a Centaur. Fire pits blazed to either side of it, and before it, at a slightly lower level, rose a set of four slender pillars of what appeared to be brass. There were cuffs of gold upon those pillars, and after my cloak was stripped away I was chained to two of them. Then my captors left me without a word, with scarcely more sound than the whisper of their hooves over the marble floor.

I studied the statue, and after a moment my eyes widened. Though the body was Centaur, the face upon it was clearly Vohanna's. I still wasn't sure that I'd ever glimpsed Vohanna's *true* form, but I'd come to think of her primarily as looking like she had when I'd first seen her on a jeweled throne in her pyramid of hate. She had appeared no more than eighteen then, innocent and fragile of body, with hair like silver turned to silk. But within her gaze of soulless black there had been nothing but lies. This statue wore that face, those eyes.

"Witch," I whispered to myself.

"The Bringer of Pain and Beauty," another voice replied.

I twisted my head to one side to see for the first time in the flesh a female Centaur. She was, perhaps, a third smaller than her male counterparts, with horns that did not curl so sharply and which were much paler in color. Her face, or muzzle, was less pronounced than that of the males as well. It made her look more human, though most human of all was the long fine hair that hung down behind her horns. The hair of the males had been curly, but hers was straight and an almost pure silver-white. She had blue eyes.

"Of pain, perhaps," I said in response to her comment about Vohanna.

She moved around in front of me, her hooves clinking delicately on the marble. If I had sought to insult or anger her with my words, I had failed in that. She chuckled.

"That depends on who you are to her," she said.

"I've never known anything but pain from her," I retorted.

"Then it must be that you resist her."

"Someone has to."

She blinked, looking suddenly surprised. But then she shook her head in what I'd come to realize was an almost universal gesture of negation among sentient beings.

"Your resistance accomplishes nothing," she said.

I was in little position at the moment to argue with her. But still I said: "At least *my* people are free."

Again my words failed to anger her.

"Do you really think so?" she inquired.

She moved closer to me then, her gaze studying. Even though this female served Vohanna I could not find myself hating her. Her blue eyes seemed guileless and I thought she must be very young.

I shrugged at her question, then asked: "Are you the priestess here?"

"In a way," she said. She did not explain in *what* way.

"So why did Vohanna go to so much trouble to have me captured and brought here? Something to do with pain, I'm sure."

"Do you always assume that *you* are the primary reason why things are done?"

I started. "No. I. Uhm...I...." My words floundered to a confused stop.

"You are here because of your brother," she said.

A chill flashed through me even in the warmth of this place; my heart jumped. "I don't understand," I said.

She did not explain but again stepped closer to me, moving gracefully on her hooves. "Would you care to see what your brother has been doing?" she asked.

I looked at her warily. "And how do you propose I do that?"

"You just have to...focus," she said, standing before me. Her blue eyes loomed in my gaze. She passed a hand through the air between us and that air shimmered and seemed to congeal. And then it was as if I were looking *through* a mirror and could see Bryce. We were arguing in the snow hut and then he threw himself from the hut and rushed into the grove of whip-trees around it.

I knew that I had followed him outside and that it was then I'd been taken by the Centaurs. But I saw none of that. I saw Bryce among the trees, saw him with the frozen glisten of tears in his eyes as he fell to his knees and fought some terrible war within himself. He was cold, shivering. But it was not the cold that tormented him. His agony came from inside.

I jerked between the pillars where I was chained, straining as I tried to lean toward the image of my brother.

"Bryce!" I shouted. "Bryce! Listen! I—"

"He can't hear you," the Centaur priestess said.

I looked at her, stricken. "Is he dying?" I asked her.

"Watch," she commanded. And I could not help but do so.

Bryce began to hammer his fists into the snow, pounding, pounding. And I could see his lips twist as he shouted and screamed words I could not hear. His body was arched, tense as a bowstring at that unbearable point just before release. He was driving himself into a frenzy.

I lunged against my bonds, shouting again for my brother even though I knew he couldn't hear me. The chains tore at my wrists but my feet were free and I began to kick wildly at the pillars. My heart thudded. The pillars rocked but did not fall. Blood ran down my arms. The Centaur female backed away from me.

And then I froze as, through the window from where Bryce struggled, there did come a sound, a sound like ice floes shearing, like mountains grinding together in an earthquake. Even the priestess seemed startled, her gaze turning from me to the scene of Bryce's agony.

My brother's body stiffened, then went into a berserk

chorea of spasms and twitches as he began to convulse. My eyes locked upon him; I bit my lip until it bled. Bryce thrashed in the snow. But in the next instant he'd fallen still again. I saw him lift his head. His eyes were closed but his mouth was open. He said a word. I heard it clearly across the distance.

"Hate!" was what he said.

Smoke spurted from where Bryce knelt. Snow flashed into steam. The very ground rippled and the nearest of the whip trees exploded into fire. A crescendo of smoke and embers whirled up; more trees erupted in flames. Bryce could no longer be seen.

My eyes felt raw with looking. I could not move.

"Please," I whispered to the priestess. "Please."

"Watch," was all she said.

The fire raged like a beast. The world was scarlet with it, and black with the darkness of smoke. But then a shadow moved within the inferno. Something took shape out of the flames. I saw it coming, saw what it was.

Bryce stalked out of the fire, embers thrown like a cloak over his shoulders, his hair wreathed with fumes. He looked up, directly into my gaze, and his once grey eyes were as silver now as if they had sucked all the moonlight out of the night. His lips twisted in what might have been a smile; the image of him winked out. The air in front of me was only air again.

I looked toward the priestess. "Get him back," I said. "Show me my brother."

She sagged, as if drained to the dregs of her soul. "I cannot," she said, her voice somber, tolling. "But it doesn't matter. Your brother is coming. He's coming here. You'll see him soon enough."

CHAPTER THIRTEEN

A DARK RETURN

How much time passed I did not know. Perhaps minutes. Perhaps hours. I stood there in my bonds thinking, for the first time in a long time, of Earth. Where Bryce had been happy. Talera was *my* home now. It had given me friends and a love I could never have found on any other world. It had given me so much that was real and good and beautiful.

Bryce it had destroyed.

And he was coming here. To this place.

I did not know if my brother were coming to kill me, or to save me, or for some other reason that I could not fathom. I did not even know, in a real sense, whether he *was* my brother anymore. The silver eyes that I'd seen through the window conjured by the Centaur priestess had not been Bryce's eyes. They had been as alien in their way as the black orbs of Vohanna when she vented her rage at her enemies. Enemies like me.

I wished so much that Bryce had never come to Talera. I wished that he was still on Earth, living outside of time in California with our mother and our father, and our two sisters. I wished many things that had no hope of ever being true.

But then there came the sound of shouts in the streets outside the pyramid. And my wishes slid away as the female Centaur lifted her blue eyes to mine and I saw them dark-rimmed with fear.

"It is he," she said, her head cocked to one side in listening. "The warriors follow him along the way but they will not touch him. Vohanna has decreed it."

"What more can she want of him?" I protested. "Has she not done him enough harm? Can't she leave him be?"

The priestess shook her head, and now her gaze looked beyond my shoulder to the entrance of this temple. "The Bringer does not explain her ways to me," she said. "Only through me."

I did not understand what she meant, but the sound of footsteps on the stone stairs of the pyramid erased any thought I might have had of questions. "Bryce," I whispered to myself, though I wondered why his tread was so heavy, why his steps did not sound quite human.

I could not turn my head far enough to see the doorway into the temple, but I knew when Bryce entered by the sudden change of expression on the face of the priestess. And now her fear was palpable. My own heart pounded and I, too, was afraid. Of something I could not name.

I twisted in my chains as much as I could, and in a moment Bryce strode into my view and paused beside me. But he did not look at me, even when I called his name. His gaze took in nothing but the priestess and the statue behind her that wore Vohanna's smirk.

Only the side of my brother's face was turned toward me, but I could still see the bleed-off of silver light from his icicle eyes. An odor of violence hung about him, and there were other changes as well. His tattoos, faded over the last few months into thin blue lines, had awakened again into brilliant streaks of ocher and cinnabar and anil. The white hair that had been dirty and unkempt when we'd come through the wild gate was fresh and pale now as a drift of new snow, and it seemed...alive in the way that it whispered around his face. There was no wind here to stir it.

"Bryce," I called again. And still he did not acknowledge me. He lifted his false hand and pointed a finger, not at the living Centaur, but at the statue.

"Vohanna," he said. "It's time for a reckoning."

My gaze followed the direction of Bryce's finger, and my heart stuttered as the smirk on the statue's stone face curved into a wicked smile that dripped shadows. I heard a moan then, a low, deep rasp of sound that ached with unbearable pain. With a sudden jolt of fear for my brother I looked back at Bryce. But he stood quiet and still, as if waiting for winter leaves to fall.

And then the moan came again and I saw that it was the Centaur priestess who gave vent to the sound. She had begun to tremble, and her eyes were closed tight as if she would deny the pain she felt. She jerked once, and again, then fell to all four knees with her body twitching and quivering. And her denial gave way as she threw her head back and screamed.

In that instant I remembered her earlier words, the ones I'd not understood when she'd first uttered them. "The Bringer does not explain her ways to me, only *through* me." I knew what was happening, knew why the priestess of this huge temple was so young and guileless. She was the kind Vohanna liked to corrupt. I didn't even need to see her eyes when they opened to know that their blue would be replaced by the cold, hard black that told of Vohanna's presence here in this place with us.

"How melodramatic," Bryce said, smirking as Vohanna rose to her new feet and stood there with her acid gaze taking in us both.

She chuckled. "The simple ones like such demonstrations. They *need* them." Her eyes locked on Bryce then. "Something *you* would do well to learn now," she added to him alone.

"I've learned enough from you," Bryce snapped.

Vohanna turned her head to one side. She blinked, and I shuddered with distaste as the lids swept from left to right across her eyes instead of up and down.

"I hardly think so," she said. Again her words did not include me.

"Bryce!" I demanded urgently. "Bryce. Free me. Let me help you against her. You don't want to face her alone."

But my brother paid me no more heed than the Witch had. He gave a low growl, his newly minted silver eyes flickering. "What you tried so hard to prevent by exiling me here has come anyway, Vohanna. I've awakened. Now we'll see who grovels, who begs."

Vohanna laughed like chimes tinkling. "So naive, my

Bryce. Tis something I've enjoyed immensely in you. Do you really think I did not know what would happen when you went through my wild gate? Nothing has awakened in you except by *my* wishes. All that I have planned for you. All that I have *commanded* of you. Is alive now in you because I willed it. We've come so far together, you and I. And you are right. It is time for a reckoning, time for you to repay the debt you owe me for what I have gifted you."

Bryce's hands closed into fists, the false one pulsing with waves of crimson hate that seemed to long for a throat to strangle.

"Bringer of Lies, they *should* call you, Vohanna. I know what's inside of me, what I'm capable of. I know exactly where you leave off and I begin. And one way or another I will be free of you tonight."

I jerked at my chains, rattling them as I called out again for Bryce to release me, to let me help him against the Witch. But he was too far gone in rage to hear or see me.

Vohanna moved, stalked forward on clicking hooves toward Bryce. For just a moment she glanced in my direction and I spat curses at her. She smiled, almost fondly it seemed. And in my mind, *to* my mind, she whispered something without words so my brother could not hear.

"Do you know. Ruenn. What a Bane-thrall is?

In the next instant she looked away again and the connection broke between us. I frowned. *Bane-thrall.* I had heard that word. Somewhere. Read it. Somewhere.

But Vohanna was speaking once more to Bryce, her voice turned as sticky sweet as poisoned honey. "Do you remember that first night in my pyramid, Bryce? When you came through the gate from your Earth with your hand sheared away and your body failing? Do you remember the kiss I gave you? How delicious it was? From that moment until this one, every movement you have made, every action you have taken, has been by my design, has been but a prelude to *this* moment, to what will happen here between us tonight."

"No," Bryce denied, shaking his head.

"Shut up, Vohanna!" I yelled. "Bryce, don't listen to her. Don't give her an opening."

Neither of them looked at me. Their eyes were like bruises on bruises, silver and black, hot and cold. Vohanna drifted closer and still closer to Bryce, and in the misted air I could smell the erotic musk that bled from her every pore. She reached a hand, brought the knuckles of it down as if to caress my brother's cheek. Bryce shuddered, retreated a pace to keep her from touching him.

"No," he said again, though his voice was weaker.

Vohanna...whispered. And the words were full of an intimacy that was meant for Bryce alone. As if I were not even here. As if they were together in that moment when lovers have shared all there is to share.

"I loved you, Bryce. In my bed of silk and chains. You begged me. Don't you remember how you begged me? What you pleaded for me to do for you? *To* you?"

It was as if the chill winds of this world had suddenly filled my veins and were congealing my heart. I saw an image of Bryce and Vohanna with limbs intertwined. I saw Bryce screaming, babbling, imploring. It was obscene. Like a holocaust. And in the frozen space of that bladed second I remembered what a Bane-thrall was.

Vohanna could possess living beings, and while she was inside them they would be like zombies to her will, aware of what was happening but unable to resist. When she left them they would return to themselves, their minds back under their own control. Only if she had implanted milkstones in them could she still monitor and influence their actions.

A Bane-thrall was different, was not truly possessed. It was a sorcerer or sorceress who was...taken by another wizard, taken and mastered so completely that it was little more than an extension of its creator. A Bane-thrall was made over in its master's image, its intelligence and courage unaltered but with its thoughts restrung so that its master's desires were its desires, its masters hates were its hates.

Vohanna had wanted to awaken Bryce's sorcerous talents all along so that she could turn him into a Bane-thrall and gain an ally who would be worth any thousand others. But first she had to *take* him, and to do that she needed him to lash out at her, needed his rage. And just as I realized this, as I found my voice to warn him, Bryce shouted into Vohanna's face.

"No!"

His hands came up and he shoved them open palmed toward the Witch. I heard a sound like bells breaking, saw the air between Bryce and Vohanna catch fire. Vohanna cried out, her own hands coming up. But too late. A wave of heated wind slammed into her, lifted her from her feet and hurled her a dozen yards away to crash heavily on the marble floor.

Bryce took two steps forward and leaped across a fire pit toward Vohanna, seeming to hang forever above the flames with his limbs flashing silver. His false hand slashed down and a spear of sound and light stabbed toward the Witch's heart. But the sorceress had her own hands up now and she swatted the blast away. And she was laughing, laughing as the energy of Bryce's attack dissipated against a nearby marble column in an eruption of dust and debris.

Bryce landed on the stone floor in front of Vohanna, his mouth screaming curses as he thrust his open hand toward her like a dagger. I didn't even see her move but Bryce's blow missed, and then Vohanna struck back. Some kind of tentacles of black fire whipped from beneath her arms and smashed Bryce aside. He went reeling to the ground, crying out in pain. But he was up again in an instant, backing away as his hands began to weave skeins of silver light before him in the air.

Vohanna came for him, stalking on Centaur hooves, her eyes looming larger and larger, swollen with power and an unearthly splendor.

"The Bringer of Pain and Beauty," I murmured.

The Witch's black-light tentacles lashed toward Bryce, one crushing aside the protective net of glowing runes that my brother had been weaving, the other striking into the floor at his feet, sending waves undulating through the marble that made him stagger and fall to his knees. Bryce's human hand seemed to lift into the air of its own volition. I saw a knot of proud flesh form in his palm. I saw that knot break open and spark with opalescent fire. It was a milkstone there, embedded within him like he'd been born with it.

Bryce rose to his feet as if dragged by the power of the

wizard's stone in his hand. Vohanna halted a dozen paces from him, her lips curved and full and crimson. She smirked, opened her arms wide.

"Smash me, Bryce. Smash your lover down and maybe it will blot from your soul what we've been to each other." She twisted her hand before her mouth and blew him a tainted kiss.

Bryce snarled as he curled his fingers into a fist. He aimed it toward Vohanna, his shoulders hunching, his body leaning forward. In that moment he looked more like an ape than a man. And his rage was a living thing whose heart hammered through my brain.

The Witch laughed. "Smash me, Bryce!" she screamed. "Show me how much you love me."

My own scream echoed Vohanna's. "No! Bryce, don't!"

Bryce released it all, all his festering hate. It struck from his fist toward Vohanna, like a lance of sun that burned my eyes. I saw the smoke, like the sinuous bodies of vipers. I heard the air cook and shriek. I felt the rumble of power surging toward the breaking point.

And Vohanna took it. She stood there, her head thrown back, shadows like wings around her. Her mouth was open; her hair crackled and streamed with fire. And she took Bryce's direst blow right to her chest, her body swallowing it, drawing it into herself.

Bryce gaped. I struggled wildly with my chains, shouting, babbling, begging for the Witch to leave my brother alone.

Vohanna reached out from a distance of yards and yanked Bryce to his knees with a tether of black. And she moved toward him, dainty on her hooves though her black eyes beat and beat with pulses of a savage venom. She dropped a hand to his chin, cupped it and drew his head up so that his gaze could meet hers.

"Mine," she crooned.

Bryce made no denial. His shoulders drooped. Vohanna curled her other hand across his face and a nimbus of light began to play between her fingers. I saw that glow brighten and dim, as if the Witch were draining him of something. Or...filling him.

I lunged into my chains once more, then sagged against them. Bryce shifted his gaze a fraction toward me then, looking like my brother of old in that moment, even through the burnt silver of his irises. I know I had tears in my eyes to match the ones in his. But with a last gesture of defiance he lifted a finger and a spark leaped the distance to strike away my cuffs.

I gasped, but before I could throw myself forward to attack Vohanna a wheel of light blossomed behind me. I felt its pull, felt the hungry void of it drawing me. My eyes locked to my brother's; I shook my head. But Bryce gave a whisper that only I could hear, a whisper full of agony.

"Go, Ruenn. A gate to Rannon. To Talera. Stop the Witch there." And. "I'm sorry, brother."

Vohanna snarled, sensing something wrong. I felt her turn one small part of her awareness toward me, felt the questing of her mind like rasping claws in my brain. And still I fought the pull of the gate behind me.

"Go!" Bryce shouted, as he turned his eyes back fully to Vohanna and reached up and grabbed her wrists. The shock of that contact whipped the air, fanned flames and mist, and shattered pillars of stone.

I let myself obey my brother, felt the void take me, whirl me away into some maw of heated white. In a flash the transition was completed and my feet rested once more on Taleran soil. Before me, in shock, stood Diken Graye, who was the anchor at *this* end of the wild gate. His body still vibrated with the opening and closing of the gate; dying twists of light played over his limbs

He gasped. "Ruenn!"

Almost instantly the light around him began to spark brighter again. He took a step toward me, his hands going out, his fingers beginning to stream with a haze of incandescence.

"By Dejhas," he said, his voice streaming echoes. "Is it really you?"

I punched him, knocking him unconscious with that one blow, but caught him as he fell and lowered his form gently to the ground. Only then did I let tears for my brother flow.

CHAPTER FOURTEEN

WHAT ALIEN HELL

I knelt beside Diken Graye where he lay unconscious on the leaf-matted loam of the forest of Vohan. Above me, the red sunlight of Talera streamed through the cathedral of trees. I felt the warmth of it on my face as I looked up, but that warmth did not touch anything beneath the skin. Even the tears in my eyes seemed cold.

Bryce was gone. Not dead. But gone from me. By now he would be Bane-thrall to Vohanna and the next time I saw him I would have to kill him. All his newly awakened sorcerous powers would be Vohanna's then. And all his earthly knowledge? Vohanna's for the milking. Unless I destroyed him. Even when he and I had fought in the Witch's black pyramid, even when he'd hated me, there had still been within him the core of my younger brother. That would no longer be true. Bryce belonged to the Witch now.

I clenched my fists, trying to fight my tears with anger. At every turn Vohanna had bested me, stealing from me that which was precious and taunting me with the ashes that were all she'd left for me to hold. Even when I'd thought her dead she'd been winning. My hate for her was strong but it had no support from hope. There was nothing more I could do against her. I had nothing left to go to war with.

Then Diken Graye groaned, stirred. I looked down at him. I remembered this man. From a mercenary who had nearly been responsible for Rannon's death and mine, he'd become an unlikely ally and a good friend. For that friendship he, too, had suffered.

I leaned down toward him. Full of despair or no, I could not let Graye awaken without an explanation for my presence or why I'd hit him. At the moment he'd seen me the light had begun to play brighter and brighter around his body, and I'd known that the gate he anchored was about to activate again. Vohanna had said that it was Graye's emotions that caused the wild gate to open. And I was not prepared to let that happen. Not after what Bryce had sacrificed to send me back to Talera. But now—maybe—if I could control my own emotions I could also keep my friend calm enough to stop the gate from triggering.

"Shhh," I whispered as Diken opened his eyes and the pupils widened in recognition. "Shhh! Diken. Stay calm." I slipped my hand over his mouth. "If you let your emotions go you'll open the gate again. Who knows where I'll end up this time."

I saw him struggle, saw a faint gleam start in his dark irises. But then he began to take deep, slow breaths. And he mastered himself. He sat up slowly and I helped him to stand. His voice was still a little ragged when he spoke.

"I...." he started, then took several more deep breaths. "I'm glad to see you alive," he finally managed.

"As I am you, old friend." I tried to put a little energy into my words but he must have sensed something missing.

"What is wrong?" he asked.

I shook my head at him. "I'm all right. Just tired."

This time he shook *his* head. "There's more than that. I know you, Ruenn." He frowned. "Or I did."

"You still know me, Diken. It's just that...right now. I can't speak of it. First we have to locate Rannon and the others who came with me to the jungle. There is one among them, Ahrethane, who might be able to help you control the gate."

He only nodded. "I saw them flee the wrecked ship when the insect queen's larva swarmed. I don't know where they went. After...." He paused to take more slow breaths.... "After what happened to you and your brother I ran in the opposite direction from them."

So, he *did* remember what happened when the wild gate opened. I had wondered. But trust Vohanna to let him be aware of the havoc he caused, even though the fault was in no way his.

"They'll be hard to find," he continued. "There's a lot of jungle here. And you've been gone nearly a ten-day."

"A ten-day!" I looked at him incredulously. "That can't be. I've passed two days at most."

He shook his head. "Then time was different where you were. This morning marked your eighth day gone."

I sighed. I knew that sphere gates *could* be time gates, though they did not normally work that way. When Bryce and I had first been drawn to Talera through a gate that had exploded in front of us, we'd been cast forward in time relative to that of Earth. Now it seemed I'd taken a trip through time again. Perhaps all wild gates acted so. I did not know. I knew only that I didn't like it, though maybe I should consider myself lucky that it was days and not years that had passed.

"Doesn't matter," I said. "They won't have left. Rannon wouldn't have."

Graye nodded slightly. And, after a pause, "It might be best for you to go alone."

I studied him, seeing his fear. It wasn't fear for himself but for those he cared about, those who might be hurt by the opening of the gate which Vohanna had cursed him with.

"No," I said. "We'll go together. But it may not be as hard to find Rannon and the others as you think. Or rather, for them to find us."

He looked at me strangely.

"Ahrethane is an efrinore. The forest is hers and she knows what goes on in it. I just have to get her attention."

"And how will you do that?"

"Watch. But stay calm. I'd think you might want to cover your ears."

With a frown that suggested he was having a hard time humoring me, he did so. I immediately threw back my head and roared as loud and long as I could: "Ahrethaneee!"

Birds startled in the branches above us and whirred away. In the underbrush dozens of small creatures fled wildly from my shout. Graye looked at me as if I'd gone crazy as he lowered his hands rather timidly from his ears.

"You think just yelling for her will work?" he asked me, his words a little on the dry side. "She could be miles away."

At another time I might have laughed at the expression on his face. Now there was not even a chuckle left in me. "I wasn't expecting *her* to hear it. But the birds and animals heard it. She'll learn of it from them."

Something seemed to click in his thoughts and he nodded. "Ah. Right. An efrinore, you say?"

"Yeah. But I don't think we should just wait here. You know the way to the wreck site? If they're expecting me anywhere it would be there."

He nodded again. "I know the way." He pointed east, then headed off in that direction without another word. I joined him and we swung along through the trees for a bit with silence lying between us. The world was rich with the smell of growth, with the bursting of pollen and the damp heatedness of mold. But even the jungle seemed strangely quiet, though here and there I saw the flitting of insects and birds within the canopy.

"Vohanna," Graye said after a bit. "When she came back here after the air battle ended. She told me that you. That everyone. Thought her dead." He shook his head as if not wanting to remember, but his words went on. "She was angry at first. I've never seen anyone that angry. But then. Then she started laughing. Especially after what she did…to me. She said you would pay. That everyone would pay. I…was wondering what she *has* done. What's happened. Outside. I've heard nothing." He gestured around at the greenery of the forest. "I've *known* nothing. Except the jungle."

I gazed at him for a bit, then decided to trust in his ability to remain calm through the telling. I explained to him how, in the aftermath of thinking we'd won the war against Vohanna, Rannon and I had decided to be married. I told him of the assassination attempts and the fiery raid on Timmuzz. I told him of the invasion from Ubai and Revenor and of our awareness that Vohanna was behind it. And, too, I spoke of our suspicion that someone in the Nysphalian government was allied with the Witch. Or possessed by her. I made no mention of what had happened to Bryce. In that case it was not Diken Graye's emotional reaction that I feared. It was my own.

"But what of you?" I asked him after. "I thought you must have been killed in the crash of Vohanna's pyramid. How did you survive? And how did...?" I did not finish the question but I believe he knew what I had meant to ask.

"I wasn't in the pyramid when it fell," he said. "I was with an attack group on saddle birds. On a Kryll."

I knew what a Kryll was, a winged predator of gigantic size, just one of the many types of saddle birds on Talera that can be ridden through the skies as men on Earth ride horses across the land.

"Vohanna had a loose control on me," Diken continued, "but during the battle I felt that connection drop away. I suspect it was when you confronted her. I intended to take my bird over to your side but as soon as the mercenaries I was with realized what had happened there was a fight. The Kryll was wounded but managed to bring me down into the jungle alive. I saw the pyramid crash and started toward the site, thinking I'd find you or some other Nysphalians there. And then Vohanna...then Vohanna took me again. She came out of another saddle bird. It had landed not far from me and I tried to catch it. I had no idea she'd possessed it."

"We had no idea she even could," I said. "Until far too late."

Graye nodded, then continued. "She only released possession of me after she found a cave where she'd hidden some of her body shells. After that I think you know as much as I do. She...implanted me. Set me loose in the jungle as a wild gate. I don't know where she went then. Apparently she's been busy."

"Yes," I agreed. "Most busy."

Graye stopped so suddenly that I walked past him several steps before realizing it.

"What is it?" I asked, my voice instantly dropping to a whisper as I glanced quickly around. My hand itched for a sword but the one I had carried to this jungle such a short time ago was lost on another planet—who knew how far away.

"It's nothing. Only...I just realized it's getting dark."

I looked around again, and this time noted the lengthening of our shadows and the gloom that had started to fill the low places in the forest. In a very real way I could smell the night gathering, for there are some things that only bloom in the dusk and the black.

"Aye," I said after a pause. "And that means the hunting begins. Maybe we'd better find a place to hole up." I was thinking, too, that the night in *this* jungle might be worse than in most, given the monsters that Ahrethane had told me were coming through the wild gate when it was open.

"Agreed," Diken said. He paused for a moment, looking around and fidgeting.

I felt myself frowning. "We could always climb a tree," I said.

He looked back at me, his lips twitching toward a nervous smile that faded before it could form.

"Well...," he said. "Maybe two trees." He looked distinctly uncomfortable. "Sometimes. At night. When I dream...." Again the nervous smile flickered about his lips, and I understood of a sudden what he was trying to get out.

"Sometimes the gate opens when you dream," I said.

He sighed. "Yes. A lot of times actually."

"Then we'd better make it two trees," I said. "What's the range on the gate?"

"Maybe twenty-five heka.[3] You stay beyond that and you should be safe."

A few minutes searching among the growing shadows revealed two suitable trees, but before I left Graye I borrowed his knife to cut and sharpen a makeshift spear.

"What happened to your sword?" he asked me

"Long story," I replied. "What about yours?" I'd noted that he didn't carry one either.

"Vohanna took it. After she put on her new body." He shrugged. "I've no need of it, though. Anything that attacks me is going to find itself shifted through a sphere gate a shri later."

"I hadn't considered that," I said.

Yet again that faintly nervous smile played around his

---

[3] About twenty feet.

lips, and I sensed the strain that this man had been under for so long. It was a wonder he was still sane.

"Sleep as well as you can, Diken," I told him.

He lifted a hand in acknowledgement, then turned and climbed his tree. I went to my own choice and soon had situated myself as comfortably as I could in the triple fork of a large bansul tree. Lying down with my makeshift spear to hand, I tried to get some rest. I didn't really expect to sleep but exhaustion soon stormed my defenses and the world went away from me.

It was hours later when I awoke to the flickering of opalescent light through my closed lids. I sat up abruptly, jerking lose the belt that I'd used to tie myself into my forest perch. Through the tracery of overhead branches I could see three moons in the sky, with Sieona far down near setting. That meant it was close to the fourth dhaur, not far from morning.

But it was not moonlight that had awakened me. From the direction where Diken Graye slept came a coruscation of fire that I knew must mark the wild gate's opening. Seen at a distance it was beautiful. Pinwheels of sparks leapt through the trees. The gate itself was like a hub of gold from which flaming spokes radiated out. I saw flashes of greenery against darkling shadows. Leaves whispered and twigs rattled.

The gate began to pulse and I felt myself frowning. Why was it staying open so long? A sphere gate normally cycles quickly. This one was lingering. I didn't like it.

I rose to my feet in the crotch of the bansul tree, striving to pierce with my eyes the interplay of light around where Diken Graye must be asleep and dreaming. And then my mouth ran dry and my heart began to pound as I saw what was emerging from the gate, what *began* to emerge.

Two by two they came, out of the whirling light to drop a dozen feet to earth. They were armed with nicked swords and ancient axes, and dented and torn shields were upon their arms. Their helmets and armor were mismatched and in tatters, rusted and holed and stained with splotches of long dried blood. They were not human but of some race I'd never seen before, built like bulls who moved on two legs. Like

Minotaurs. And all of them were dead and walking.

I saw bodies in all stages of decay, some barely rotted, some with the skin sloughed away to reveal the blackened jelly of fat and muscle beneath. I saw faces with missing jaws, saw ribs through corrugated flesh and skulls gleaming through sparse scalps of lank hair. It was if some alien world's hell had opened and was emptying itself onto the soil of Talera.

Dozens of the beings there were. Then hundreds. Then an army. Marching. Marching. I did not think it an accident that they headed south through the darkness toward the Nyshphalian capital of Timmuzz. For surely it must have been Vohanna who called these bull-men up for use in her war against my adopted homeland.

The proof of my conjecture came when the gate closed and the last six of the dead warriors turned to look in my direction with the glittering red eyes that always marked Vohanna's servants. I did not know if they could see me through the night and the thick spread of jungle between us. But they sensed me; they came for me.

My lips curved. In the near darkness, I smiled.

CHAPTER FIFTEEN

KILL THE DEAD!

Grasping my spear tightly, I dropped quickly down through the bansul tree to a limb some twelve feet above the earth. The six dead warriors came stalking, blades and axes tight in rotted fists. In the dim light cast down through the jungle by the three moons the beings looked almost human except for bull heads and hooves and the strange arrangement of leathery musculature across their broad frames. But any otherness they *did* possess was magnified by the fact that bones and tendons and bloodless veins showed through their tatters of skin.

I did not know whether Diken Graye would awaken from his sleep after the closing of the gate, but I did not think he would be able to help me against these enemies, not without the risk of reopening the gate and sending me away with them to some far realm. The coming fight was mine. I welcomed it.

Vohanna's minions spread out as they approached. They made no sound from throats that surely ran more with sand than with words, but their intent to surround me was clear. I chuckled. They hoped to keep me from escaping them. I had no thought of such flight. These beings had died once; they would die again if I had to hack them into gobbets.

Rising to my feet suddenly, I sprinted lightly along a thick limb of the tree and vaulted downward toward one of the bull-men who carried a sword that was rusty but not as time-worn as the others. It was the blade I coveted. The creature wielding it tried to raise it as I dropped upon him, but he had no chance. With my spear held tight in falling I rammed the thick wooden shaft through the slitted visor of the helmet from which his sorcerous red eyes peered. His head exploded with dust, smashing backward from his neck in a rupture of shredded muscle and sinew.

With the remnant of his desiccated brain shattered around my lance, the bull-man dropped as if pole-axed. By that time I'd already scooped up his fallen sword, had felt the haft socket itself firmly in my hand. It was a broadsword, heavier than I was accustomed to. But hate gave me plenty of strength.

The closest of the bull-men lashed at me with his axe. I knocked it aside with the sword, then spun off my right heel, bringing my blade around. He tried to get his shield up. He almost made it. Sparks shrieked as the edge of the sword struck the edge of the shield and slammed past. His neck took the blow, was sheared nearly through. Hanks of mag-got-ridden hair went flying.

The being staggered, twitching madly, his head hanging off to one side by threads of dried meat. I planted a boot in his chest and kicked him backward. He fell, but the other four were coming. And they did not move like dead men. They were quick.

I charged them.

The beings were taller and broader than I. In life they would have been much heavier. But now in their dryness they were probably close to my own two hundred pounds. The first pair barely had time to raise shields before I plunged into them, their weapons useless in the surprise of that instant. The impact was like hitting a wall; I heard the brutal slap of flesh on bone. But pain wasn't registering through the anger surging inside of me.

The two went down, hands and shields up to block my boots as I tried to stomp their bull faces. Mostly I missed, then had to leap aside as the two who were still on their feet rushed in. A wild blow from a filthy axe connected with the sword that I flashed in defense and the impact knocked me sideways into the path of a second attack. Barely did I man-age to duck under the spikes of a ball-and-chain mace as they slammed into a tree by my head.

But for just a moment those spikes lodged in the wood of the tree. I slashed up with my blade, chopped through the mace's rusted chain. Oxidization cracked away along the length of my sword and the steel beneath burst into a gleam of silver in the moons' light.

The bull-man whose weapon I'd hacked in twain staggered back. The other came charging and I ducked beneath his strike. He overran me, and from behind I snapped the haft of my sword up beneath the rim of his helmet and into the base of his skull. The half rotted cranium exploded and the creature smashed face first into a tree and dropped. I spun the blade through my fists and slashed down at the other dead warrior. He lifted a hand in vain and the steel cut through his fingers as if they were half melted butter and split his skull to the shoulders.

The last two of my enemies had risen again from where I'd knocked them down. But they had not attacked. Their red eyes flickered from beneath dark brows; they looked unsure. I snarled, stalked toward them, the now-bright blade swinging in my hands, its length shining with moonlit runes. Vohanna had bested me at every turn. But if I could not take my rage out on her then I would make her servants pay. And pay.

I leaped forward, my blade rising. The two foemen locked shields against my attack, their own weapons coming to guard position. But just before I reached them I dropped into a slide on my knees and slashed across with my sword just below the level of their defenses. Steel took on bone and dried tendons. Steel won. The legs of one bull-man sheared completely away from his torso. The other took a cut halfway through one thigh. Both of them collapsed, face first.

I had already rolled to my feet. The one who'd lost his legs jerked on the ground and I stepped forward to straddle him, both hands around the sword's hilt as I put the tip of the blade right through the back of his nearly fleshless skull, shattering sutures and bone and driving nearly a foot of steel through into the soft forest loam.

For just an instant I glimpsed some tiny pearl of light escaping from the wrecked braincase into the night. But then I heard the sound of my other foe, my last foe, scrabbling in the dirt. I turned. He reached his feet at the same moment, tried to hop away from me with one leg dragging.

I twisted my sword free of the earth, lifted it and threw it like a lance toward the being's back. The steel split him between the shoulder blades and six inches of it erupted out through the front curtain of his ribs. He fell and I leaped across the few yards that separated us to drop on top of him. Face down, he writhed, bony fingers clawing up twigs and dead leaves. I cupped his chin with both hands. My mind was a dark hell now, unforgiving, without mercy. I gave a savage wrench, heard the vertebrae shriek as they were torn apart.

I rose with the head in my hands. The teeth clacked; the neck trickled dust. With a growl I hurled the flame-eyed thing into the broad trunk of a nearby carbaxus tree. It split into half a dozen pieces, and again I saw a firefly spark as it leaped from the skull toward the heavens. And I smelled something then, something alien for which I had no name.

Behind me came a low hissing, and when I turned I saw the bull-man whose neck I'd hacked almost completely through. He lay on his back, his gaze burning up at me like a raw wound. I took up my new sword and moved over to him, stood looking down. This one still had its tongue, like a black and rotted fig, and it was the tongue moving over the teeth that made the hiss.

I lifted a foot. For a bare moment the thought of mercy licked my lips. Then some voiced whispered: "Think of Bryce." I stomped down, smashed the thing open and ground my heel in until there was nothing but shards left. Then I turned away.

I walked toward the tree where Diken Graye had gone to sleep, but at the base of it reaction hit me and I suddenly vomited up the few berries and nuts that I'd eaten since returning to Talera yesterday. My body shook and I half fell, half leaned against the bansul's trunk. I had killed before. But only once had I enjoyed it, and that emotion had been so distasteful and so frightening to me that I'd vowed never to allow it inside myself again. In that I had failed. For just now I had enjoyed killing again, had reveled in it. Without pity.

I shook my head, trying to regain control of my roiling

thoughts—thoughts of hate for Vohanna, of love and fear for Bryce and Rannon, thoughts of self loathing and despair and the wish for hope that I could not find. I believe in that moment that it was only the image of Rannon that kept me sane, that convinced me I had to keep trying even though every nerve screamed at me to sit down and not get up again. The very existence of Rannon gave me no choice but to keep going. To stop would be to disappoint her. And that I could not do. Perhaps, I thought, looking around at the carnage I had wrought, it was the *only* thing I could not do.

I turned my face up to the sky. The moon Sieonna, she who was sometimes called the Storm Queen, had sunk from sight, and the orb of Tisiminna lay upon the horizon. Only the scarlet face of Rath still floated above the canopy, its angry light tempered by the coming of a grayness into the world that marked the dawn. There was much that I had to do this day.

I started up the side of the tree to awaken Diken, my soul as red and gray as the light in the forest. I thought of Rannon. And salvation.

CHAPTER SIXTEEN

GHOSTS IN THE FOREST

Graye still slept, nestled in a hollow among limbs of his tree. Perhaps it was sorcery that had kept him so dead to the world while I'd fought among the shadows below. I did not know, but in the aftermath of the dream that had unleashed new invaders on Talera his face looked at peace. It was the first time I'd seen it so, and I hated to awaken him. I envied him.

But we had to get moving toward the site where the *Aestor II*, Rannon's airship, had been wrecked. I hoped to find Rannon and Ahrethane there. I needed to see Rannon, to hold her. And perhaps she or one of the others would know of some way to get word to Timmuzz about the army marching upon the city.

"Diken," I called softly. "Diken."

He sat up suddenly, eyes startled. Some faint white bloom unfolded in his dark pupils and I backed away. But he got control and the light died. With a sigh, he untied himself from the tree and rose slowly to his feet. I heard the creak and crack of his bones and muscles as they reaccommodated to each other.

He looked at me, and then away. I wondered what he had seen.

"Did I dream?" he asked.

"Yes," I said.

He jerked, then started to take deep, slow breaths. "Tell me," he said when he was calm.

"You dreamed an army," I told him. "And they march

now on Timmuzz."

He gave a tiny moan. I saw his jaw work, but he fought the tension down. It took him a while. Finally, he looked at me again.

"You should kill me, Ruenn," he said. "Do it when you can surprise me. So I won't know. So the gate won't open. I can't do it myself. I've tried."

I shook my head. "No. We'll find Ahrethane. She should be able to help. I'm sure...she can."

His haunted eyes seemed to accuse me; any peace he'd known while sleeping was long gone. But he turned without further words and started to climb down the tree. I followed him to the ground.

Saying nothing of the signs of destruction that I'd left scattered around, Graye headed off to the east in the direction we'd been going yesterday. I relieved myself, then followed. A handful of porphit berries made my breakfast. And after a bit I began to jog, feeling the goad of passing time stab at me. Diken Graye kept pace but still did not speak. His thoughts were a blank to me.

Just before the tenth dhaur, the Taleran noon, we passed beneath a stretch of rope bridge running through the trees in the same direction as we were going. I recognized the area, remembering the time in Ahrethane's tree house and the rope bridges around it that marked a once thriving settlement in the jungle canopy. That had been before Vohanna.

Bidding Diken Graye wait, I went forward on my own for several hundred taung (a taung is just over a yard). Soon, I came upon bits of shattered trees thrown like flotsam through the forest, and ahead within the gloom I saw the brightness of a clearing. Even before I stepped into that clearing, where Vohanna's pyramid—and later Rannon's ship—had crashed, I heard Ahrethane call loudly my name.

And then I was free of the screening trees and I saw Rannon standing near the stern of her smashed airboat. Rhandh and Ahrethane and three gray-cloaked guards stood with her, but it was Rannon my eyes devoured. She was looking my way, and with a cry of joy she suddenly came running, her dark hair streaming. I met her beside a jagged black boulder left over from the fall of the Witch's dark lair.

She leaped against me, laughing and crying, smothering my face with kisses. I held her tight, feeling and tasting her tears against my face and mouth.

"I thought you were lost forever," she murmured.

"So did I," I murmured back, squeezing her, blinking away my own tears.

Finally, Rannon released her arms from around my neck and I let her slide down until her feet touched the earth. She studied me. She knew immediately that something was wrong.

"Bryce?" she asked. "What happened?"

I looked up. Ahrethane and Rhandh had come closer, though not so close as to intrude. But when I answered Rannon's question I spoke loud enough for them all to hear. I told them of Bryce's battle with Vohanna in an alien temple, on an alien world. I told them of how at the last he'd opened a sphere gate and sent me through.

"Before," I added. "Before the Witch crushed the last of his will and made him her Bane-thrall."

There were more tears in Rannon's eyes now. These weren't joyous. She glanced from me to Ahrethane, as if the fiery-haired efrinore might have an answer. But there were no answers anywhere. I squeezed Rannon again.

Ahrethane sighed. I saw her shoulders slump.

"I've brought someone else with me, though" I said to the druidess. "A friend named Diken Graye. I thought... maybe you could help him. *He* is the wild gate. Made so by Vohanna."

Ahrethane's jade eyes quickened as she glanced once more to me. "Ah. That would explain much. Not least of which is why I did not know when you returned to the forest."

I frowned. "I wondered about that," I said. "I tried shouting. To startle the birds. I thought you might be able to trace me that way."

She shook her head. "I sensed a disturbance but not the cause. You remember that I could not locate the wild gate? Its magic is alien to mine. As long as you were close to its source I could not see you."

Her words made sense to me but hardly seemed important now. I looked back at Rannon and gave her a harder squeeze. Then I pushed her gently to arm's length and held her there.

"There's more that I must tell you all," I said, without taking my gaze from Rannon's blue on blue eyes. And I described for them the army of the dead.

Rannon gave a low cry, gasped out a "no," then sagged against me. Rhandh grunted an oath, his hand going white on the hilt of his broadsword. Ahrethane and the others, too, seemed devoid of breath.

Finally, Ahrethane moved forward to rest her hands on Rannon's shoulders. She looked at me. "We have to warn the city," she said. "But at the same time we must stop the wild gate inside your friend. Before it opens again and *another* army comes through. Or something worse."

Rhandh grunted. "Even if we left this moment," he said, "we'd not be able to reach the city in time to warn them. We have no transport. On foot we'd do no better than our enemies."

"There's a way," Arethane said. "After the battle here against Vohanna, many of the surviving saddle birds settled in the forest. I can call them."

Hope leaped in Rannon's eyes, and in Rhandh's and those of the other guards.

"But Diken Graye cannot leave the jungle," I said. I glanced at Ahrethane. "If we went to warn the city, could you help him?"

The efrinore licked her lips. Her eyes looked scared for a moment, but then she took a breath and I saw her composure return. "I may be able to," she said. "But I will need help. At least two people. One should be you, Ruenn."

My heart pounded at the thought of more sorcery. Give me a sword and I was brave enough to use it. But even the hint of magic turned my blood weak. Yet, I had no choice. Diken Graye was a friend.

I took Rannon's hands. "You should go," I told her. "Your peop—"

"No, Ruenn! I can't leave you so soon after finding you again. I...." She trailed off as she realized what she was saying. She was a princess, daughter to the emperor of Nyshphal. The people of this land were her responsibility. She could not shirk them, not for love or for any other reason. Her face was stricken.

"I will go," Rhandh said. He turned to Rannon. "I can warn the city as well as you, Jhesana. "You and Ruenn stay to help the druidess and come when it is done."

I knew what it must cost the big Vlih warrior to offer up his place at Rannon's side for even a moment. And to do so for me must have galled him. We had never become close friends. I did not think he believed me worthy of his princess, his Jhesana. Well, in that he was correct. Yet, it was clear to me from his words that his love for Rannon was pure and strong.

"How long will it take to do what we must for Graye?" I asked Ahrethane.

"A few hours. We must wait until night, though."

I nodded, glanced at Rannon. Any orders here would have to come from her. She was the daughter of Hurnan Jystral.

Rannon had moved to clasp Rhandh's wrist. "Thank you, old friend," she said. "Such service can never be forgotten." She turned to look at Ahrethane. "Please call the birds. Rhandh and the Gray-Cloaks who are left," she gestured at the three bodyguards who were all that remained of the twenty that had accompanied us when we left Timmuzz, "will go to alert the city as soon as their mounts get here. The rest of us will follow after Diken Graye is healed."

Ahrethane nodded and moved away toward the edge of the jungle. Rhandh was protesting that the Gray-Cloaks should stay with Rannon. I did not think he would win that argument.

"I'll fetch Diken," I told them both. They scarcely seemed to hear me.

By the time I returned with Graye in tow, the black dots of distant saddle birds were already growing wings in the scarlet sky. Soon we had a dozen hawk-like sabruns fussing and strutting in the clearing, though these hawks were big enough for men to ride. And not long after that, Rhandh and the others were mounted and ready to go. I'd been right. The Vlih hadn't won his argument with Rannon. The Gray-

Cloaks went with him.

After Rhandh and the others were gone, Rannon and Diken and I tethered the rest of the sabruns and then set to building a hut following Ahrethane's instructions. There were axes aboard Rannon's ship, and with them we cut limbs from some of the many fallen trees that had been killed when Vohanna's pyramid crashed here. The limbs made the skeleton of the hut and we fleshed it with huge leaves from the juujum bushes that grew in the clearing.

Our quick construction wouldn't keep out rain or insects but it seemed to satisfy Ahrethane. She disappeared inside as soon as it was completed, telling us that she'd call when she was ready.

Diken wandered off to brood. He had at first insisted that we leave him here, but he'd understood when I explained why we had to try and shut the wild gate permanently. He'd understood, and then felt even guiltier. There was nothing I could say to make him feel better.

Depressed, I leaned with Rannon against the twisted hull of her aircraft. We talked quietly. I told her what I had seen through the mouth of the wild gate, of the many strange battles and of the moon where we'd seen Talera rising. The battles surprised her, though not the fact that there was life on Talera's moons. Such had long been rumored.

To keep the topic off of Bryce, I asked her: "What happened with the insect queen's larva? Were you able to outrun them? Or did you have to fight?"

"We fought. They killed several more guards before Ahrethane was able to set them a trap. She lured them to a place where the ground collapsed under them. I imagine they're down in the caverns beneath the jungle where once you were."

I nodded, well remembering those caverns. "I'm sorry I wasn't...here," I said.

She half smiled, kissed me on the cheek. "You had to go after Bryce. There was no other choice."

And so the topic came back around to Bryce anyway. I was relieved when Ahrethane chose that moment to call us to her. Night had fallen.

Inside the hut there burned four small fires, each producing a different color smoke—one red, one blue, one green, one brown. I could smell herbs, moonrose and hysis and whitethorn, a dozen others I could not name. The crackling of the flames seemed loud in that quiet place, and though the smoke was steady it did not fill the room but spiraled out through gaps in the leaf covering as if it were being pulled.

Ahrethane had arranged a thin bed of moss in the center of the hut and she knelt at the foot of it. She was naked save for the fall of copper hair over her breasts. Her eyes were closed but she seemed to know where the three of us were when we stooped and entered. Her blind gaze turned to Diken Graye and she motioned him to lie on the moss. He did so, and Rannon went to kneel behind his head as if she knew what she was doing. I hesitated, until Ahrethane spoke in a soft and hollow voice.

"To his right, Ruenn. We must leave the left open."

I obeyed her, sinking to my knees where she indicated, feeling the faint damp coolness of the soil bleeding through the leather of my breeks.

From between her knees, Ahrethane picked up a cup woven of grass and bark, and she leaned forward and offered this to Diken. I smelled sage and verhlis and something else, something bitter—kahurra perhaps, or chirik root. She bade Diken drink and he lifted the cup to his mouth. The liquor inside was black, viscous, and Graye made a face as he tasted it. But he swallowed it all down.

"Sleep now," Ahrethane told him. "Sleep and do not dream."

Diken's nervous smile played across his lips, but he lay back and closed his eyes. Within moments he was unconscious. I looked up at Ahrethane. She had braided twigs of willow and oak through her hair, I saw, and there were symbols painted upon her belly and across her breasts with the purple juice of porphit berries. There were other symbols that had been cut into the soil around the moss bed with an oaken stick. Runes, they were, like bolts of lightning, and moons, and suns.

"Rannon," Ahrethane said, opening her eyes. "You will be my hands tonight. I cannot touch him. The magic that afflicts our friend here is alien to me and to this forest. To bring that magic and mine together directly would be...unfortunate." She gave a crooked smile to make it clear that "unfortunate" was an understatement.

Rannon nodded as I turned to study her. She looked calm, and beautiful. It was hot in the hut. Sweat beaded on her face and the gray silk of her shirt clung to her skin. Tangles of dark hair hung across her face, and there were streaks of dirt upon her from her days in the forest. But she was beautiful.

Ahrethane closed her eyes again and the world inside the hut grew warmer still, and darker. And then the efrinore began to chant in a tongue I did not know, the words coming slowly, but powerfully, as if from some deeper voice than this one small woman could possess. I saw, or thought I saw, the smokes from the four fires coil around Ahrethane and then drift across Diken Graye's recumbent form to flow into Rannon. At that moment Rannon picked up the chant herself, and I shivered despite the heat of the room. For I did not think my love knew this language.

The intensity of the chant doubled, and doubled again. The sound pounded in the tiny space. I wanted to cover my ears but could not seem to move. Then Rannon reached out to stroke Graye's temples, her fingers drawing circles there. Graye's mouth fell open, and I jerked as now I heard the sound of the chant coming from *his* throat. Even though his lips did not move.

Things got stranger. Rannon's hair lifted from her shoulders, floated in the air on wisps of smoke. And the blueness of her eyes became as green as the owl-eyes of Ahrethane. I stifled a cry, not daring to interrupt now, though my hands were clenched into bloodless fists on my knees.

From Rannon's wrists there sprouted dozens of earth-brown tendrils. Roots they were, growing, twining. They curled over Diken Graye's face, slipping into his mouth, up his nose, through his ears. Graye suddenly stopped chanting, mumbled some word I could not make out. He began to twist back and forth on his mossy bed.

Rannon and Ahrethane leaned further forward, chanting harder now, faster. The four fires, burning in the cardinal directions, sparked higher. Their smoke rose and billowed. It was all around me. I breathed it in, tasted and smelled it. But it did not choke me. It was faint, almost unreal.

Even the hut began to change, began to...dissipate. I glanced up, found myself looking through the leaf walls at the forest. The vast trees stood like brooding soldiers, and among them was a gathering. I saw shapes coming closer and closer, drifting, running, crawling. Some were human, with copper hair and green eyes and features like those of Ahrethane. Others were beasts, wolves with yellow gazes, panthers and black ghyres, winged reeths and pythons.

"Ruenn!"

I did not know who had called me. Ahrethane or Rannon? Or some other? But I jerked my gaze from the forest, found myself back in the hut. The temperature had spiked higher still. I felt it like a fist in my chest. Diken was grunting, struggling as if to throw off the tendrils that were burrowing into him.

"Hold him!" I heard, the command ringing in my ears.

I obeyed, throwing myself across Diken Graye, my hands on his shoulders as I tried to press him down. He struggled harder, began to thrash. I fought him. The chant tolled, and other voices entered in now. Voices from the forest. Human and not human. I tried not to hear, gritted my teeth as I fought Diken to stillness.

The chant surged, surged, surged. Graye arched his back, began to scream. I heard my own voice crying out, felt my muscles shaking and shaking as if they were about to rattle apart on my bones.

And silence exploded within the hut, rippled out through the walls. The jungle went quiet in an instant. Diken Graye collapsed beneath me. I glanced up, saw the whip of the tendrils withdrawing into Rannon's wrists, saw her slump, her eyes rolling back in her head.

"Rannon!" I shouted, pushing myself to my knees. I reached toward her.

"No, Ruenn!" I heard.

I paused, turned to look at Ahrethane. She was standing now, with the smoke of the fires over her shoulders like a cloak. She was not looking at me, but toward the forest. I followed her gaze, saw there the shapes I'd seen before, saw them turn away, saw them fade into the trees like the ghosts they must have been.

"My people," Ahrethane said. And, fiercely: "Vohanna could kill their bodies but not their spirits."

She turned then and gazed down at me. With her chin she gestured toward Diken Graye, and when I looked I saw that upon his chest there rested a single oval stone of palest glowing white. My skin crawled. It was a milkstone, a toir'in-or.

"Pick it up, Ruenn," Ahrethane whispered.

I hesitated.

"Pick it up for I cannot."

I nodded, reached out and pinched the stone between my thumb and forefinger and lifted it from its place. I expected it to be hot but there was no sensation at all except a smooth oiliness. I closed my palm over it, shutting off the wicked gleaming that I could not stand to see.

A sudden breeze caressed my back and I spun around to find that Ahrethane had fled the hut. I did not know why. But my first thought now had to be for Rannon. Diken Graye seemed merely to be asleep.

Tucking the milkstone into a pouch at my belt, I moved to lift Rannon and carry her out into the cooler air of the night. She stirred in my arms and when her eyes opened they were the old familiar blue. I smiled and kissed her, and lay her down upon a swatch of soft grass.

She smiled back. "Did it work?" she asked.

"Yes," I said. "It worked. Diken is free of Vohanna's control."

"Good," she said. She closed her eyes. She slept.

I sat there beside her, holding her hand but looking off into the forest where the ghosts of Ahrethane's people had gathered, and aided us. The night was lonely without them.

Chapter Seventeen

The Rasp of Leathery Wings

I found Ahrethane at the heart of the clearing petting a sabrun saddle bird. And though sabruns are normally full of peck and venom, this one stood quietly while the efrinore curled her slender fingers through the steel-gray feathers at its neck. The Druidess's eyes were luminous when she turned toward me. It was clear she had been crying. I hesitated, embarrassed at intruding. But she smiled.

"You were wondering how long we should let Diken and Rannon sleep," she said, and I nodded. I'd tried to make the two comfortable with pillows and blankets from the wrecked airship, but I was very conscious of the passing time as the army of the dead marched closer and closer to Timmuzz.

"In a dhaur or so they should awaken on their own. Refreshed. Then we will ride." She looked off into the forest and said with a quiet ferocity that resonated: "Vohanna's plans for Nyshphal can*not* be allowed to come to fruition."

"I agree," I said quietly. I left her to her thoughts then, went back into the wrecked airship to fetch the tack that I'd need to saddle and rein the birds.

True to Ahrethane's prophecy, both Rannon and Diken were soon up and around and the four of us were underway, winging south beneath an early night sky in which only the first moon, Nimeru, shone. The jungle of Vohan lay about a hundred and fifty verlangs (300 miles) from Timmuzz. In the *Aestor II*, Rannon's flyer, we'd covered that distance in a little over six dhaur, averaging in Earth terms about fifty miles per hour. Though sabruns could fly that fast for short distances, they could not keep it up for long, and so it took us all of what remained of the night period of ten dhaur to reach the city.

Only the last moon, Rath, still held the sky as we came down the Nyshphalian plain toward the conflux of three rivers where sat Timmuzz, the capital city. The horizon was already peeling away in a faint rind of pale russet light, and in the coming grayness Rannon urged her sabrun to greater speed, leaving me trailing behind with Diken Graye and Ahrethane even farther back.

I had just goaded my own bird ahead to catch up with Rannon when my love suddenly hauled back on the reins of her mount and stood up in the stirrups with the sabrun slowing beneath her. I frowned, drawing back on my own mount's reins, then glanced beyond where Rannon hung in the sky toward what should have been the sleeping city of Timmuzz.

The earth was still in darkness there, but the city was not...dark. Flames leaped in a dozen places, and above those fires now, against the quickening sky, I could see columns of black smoke rising.

Across the distance from Rannon I heard a faint cry breaking in the dawn, and then she kicked her bird into motion and raced away from me toward the smoke. I shouted after her, then loosed my own bird's reins and booted it beneath its wings. The sabrun leaped ahead, screeching like an angry hawk.

We swept forward, the beat of the wings rising to either side of me, throbbing with power. The light of dawn had gathered along the River Vehr and now it pounced across the water into the city. I saw in that light the wharfs and the merchant district and the palace intact. The flag of Nyshphal still flew.

But to the north side of the city, where the fires burned, many buildings were in rubble, and there was a wall where no wall had ever been. No, not a wall but rows of demolished buildings with the fallen blocks piled up hastily and haphazardly. That makeshift barrier continued to the east and west sides of the city, and in each of those three compass directions there smoked the fires of an army encampment.

Timmuzz was under siege!

But that was not possible. The dead army that I'd seen come through the gate in the jungle could not have reached here so quickly. The explanation struck me like a hailstorm. Vohanna must have other gates. And through them had come *other* armies. And why not? Why had I not conceived of such?

I shouted again for Rannon, my words whipped away by the wind. My boots drove a staccato rhythm into the sides of the sabrun as I urged it on. But Rannon's bird was faster than mine. She was pulling away, leaving me behind and above her as she angled downward like an arrow against the rising sun.

Then, from what must have been far above us both, a shadow dove upon her. I glimpsed wide spread wings supported by stretched bony fingers, a long whip of a tail with a spade of flesh at the end, and a savage beak curved like a sickle. The whole of it was without feathers. It was some kind of reptile.

There were two riders on the back of the beast, also winged, also reptilian. I saw one raise a tube to its mouth, heard a call peal forth, the sound of it like brazen chimes thrashing together. Rannon looked back and up. Her face whitened as the riders swept down upon her.

The one who had sounded the horn released it to hang around his neck and drew from his hip a weapon. I saw the ugliness of it, an ungainly thing of pipes and a handle of black wood. He fired it at Rannon. Puffs of smoke erupted from the pipes. Four of them. I heard a sharp crack even as I screamed a warning that was far too late.

Something hit Rannon in the back, slamming her forward over the neck of the sabrun. She cried out, and the bird joined her as its wings stuttered in mid-beat. I dropped the reins around my own sabrun's neck, leaned hard and low over its shoulder as I shouted it into a dive. My right hand dipped, hooked around the hilt of my sword. I drew the steel flashing into my fist.

The huge flying reptile pulled up to avoid slamming into Rannon's struggling mount. I saw one of its riders sawing back and forth on long reins that glinted like strands of barbed wire. The thing shrieked. I was close, close enough to hear the rasp of the beast's leathery wings as they bit harshly at the air.

Both of the alien riders seemed to sense me at the same moment. They looked up. Their faces were round black pits full of needle teeth, but they had eyes above those awful mouths and in those eyes I saw awareness. Of death coming.

Far over the neck of the sabrun I leaned, and chopped down hard with the sword. This was the same weapon that I'd taken from a dead man in the jungle of Vohan. Its three foot blade gleamed in silver, marked with strange, inhuman runes. Its edge was sharp and terrible and it sheared off the side of one rider's face, sliced on across the neck of the other to send the head tumbling away. Gore spattered, luminescent green in the gray of morning. I could smell it, like burning mold.

The right wingtip of my sabrun brushed the beak of the flying reptile and then we were past as the monstrous beast wheeled away in startlement, its riders hanging dead or dying in their saddle straps. From above, I heard more of the wild horns sound, knew they were sounding as a signal to a fresh assault. On me. But my only need was to see Rannon.

And there she was, just below me. She was alive, half standing in the stirrups as she hauled back on the reins of her mount. I saw wetness across the leather at her shoulder. But she was alive.

Her bird was not so lucky. Even as I watched, its wings beat a last desperate measure and folded. My love and her sabrun fell straight down toward the plains below.

CHAPTER EIGHTEEN

LONG FALL TO EARTH

They fell! Rannon and her sabrun. Down and down toward the still dark lands below. At the end of that drop would be nothing but death for them both. Above me I heard the brazen horns, the call of the hunt. Ahrethane and Diken Graye might be targets for that hunt. Surely I was a target. But none of that could matter to me now. Rannon mattered.

I sheathed my sword, leaned forward to shout a word in my sabrun's ear. That word was, "rish." If the bird knew it then Rannon might have a slim chance to live. Sabruns are among the smartest of the saddle birds. When fully trained they may recognize a vocabulary of dozens of words. But was this bird so trained?

The answer came as the sabrun immediately folded its wings and plummeted headfirst toward the earth. I was thrown hard against the straps that belted me into the saddle. They held.

I tucked my head down, slid my arms around the bird's neck. The wind screamed around me as I pressed my face close to the sabrun's shoulder, close enough to smell the ammonia given off by the feather mites that had infested it in the jungle of Vohan.

A glance around the saddle bird's neck brought wind-tears to my eyes, but it also showed me Rannon. Her bird was not quite dead. It struggled, wings fluttering, and Rannon struggled with it, standing in her stirrups with blood across her back, her hands working the reins as she tried to coax some last miracle of flight from her mount.

Morning light rushed across the earth below, and the earth rushed up toward us. I whispered another word to my mount, "jehas," and it shrieked a sharp savage cry. Rannon could never have heard *me* above the shout of the wind, but she heard the bird. She looked up and back, her face a pale oval, her mouth and eyes wide. Over her shoulder I could see trees and plowed farms and the river curving through them. So close.

We would only have one chance at this. I dropped the reins from my right hand. A tug with the left turned the sabrun's head, changing the angle of our dive. Our fall slackened just a bit. I hoped it was enough. But nothing that I did mattered if Rannon did not....

She did! I saw my love's hand slip to her waist. She drew a knife, slashed across her body to hack away her own saddle straps. For a moment the only thing holding her in the saddle was the grip of her feet in the stirrups. And then we were on top of her, almost beside her with the ground just below.

I jerked the reins to bring my sabrun's head up. Rannon kicked free of her stirrups at the same time and leaped toward me. Her pupils were huge, dilated with fear; her face was as white as bone.

A flash of my sabrun's wing fanned Rannon's hair. Her hands reached desperately. She flailed, missing my grasp, the wing brushing her flank. But then she slammed into my side just below the shoulders. She started to slide, her hands grabbing, grabbing, her feet kicking off in the air. My mount shrieked again, in its own fear now as the sudden new weight drug it to one side. Rannon's saddle bird hit the ground like a broken fist, with the sound of bones snapping.

I snatched at Rannon's slender frame. My fingers caught in the leather of her sword belt, latched on. For an instant I took her whole weight, the muscles of my arm straining as if the tendons were going to tear lose from the bone. But Rannon got her arms about me, locked them in a death grip around my waist, and I pulled her up and into the saddle so that she faced me. Her shocked eyes loomed into mine. I could feel her heart pounding through her chest where she was pressed into me. There was no time to kiss her, though I

126

thought of it.

I grabbed the sabrun's reins with both hands, but the bird was already pulling up on its own, skimming so close above a grove of oaks that I heard the breeze of our passage stirring the leaves. A sudden hornet's buzz slashed past my ears and then I heard the report from one of the reptile rider's guns. Instinctively I ducked, and so did Rannon. I had forgotten about our hunters. They *hadn't* forgotten us.

The sabrun responded instantly as I jerked the left and down reins at the same time. We swept below the level of the trees as more shots from enemy guns whipped past above us. Below us were fields of grain, of wheat and yellow cymer. Most of it was trampled now, torn up under the boots of the city's besiegers.

"They're diving," Rannon shouted, her gaze looking above my shoulder at the coming attack.

I took the sabrun to the right, down into the channel of the River Vehr where the muddy current churned. We skimmed the water, close enough to feel its coolness washing up and over us. More enemy bolts slashed past us to dimple the surface of the river. I saw a huge shadow swoop between us and the rising sun. But the sabrun was faster in the stretch than the reptiles. We began to pull away with the horns sounding havoc behind us and the massive stone quays of Timmuzz's harbor growing closer before us.

I glanced up, cursed as I saw a flock of some dozen of the reptiles diving from above to cut us off from the city. They had the angle on us. We would never beat them to a place of safety.

I looked at Rannon. She'd seen the same thing I had. Now she looked back at me. And I swear there was a smile tugging at the corners of her lips.

"Jump when I say," I told her softly. "We'll swim for it."

She nodded.

But in the end we didn't have to jump. Or swim.

Out of the city came a sortie of patrol flyers, the maroon and gray flag of Nyshphal snapping at their prows. The outnumbered reptile riders didn't even try to fight but turned tail and ran. No doubt, they knew they'd have another day.

The Nyshphalian flyers swept down around us, turned to escort us toward the palace. I wasn't sure how they had known who we were. Unless Rhandh had gotten through and they were watching for us. For the first time in a while I had a moment to worry about Ahrethane and Diken Graye. Had they made it through as well? Or had they become prey for the enemy? I ground my teeth, knowing that there was nothing I could do to affect either outcome.

In another few dhorrin we were coming in to land on the roof of Hurnan Jystral's palace, where the sabrun mews were located. I noted that landing space had been hastily cleared for flyers as well, and two of our escorts settled to rest with us while the others turned away to resume their patrols over the city.

As soon as we were down I dismounted and pulled Rannon from the saddle into my arms, turning her about to look at her back where I had seen her struck by at least one shot. Her leather jerkin was sliced open over the shoulder and something—I couldn't tell if it were a bullet or a bolt—had cut a shallow groove through the flesh beneath. She had bled a lot, enough so that the injury looked much worse than it really was. But already the wound had clotted and the blood was drying. She was going to be all right.

I breathed a sigh of relief and Rannon turned to face me. Her hand stroked my cheek, and the blue in her eyes was more brilliant than the clearest sky of the clearest day on the planet of my birth.

"I'm fine, Ruenn," she said. "But thank you once again for saving me." She paused, and a small smile curved her lips. "This time I really did need it."

A voice preempted any response I might have made.

"Jhesana. Thank Sevarian."

We both turned, and I was surprised to see that Rajan Critus had been aboard one of the flyers that had come to our aid. It was he who had spoken, and now he offered Rannon a salute. She acknowledged it, but I could not help wondering why the lean commander of the Imperial Guard had been risking himself aboard a patrol flyer. With Rannon and I gone, and with Kuurus accompanying his father to the coast, Critus had been placed in charge of the entire city. That had been mere days ago.

"Thank Sevarian," Critus said again. "I—"

"What happened here, Commander?" Rannon interrupted. "We are gone only a week and return to find the city besieged. And what of my father? Have you heard from him?"

Critus sighed, rubbed at his tired black eyes with a grimy hand. Smoke had smudged his dark-complected face and there was a rip in one sleeve of his usually immaculate uniform. I had never seen Rajan dirty and unkempt before. It was a worrisome sight.

"Barely two days after you and your father left Timmuzz," he said, "the Reploids attacked."

"Reploids?" I asked.

He waved a hand toward the dawning sky beyond the city. "You saw them. The ones who tried to kill you. The reptile riders with wings. But there is another kind as well. Non-winged. And there are more of those. They came out of the northern prairie riding some kind of huge beasts that had never been seen before. With the flying ones overhead.

"They attacked into the city. In the northwest quadrant. Tough as ironwood they are. It took us three days to drive them out again. By that time two more armies had arrived, each from some unknown race. Unknown to us at least. We had managed to get up a kind of rough barricade. You probably saw it flying in."

Both Rannon and I nodded as he continued.

"The newcomers didn't seem intent on attacking. They threw up camps and we've been exchanging skirmishes with them since. They haven't completely encircled the city yet. We can still get supplies in along the upper river. If we escort those supplies with flyers. And to the south the prairie is open."

"It may not be for long," I said, telling him then of the fourth army that was marching our way. I didn't tell him that *that* army might be even harder to kill than the others. Seeing as how they were already dead.

He nodded. "We've been expecting some such." He looked at Rannon. "Your brother thinks we can hold the city against them all."

Rannon blinked. "My brother? Kuurus is here?"

Critus inclined his head slightly. "Yes, Jhesana. Kuurus is here. He returned two days ago. For reinforcements. But...." Critus shrugged. "He felt that, with the attacks, he should stay. And take charge."

I saw Rannon frown at this unexpected news. "And what did Kuurus say about my father? About the battle at the coast?"

"I am sorry, Jhesana. But he said the battle had gone hard for Nyshphal and that your father was fighting a slow retreat back up the river toward Timmuzz." He paused for just a moment before adding. "Pursued by half a dozen Ubain legions."

Rannon swiveled her head to look at me. Anyone else might have believed her calm. But I knew the truth. I could see her worried thoughts shifting across her eyes like drifts of dark birds.

My own thoughts were equally troubled, but perhaps for a different reason. Something about what Critus had said did not add up. I just couldn't quite figure out what. And there were too many other concerns on my mind at the moment to spend time thinking on it.

"I must talk to Kuurus," Rannon said, her words rushing. "We have to get in touch with my father. Find out what he needs us to do."

"Of course," Critus said, turning to lead us into the palace. "I'll take you."

"One more thing," I said, drawing the guard commander's gaze back to mine. "Did any other bird riders come in? Just before or after us? We had companions. A woman and a man. But we lost sight of them when the Reploids attacked."

Critus shook his head. "I saw no other riders," he said. "But perhaps some of the other patrols...." He trailed off, shrugging helplessly.

Rannon studied me, reached to give my arm a squeeze. "Have someone check with the other patrols," she ordered Critus. "And if there's no sign send out search parties. Bring us word as soon as you have any."

Critus nodded, glanced meaningfully at one of his lieutenants who hurried off to obey. Then the commander, and Rannon, and I strode into the palace. Above Timmuzz the early morning sun stood scintillant, shedding its crimson light. A new day had begun, a day that could have been beautiful but was stained instead with the darkness of smoke and war.

My soul felt just as dark.

I hoped it was not as stained.

CHAPTER NINETEEN

THE SOWING OF DOUBT

From the roof where the clangor of a city at war pounded the ears, Rajan Critus guided us into the hush of Jystral Palace. When Hurnan Jystral dwelt within these walls there were always the sounds of life being lived, the rush of feet on the marble stairs, the clatter of pots in the kitchens, the laughter of women and men going about their daily tasks. Now it was as if a funeral had passed by and left its somber mood behind. But perhaps my metaphor was more apt than I had intended. Who knew how many had died in the past few days, how many *would* die in the next few.

It was to the main throne room that Critus led us. I was surprised, though perhaps I shouldn't have been. Rannon's father, the emperor, typically used the royal chamber only for ceremonial occasions, preferring to hold most conferences and make most decisions from within his more comfortable and more approachable home quarters. The emperor's son, Kuurus, seemed of a different mind, although he too had sumptuous rooms given over to his use within the palace.

Soldiers in maroon and gray ushered us past doors of gold and white into Kuurus's presence. The prince wore the coal black uniform of a captain in the Imperial Guard, though it was not, in truth, an office that he held. The clothes fit him well, though. He'd set up his command post before the snow-wood throne of his father, and there upon a table of mahogany I saw scattered maps and small figurines that represented troops and lines of defense. Many more soldiers hung about the room, their weapons at the ready.

Kuurus stood behind the table with Arca Heskern, Nyshphal's chief scientist, and with Taskin Bhent, general of the Nyshphalian armies. He and the general were arguing. About what I could not hear. But when Kuurus saw us enter he shook off Bhent's complaints and put a smile on his face, and he came rushing around the table as if glad to see us. I noted that he alone of those present did not look exhausted. There was no grime on *his* face, no dark circles under *his* blue eyes.

"Rannon! Dear sister." He gave her a hug, no doubt astonishing her as much as he did me. Even more shocking was when he turned and grasped my shoulder in a comradely way and said with a smile: "Thank you for seeing my sister safely through our besiegers, Ruenn. Such will not be forgotten."

I think my mouth must have dropped open wide enough to insert a small anvil, but Kuurus did not see it for he had turned back to Rannon, linked his arm through hers, and was guiding her toward the map table. Haltingly, I followed, wondering if I had somehow been transported to yet another strange world, one where Kuurus Jystral was kind and considerate rather than rude, pompous, and insufferable.

I shook my head at myself. *Impossible!* Some things are just *too* far fetched to ever be true.

Arca Heskern and Taskin Bhent each gave me a nervous smile as I approached the table. Each stepped back to clear me space. I nodded a greeting to them; their responses were tepid, short inclines of the head that did more to suggest uneasiness than friendliness. Yet, I had known each of them for some time and we had always gotten along. One would think, at least, they would be happy to see Rannon return to the city.

Something was wrong here. And it was not just Kuurus's newfound graciousness.

I glanced about. For the first time I noticed some troopers who did not wear the maroon and gray of the palace guard. Instead, they were dressed in rust-brown leathers and stugah-hide boots, attire commonly seen among mercredi. That is, among mercenaries. These—and there were six of them—lounged in the background, though their seemingly relaxed postures were clearly an act. I could see the predators in their eyes as they watched the room. All six were human, and two were black, though it is unusual to see blacks among the northern companies of mercenaries.

One of the mercredi was staring at me. I met his gaze, studied him. He was powerfully built, with muscles bulging his bare and tanned arms. His eyes were a very intense brown, almost yellow, and there was a scar left by some bladed weapon across his lower lip.

My glance found the other mercenaries in turn then, and the small sense that I'd had of something being wrong intensified. Warning bells began to clang in my head, though still I could not be sure why. It was only that...their stances were wrong. Although each of the six warriors carried a sword and daggers at their belts, their hands were not quite in the right places.

A right-handed swordsman normally wears his blade at his left side. Even when at rest his hands will fall a certain way when he lets them hang. His left hand usually grasps the upper part of the sheath, just beneath the quillions of the blade. The thumb of his right hand will often be hooked into his belt, the fingers curled toward the hilt for a quick drawing of the weapon. Even if his right hand rests near a dagger at his right side, his hand will be curled a little toward the left.

One of the mercredi had his *left* thumb tucked into his belt, even though he wore his sword on that side. In several of the others I noted that their right hands hung almost flat at their sides, palms parallel to their thighs with the fingers curled just slightly inward.

I frowned. A thought nagged at me.

"But we must!"

The words fell loudly into the room and I turned. It was Rannon who had spoken, and in her face was written some admixture of worry and anger. I moved to her side, having missed most of her conversation with her brother. For his part, Kuurus looked at me with what could almost have been an appeal.

Rannon's blue eyes were turned toward me as well. And

in her face now, the worry was clearly winning over the anger. My heart suffered for her. I knew what must be terrifying her. I took her hand.

"Ruenn," she said. "Tell Kuurus that we must get word to my father. We have to warn him of the armies that await him here as he retreats. We...." She broke off, looking back at the war table and its complicated map. Downriver to the west of Timmuzz, that map was frighteningly empty. We had so little information about what was going on toward the coast. We did not know where Hurnan Jystral was. We did not even know—I tried not to look at Rannon—if the emperor still lived.

I glanced at Kuurus.

"I've already sent a dozen bird riders," he protested. "More went out this morning. It would be foolish to send others until we know what happened to the first ones."

"A reconnaissance in force, perhaps," I mused.

Kuurus sighed. "I had thought of that. But now." He shrugged. "With the news that Rannon just told me! A fourth army marching to besiege us! There's been enough activity in the enemy camps to suggest that they are readying an assault. It must be the arrival of the fourth army for which they await. When the new attack comes, I'll need every man I can muster. Our barricades will barely slow them down. We'll be fighting in the streets. Can you imagine what our father would say if he found out we'd stripped the city's defenses in order to send him a message?"

Rannon's shoulders slumped. She knew what their father would say. I squeezed her hand more tightly, wracking my brain for a solution that would not come.

"Where's Rhandh?" Rannon asked, suddenly. "He did make it through did he not?"

Rajan Critus had come up beside us while we spoke. I thought I saw him stiffen at mention of Rhandh's name. But when his gaze met mine, his face was bland. Perhaps I'd imagined a reaction on his part. Damn, but I was jumpy.

"Yes," Kuurus replied to Rannon's question. "Your Vlih bodyguard made it through. That's why we were watching for you. But he left again right after. Said he would return to your side." The prince's lips pursed in a moue of petulance that was almost refreshing. "He disobeyed my orders, in fact."

Rannon shook her head, looking down at the floor. I put an arm around her, felt her shoulders trembling as she fought for control. First her father she had to worry about. And now Rhandh, who had been her protector and her friend for a very long time. Yet, I suspected the big Vlih would survive if anyone could.

"I think the princess and I need a little rest," I said.

Kuurus looked stricken, as if he'd somehow forgotten his manners. "Oh, of course." He gestured. "Rajan. An escort if you please."

The commander stepped forward and detailed half a dozen soldiers to accompany us. I almost started to protest, wanting more than anything to be away from military matters for a moment. But...we were at war. There was no escaping that.

The palace corridors were largely empty of servants. I supposed many of them were either manning the city barricades or were providing logistical support for those who did. Our passage to Rannon's apartment went unhindered, and once there our escorts set themselves up at the door as a guard detail—all except for one who I sent off to fetch me word as to the health and whereabouts of Valyan and Kreeg. I'd forgotten to ask Kuurus about them, and none of our guards seemed to have any idea where my old friends might be. I did not like that. But then, there were quite a few things about this new palace I did not like. Or trust.

"So, what angel did Kuurus kill for its wings?" I asked Rannon after we were ensconced in her room and she'd flopped onto her bed with an exhausted sigh. "Surely he's not become as sweet and thoughtful as he seems." I noted that the glass had been replaced in her balcony doors from where I had kicked it in on the day the assassins had come for us

Rannon smirked at my comments. "I think he's just enjoying playing at being emperor," she said.

I nodded. Kuurus was Hurnan Jystral's only son, and in most places during the history of Earth that would have meant he was first in line for the throne. But this was Talera.

The elder Jystral had made it clear that Rannon, his daughter, was his chosen successor, not because she was the older of his two children, but because she was in his eyes—and mine—most fit to rule. It was clear to me that Kuurus had long resented his father's choice, though he had never spoken publicly against it.

I moved over to where Rannon lay and leaned down to kiss her.

"I want you to rest, Saysa," I told her softly. "I need to fetch a few things from my room. And check on Valyan and Kreeg if anyone can tell me where they are. I'd also like to get a look at the barricade. See what kind of defenses are set up there."

She nodded, then closed her eyes with a sigh. The fact that she'd not sought to accompany me proved how tired she was, and almost instantly she was asleep. I was glad. I did not think she'd fully recovered from acting as a conduit for Ahrethane's magic when the druidess had pulled the milkstone from Diken Graye's body.

Thinking of milkstones, I reached suddenly for the pouch at my belt where I'd tucked the one that Ahrethane had removed from Graye. The pouch was gone and I felt a momentary chill. I'd once been able to use a toir'in-or stone against Vohanna. I'd thought, perhaps, that I might be able to do so again. But now there was no chance of that. The pouch must have fallen off during our long flight on the sabruns. I hoped the loss wouldn't become the dog that bit me.

Leaving Rannon sleeping and with the guards outside her door, I headed for my own room within the palace. This time I took the corridors and stairs instead of jumping the balconies as I had a week ago. It might not have been as fast but it was a lot less brutal on the old body.

My apartment was just as I had left it. Had it been only a ten-day ago? I crossed immediately to a corner table where a haphazard collection of old weapons lay piled, and reached for a worn quiver that held only two arrows. And I found that not *everything* was as I'd left it.

In the meeting that I'd had with Hurnan Jystral after the assassination attempts on myself and Rannon, I had shown the emperor two Smith & Wesson .38s that had obviously

137

been brought from Earth to Talera. One of those had been given to Arca Heskern for study. The other I had brought back to my room and hidden in an arrow quiver. That one was missing.

I felt a frown pulling at the corners of my eyes. Though not common, there are locks on Talera, bulky but simple affairs of iron and wood. I had used one of them on the door to my room when I'd left Timmuzz, and it had still been there when I'd returned just a few minutes before. Clearly, someone had managed to bypass that lock. I supposed they must have used another key, though there wasn't supposed to *be* any other key.

So, who could have found the way?

The door creaked behind me and I spun on my heels, grabbing for the hilt of my sword. Rajan Critus stood there. And in his hand was an answer to my question of the instant before. The pistol wasn't quite pointed at me, but it wasn't quite pointed at the floor either.

As if for the first time, I suddenly noticed how black Critus's eyes were. Almost Vohanna black.

CHAPTER TWENTY

OF TRUTH AND DECEPTION

"Looking for this?" Critus asked.

My gaze swept from Rajan's black irises to the dark clot of the pistol that he held loosely in one hand. His finger was not on the trigger and I wondered if he knew how to use the weapon. I had to assume that he did.

But...even if he knew how to use it, could he hit what he aimed to hit? Putting a bullet into a target with a pistol is not as easy as most people think. Especially if the target is moving. My uncle had been Quentin Maclang, known in the Old West of the 1860s and '70s as a shootist, a gunfighter. He'd told me of fights where two men as close as a dozen yards to each other blazed away until their revolvers were empty without hitting a thing they were shooting at. Like with a sword, it takes talent *and* practice to learn how to use a gun. I wondered how much practice Rajan Critus might have had.

I wondered what he would do if I rushed him.

"Indeed, I was," I said in answer to the guard commander's question. "Interesting to find it in *your* hands. I'm wondering why?"

Critus stepped the rest of the way into my apartment and closed the door carefully behind him. I tensed as he lifted the pistol, but still his finger did not curl through the trigger guard. And then he was turning the weapon about in his palm, offering the butt to me. I walked across and took it, stood for a moment studying him. He was about an inch shorter than I, perhaps a few pounds lighter. It was said that he was an incredible swordsman, though of that I could not be sure, never having had a chance to fence with him.

"I took it before someone else did," he said. "Someone who I didn't want to have it."

I arched an eyebrow in question.

He left any answer unvoiced, but instead walked past me into the room to gaze out through the glass doors that fronted my balcony. The morning sky beyond that glass was blushed with rose, and there was no sign of the smoke that had stained it earlier. It might have been a typical day in Timmuzz. But I knew it wasn't.

When Critus did speak, it was of a different matter. "One of Rann—one of the Jhesana's guards said you were looking for your companions. The gladiator and the Green Llurn."

"Yes," I said, moving eagerly toward him. "Kreeg and Valyan! Do you know where they are? Or if they are well?" His comment about the gun was not forgotten but at the moment I was more interested in hearing news of my friends.

Critus turned to face me, linking his hands together behind his back. His face was as expressionless as fired clay.

"They were removed from their rooms here," he said, "but are still on the palace grounds. The temple of Sevarian has been set up as a phorosnex. We'll almost certainly require such when the fighting starts in earnest."

Phoros is a Taleran word meaning healer or physician. Nex means place. Critus was telling me that Valyan and Kreeg had been taken to a hospital. And I imagined he was right in saying that we'd need hospitals once our enemies attacked in force.

As if he'd seen all he cared to see through my balcony doors, Critus turned and walked back past me, pausing only at the opening into the hall. The glance that he gave me from there was inscrutable.

"Perhaps you would care for a more complete aerial view of the battlefront," he said. "After you've seen about your friends, if you would join me on the roof of the palace, we can take a flyer."

I nodded. Critus's voice had been casual, but there was something…not casual behind his words. Or at least I felt that there was.

"I'd hoped to get a better look at our enemies," I acknowledged.

It was the commander's turn to nod. "Then, shall we say in a dhaur?"

"Agreed."

A small smile flicked across the man's lips and was gone just as quickly. He shut the door behind him as he went out.

What had just happened here, I wondered. Had I been threatened? Or was Rajan Critus trying to warn me of something? I shrugged. In a little over an hour I should find out. For now, I wanted to see my friends.

I snapped open the cylinder of the Smith & Wesson .38. There were six cartridges but one had been expended. I remembered the single shot that a Kaldi assassin had fired at me. This was the gun he'd used. Plucking out the spent shell casing, I tossed it onto my bed, then closed the cylinder and eased the hammer down over the empty chamber. I tucked the weapon under my sword belt at the small of my back. It seemed like a good idea to take it with me.

Although it wasn't yet a cold autumn, there was enough chill in the air that wearing a coat would not seem amiss. I slipped on a long rawhide duster, the kind often worn by saddle bird riders, then went out the door and down through the rooms of the palace. The coat would hide the pistol.

* * * * * * *

Sevarian is the primary god worshipped by the people of Nyshphal. He is a god of good harvests, a god of brotherhood and peace. Although I imagined there were other gods being prayed to in Timmuzz these days, darker gods meant to serve more violent passions, Sevarian was still the one to which most of the people turned. There were thirty or more temples dedicated to him across the city, but the one to which Rajan Critus had referred to as a phorosnex was on the grounds of Jystral Palace. I had been there many times.

The main chapel area of the temple had been left untouched, I found, but the greater part of the building had been converted into rows of simple beds and small rooms for surgeries. All floors and surfaces were meticulously clean, for the germ theory of disease was well known in Nyshphal, if not generally on Talera.

It was good to see that most of the beds were still empty. My footsteps echoed as I passed among them. A workman finally pointed me toward a corridor where I might find a phoros, a doctor. I went looking.

Physicians on Talera do not wear white coats and carry clipboards. But they have the look and the presence, that combination of empathy and intelligence, of concern and a confidence that may—in some—border on arrogance. Even without seeing his face, I could tell that the Kaldi I found speaking to a patient in one of the beds was a healer. His body telegraphed it, though there was nothing of arrogance in his stance. I waited until he finished talking to the young soldier, who had one arm in a sling, then stepped forward to catch his attention.

And I stopped. I knew this phoros. Though he looked older than I remembered and had grown almost painfully thin, I knew him.

"Vriun!" I said.

"Ruenn!" His smile was wide as he came toward me and we clasped arms. "By Venghi's withered paps, it's good to see you. It's been far too long."

"Aye. It has. But I thought you had retired."

"I did," he said, chuckling. And then more seriously: "Planned to spend my waning years growing wine-grapes along the Upper Vehr. But," he glanced toward the soldier with the injured arm, "I'm needed now. Or soon will be at least."

Vriun's last statement was very close to what Rajan Critus had also said. I was very afraid that both of them were correct, and it made me wince. But still, it *was* good to see a friend. I'd met Vriun in the lava mines of the Klar pirates not long after I'd arrived on Talera. We'd both been slaves there, and had fought free of that slavery together. Afterward, he had returned to Nyshphal with Rannon and me and had taken up the duties of a court physician. Barely a year later he had retired, less because of his age, which was considerable, and more from the accumulated injuries he'd sustained over years of harsh imprisonment by the Klar.

Vriun lifted a hand to rest on my shoulder. "I heard about Heril's death," he said, his tone somber now. "I'm sorry. He was a fine man. A good friend."

"He was that," I agreed, nodding at his words. "I suppose Valyan or Kreeg told you?"

Heril, and Valyan, and Kreeg had been with Vriun and I in the lava mines of the Klar when we fought the slavers for our freedom. None of us would have made it without the others.

Vriun frowned, shook his head. "No. I haven't seen Valyan or Kreeg since I returned. I forgot who told me about Heril. Another phoros, I think."

My heart thudded; a chill slid beneath the skin at the back of my neck and burrowed downward.

"But aren't they here?" I asked. "I was told...."

I trailed off as Vriun's frown kept growing. He shook his head again.

"There aren't that many patients here at the moment. I've probably seen them all." He paused. Then his frown began to fade as a thought seemed to occur to him. "But I've only been at the hospital two days. I suppose they could have been released before I arrived."

Kreeg, perhaps, I thought. But Valyan had been badly hurt. He hadn't healed broken ribs in a ten-day.

"Is there a way to find out for sure?" I asked.

"I should think so," Vriun said. "We'll have a look."

The vestment chamber where the priests of Sevarian normally changed into their ritual robes had been converted to a hospital office and it was there that patient records were kept. Those records were maintained on neatly inscribed sheets of wax-cane parchment, in separate folders of vellum. It took Vriun and me only a few dhorrin to realize that there were no folders for either Valyan or Kreeg.

The Kaldi's frown was back. "Are you sure they were brought here?" he asked.

"So I was told," I said. "Are there other hospitals?"

"Several. But if they were being carried directly from the palace they *should* have been brought here. It's not as if we lack room at the moment."

"It would appear, then, that I've been lied to."

Vriun must have heard the grim river running beneath my words.

"I'm rather glad I'm not the one who told that lie," he said. And: "I can see that the records are checked at the other phorosnexes. You're staying in the palace?"

"Aye," I said, reaching to grasp his arm. "I appreciate it."

"Of course. As I appreciate the chance to *be* of help instead of wielding a pick in the lava mines of the Klar."

Our gazes met. We understood each other. Now he, too, would be searching for our friends. And thin and old though he might be, I remembered him with a blade in his hand as we charged into the Klar lines those long days ago. Vriun the Kaldi was still a man to beard the devil with, and a dangerous foe to have as an enemy. As *our* enemies might soon find out.

Leaving Vriun to his investigations, I made my way toward my meeting with Rajan Critus. There was much I had to ask him. And yet, confusion reigned in me. If Critus had lied deliberately, why had he done so? And why such an obvious untruth, one so easy to uncover?

In a few dhorrin I was stepping onto the roof of the palace in search of the guard commander. There were no flyers to be seen. But there *were* four men waiting for me. Two of them were not human. Neither of the others was Critus. All four were smiling, with naked blades gleaming cold in their hands.

CHAPTER TWENTY-ONE

A SWORD FOR TALERA

The leader of the four assassins—for so I assumed them to be—was a lean and battle scarred Vhichang. Beside him stood an Ss'Korra, and behind them were two humans who were alike enough in their red hair and ruddy faces so as to be brothers.

Though they have two arms and two legs and lack wings, the Vhichang evolved from avian ancestors. Their faces are beaked, the tip cruelly curved, and above the beak are small eyes, like wicked yellow rosary beads. A pelt of downy feathers covers their bodies and their shoulders are humped with the muscle that is a legacy of their flying forbearers. An occasional baby is even said to be born with vestigial wings on its back. The legs of a Vhichang are curved almost into the shape of an unstrung bow, seemingly built more for perching than striding. But they are quick.

The Ss'Korra are sometimes called the dog people, and perhaps they resemble a two-legged version of such beasts. They are furred, except on their bellies, and their faces have muzzles. Their feet look much like paws, though they have human-type hands. Many of them have blue or green eyes.

Neither Vhichang nor Ss'Korra are common races in Nyshphal, which, as I may have said before, is largely a human country. Both of these were probably mercenaries who had come here seeking employment in the war. Or at least that was the impression they meant to give. No doubt, the two redheaded humans were cast from the same set of dies. It would seem that all four had found ready employment for their swords.

I wondered who had hired them.

I doubted they'd volunteer to tell me.

"Where's Critus?" I demanded.

One of the redheads chuckled. The Ss'Korra smirked. Or snarled. It was hard to tell on his muzzled face.

"I'm afraid Commander Critus isn't giving tours today," the Vhichang said. He started walking slowly toward me, bringing his sword up in line with my body. The others came too, fanning out to either side of their leader.

"And are any of *you* giving tours?" I asked.

The Vhichang paused, momentarily confused by my question.

Again, one of the redheads chuckled. I thought it was the same one as before. "Our swords are gonna have a bloody tour of your guts," he said.

I smiled. "Such colorful language. You should have been a poet."

The Ss'Korra had paused when the Vhichang had, but now he started forward again. "Enough," he snarled. "Let's kill him and be done. Before someone comes."

I had not yet drawn my blade. Now, instead, I slipped my right hand under my coat and behind my back, brought it out again with the Smith & Wesson .38 held in my grip.

The four assassins kept coming. Yet again, one of the redheads snickered. And I caught a swift and withering glare sent his way by the Vhichang leader.

My eyes narrowed. Perhaps none of the four had seen a gun before. Perhaps, with their being from outside of Nyshphal, they had not even heard of them. The quick little snicker of the redhead could be dismissed as an emotional tic. But that glance from the Vhichang? It bothered me.

I looked down at the pistol in my hand. Its blue-steel barrel pointed like the finger of death toward the assassins. Or did it? A worm of doubt had crawled in through my eyes with the Vhichang's glance. It began to burrow.

A low stone parapet bordered the rooftop area. I placed the pistol carefully on its flat granite surface, then drew my sword and started walking forward to meet my enemies.

"No need for a gun to deal with you four," I said, smirking at them.

The Ss'Korra growled savagely, his green eyes brightening, his body going tense. I'd expected him to be the most volatile, the least able to take an insult. I pointed the tip of my blade at him.

"I'm going to kill you first," I told him. "Get the easy stuff over with." My gaze was locked on his, my mouth filled now with a smile.

"Don't let him taunt—" the Vhichang started.

It was too late. With a howl of rage the Ss'Korra hurled himself across the last few steps separating us. His blade was out, but though he was furious he was not stupid. He didn't slash with his sword. He came in thrusting, his weapon in line for defense in case he missed his strike.

But I didn't do what he expected me to do. I didn't parry, or dodge, or backpedal. I leaned into his attack, my runed blade leaping out to meet his, but not to block his thrust.

He carried a rapier with a basket hilt, that hilt woven from finely filigreed wires thickly wrapped about each other. It was pretty. And dangerous. My sword was longer than his by about four inches. Our blades slid together, shrieking, the tip of my weapon scraping sparks along the blood runnel in his steel. Then, with a tremendous jar, the point of my blade stabbed into the grillwork of his hilt. The weapons locked and I twisted my arm from the shoulder.

I was ready for the shock; he was not.

The impact must nearly have broken his wrist. It certainly ripped the blade right out of his grasp. He cried out, tried to halt his rush. I whipped my leg across to take his feet from under him. He went down, hands out to break his fall. I heard him cry out again as the flesh of his palms tore on the harsh stone of the palace roof.

The two redheads came rushing, the Vhichang a step to their right. I snapped my wrist upward, flipping the rapier off the tip of my blade. It spun, winking in the red sunlight, and came down. I plucked it from the air. The redheads were almost on top of me. I parried their thrusts, a sword in each of my fists. Metal clanged.

The Vhichang lunged, his blade parallel to the earth, the steel humming as it came. To hesitate was to die spitted on three swords. I leaped forward from between my foes, a desperate leap that I could never have made without the threat of death goading me. Two razor sharp edges carved air where I'd stood. The Vhichang's blade caught the whipping tail of my coat and sliced through.

I spun off my right heel, lashing out with my rune-blade. One of the redheads was there and he got his sword up to block, but the blow hammered him back a step. Again, steel rang on steel, like savage bells. I fenced with the rapier, holding the others off for the moment.

The Vhichang was good. He got his blade inside my guard, sliced a blazing line of fire across my left arm. But the cut was shallow. It wouldn't slow me. I let it light the flame of my anger instead.

But I couldn't stand motionless against four opponents. And by now the Ss'Korra was back on his feet, had drawn a dagger and was looking for an opening. I ran to my left, skirting my attackers, trying to draw them apart.

The Vhichang leaped toward me, his blade hacking madly as he tried to finish me. He was good, but not that good. Our weapons sang, and crossed, and clanged. And he went reeling back with the very tip of his beak sliced cleanly away.

The redheaded brothers were both on my right now. They came boring in but I didn't wait for them. I charged, my blades weaving. In the next instant we all met, our swords flaming, coming together, drawing back and away in a wild clamor of sound. I could see the sweat on the two's faces, see their pupils dilated widely. They each had hazel irises.

But we were too close together, the three of us. Their nerve broke before mine and they jumped back. For a moment there was a pause, a lull in our little war. I was breathing quickly but easily. So were the assassins. No one was tired yet, and the Vhichang's wound wasn't serious.

I smiled, glanced at the Ss'Korra.

"My mistake," I said to him. "I guess I'm going to have to kill you last."

He roared, a predatory sound, and whipped his arm up and forward, the dagger leaping from his fingers like a burning streak of chrome light. I dropped to my knees. The knife wheeled past over my head. One of the redheads had expected me to dodge. He lunged forward, slashing his sword through the place where I would have been had I done so. It left him open and I put my rune-blade into his stomach just where his navel would be.

The steel tore him up. Blood spewed from his belly and mouth. And I ripped the sword free with an awful sucking sound as I rose to my feet. His brother charged me, snarling. I parried with the rune-blade, the blow jarring, scattering droplets of crimson across the gray stones. The rapier seemed to spin on its own in my left hand and I slashed upward in an arc from right to left that opened the man's throat and spilled his life away.

The Ss'Korra looked scared.

The Vhichang sighed, reached up to rub at his injured beak. I glanced at him. His yellow eyes were hard. He hitched up his sword belt and drew a dagger into his left hand to give himself two blades to match mine. He started walking toward me.

"It doesn't have to be this way," I told him.

"I took the gold," he replied.

"A hard way to make a living," I said.

"Aren't they all."

He lunged for me then, blades winking with light, his movements smooth and fluid, his technique nearly flawless. Nearly.

My rune-blade licked out, met his dagger, hacked it free of his hand. My rapier hooked up and inside his sword, driving it out of line with his body as his thrust brought him a little too close to me. I stepped into him, looping my arm around his, locking my elbow to catch his wrist and sword against my side where they were useless to him. I wrenched upward on the Vhichang's arm, heard him grunt as his shoulder came out of its socket.

I lifted my other sword, the runes glimmering along its length as I brought it high. The Vhichang snarled, spat at my feet. I didn't hold it against him, but I killed him anyway, bringing the blade down hard, hacking into the soft juncture where the shoulder met the neck. He sagged, collapsed against me with what sounded almost like a sigh, and I released my grip on him so that he fell like a sack of feed at my boots.

The Ss'Korra had not moved. I saw him shiver, and I tossed him the rapier that I'd taken from him only moments before. He caught it reflexively, breathing hard, his green eyes skittering from side to side like minnows fleeing the approach of a shark.

"Tell me who hired you and I'll let you live," I said.

He groaned, and if it were possible his pupils dilated even more widely. "No!" he screamed, and threw himself toward me.

Our blades linked, slid together in a rasping burst of sparks. I stepped back and away. The Ss'Korra stood for a moment, then collapsed to his knees, dropping his sword in a clatter on the ground as his hands came up to try and stuff the pouring blood back into his chest. I turned away, heard the thud of his body on the stones as he fell the final distance onto his face and died.

Walking back across the roof, I picked up the .38 from where it lay. I turned the weapon over and over in my hands, then snapped open the cylinder, looking for some…thing that was wrong. I found it when I glanced down the muzzle. With the cylinder open I should have been able to see light through the barrel. I couldn't. The barrel had been packed with something, a nail by the shadowy outline of it. Had I fired the pistol it almost certainly would have blown up in my hand.

Vohanna's work! It had to be. Who else would want to make sure I lost a hand before I lost my life, that I lost a hand just like my brother Bryce had lost *his* hand when a pistol had blown up in his fist.

Vohanna was here. In Timmuzz. I could smell her. And she had said as much after Bryce and I were sucked through her wild gate to the world where she was known as "the bringer of pain and beauty." She had spoken in that place of "revealing" herself in Timmuzz at the end. She'd said we would be "surprised."

So who had she possessed? What body did she inhabit here in my adopted homeland? Who wielded the knife that was pressed unseen at my back?

I thought of the one who had given me a spiked pistol, of the one who had arranged with me a meeting for which only assassins had shown up. I thought of Rajan Critus and his black eyes.

CHAPTER TWENTY-TWO

ALARM!

I returned to Rannon's apartment to find that my love was awake and had even managed a bath. Her torn and bloody black leathers had been stripped away and replaced with similar garments in scarlet. She was gorgeous with her dark hair hanging long and still damp over her shoulders, and with her blue eyes alive with the inner fire that always marked her. Upon her feet were boots of gray made from the soft leathery shells of the turex, and at her hip rode her sword, its slender hilt carved from tasaber horn and with scarlet feathers dangling from the quillions.

Those feathers! I had once thought them a mere affection. When Rannon lifted her sword to the guard position they fell about her small fist like a cloak of crimson. And when she fought they danced like mad moths around her hilt and hand.

It was a brave display. Yet, I had considered them no more than a vanity, an adornment without a purpose. I should have thought better of my love. And I learned better the first time I fenced with her. It was only a practice session, the tips and edges of our blades covered in cork sheathes. But on that day she had beat me because of the feathers.

As she moved with the sword, parrying, thrusting, launching a riposte, the feathers had woven a surreal sketch of color and shadow in the air before me. I could hear the snap of them twining about her hilt. And for just a moment I lost the sense of where her blade was and felt it tap, tap along my ribs.

I had smiled and saluted her, and she had come into my arms to be kissed.

"Was it my feathers or my form that so distracted you, my love," she asked softly in my ear.

I remember that I chuckled.

"The feathers were only a temporary distraction, Saysa. Your beauty is a constant one. 'Tis a wonder I can put one foot in front of the other when I'm around you."

She, too, had chuckled. "I see you are better with words than steel this day."

"And did my words win me another kiss?"

Her laughter had been sweet and teasing. "Men. So easily beaten at swords and at love."

I had agreed, of course.

Now, as Rannon saw me come into her apartment, she gave me another brilliant smile and came to greet me. But her smile faded as she saw the tear in my rawhide coat from where the Vhichang assassin's blade had ripped it.

"Ruenn? By Sevarian, what happened?"

Her hand lifted the coat by the tail. Her gaze examined me minutely for injuries. She found only the scratch on my right arm and winced as she ran her finger lightly along it.

"Another assassin?" she asked.

I told her all of it, of meeting with Rajan Critus in my room, of the wasted search at the phorosnex for Valyan and Kreeg, of the four assassins and the spiked pistol. She sighed, shook her head.

"First the commander of our navy falls under suspicion. And now Rajan Critus. But it sounds like we have more than enough evidence on Critus. We need to speak to Kuurus. Have the man arrested."

"Not just yet," I said.

She arched a delicate eyebrow. "And why not?"

I know all the evidence seems to point at Rajan. But isn't that in itself suspicious? I never thought of Critus as stupid, but his moves here have *been* stupid. *If* they are his moves."

Rannon frowned. "The note," she said after a moment.

"What?"

Rannon looked at me, then looked away. Her cheeks were flushed, and it seemed suddenly as if she were embarrassed.

"The note," she said again. "Less that a year ago. When...." She trailed off, fidgeting.

I knew then what note she referred to. When the first war against Vohanna had been barely started, before we even *knew* it was Vohanna we faced, I had been implicated in a plot to overthrow Nyshphal and betray Rannon. A thin strip of parchment had fallen into the Emperor's hands, and on that parchment there seemed to be proof of my traitorous ambitions. It had taken many months and the sufferings of many innocent people before the truth had been uncovered.

"Critus is being framed," I said, my suspicion blossoming into knowing. "Just like I was. And probably like Horlis Kazhian of the navy was."

Rannon nodded. Her cheeks still blushed, but her words were angry. "So it would seem. And it sounds like Vohanna's work. The sick games she likes to play with people's lives."

I stepped forward and slipped my arms around Rannon, pulling her against me. She turned to push her face into my shoulder.

"I'm sorry," she said. "For doubting you...then."

"Shhh," I said. "We've already apologized to each other for our mistakes in that time. It is forgotten."

I felt her nod against my shoulder, and I kissed her on top of the head. At that moment alarm tocsins began to blare. Rannon and I nearly jumped out of our skins, then raced out onto her balcony.

Explosions rattled in the distance and we saw smoke and dust rising over the makeshift barrier that had been thrown up at the city's perimeter. That barricade and the thin line of warriors who guarded it was all that stood between us and the besieging armies of our enemies. Now it was engulfed in flames, and above it in the smoke-stained sky writhed black knots that could only be saddle birds and flyers and winged reptiles locked in lethal combat.

"The attack has begun," Rannon cried out. And she turned and rushed back into her apartment with me at her

154

heels.

We each began grabbing up weapons and pieces of armor and buckling them around us. Rannon strapped a bow and quiver of arrows over her shoulder. I did the same, then found extra daggers and helmets for us both.

The door was flung back and one of Rannon's Gray-Cloaks burst in. As soon as they'd found out about Rannon's return, the princess's own guards had taken over from the men that Kuurus had initially assigned to watch her door. I'd been happy about that.

"Jhesana," the man said, his voice cracking. "The attack! A new army. Just arrived. The enemy is breaking through at the barricades!"

The bull men, I thought. It had to be the Minotaurs who I'd seen come out of the wild gate in the forest of Vohan. They must have marched swiftly to get here so soon. But then, I suppose the dead had no need to stop for rest or food. How were we going to fight them?

Rannon's words to the Gray-Cloak knifed open my thoughts, drew me back to the moment. "I know," she said. "We must get to the fighting. Rouse the guard and send someone for saddle beasts." She was already heading through the door where others of her men milled about. Warriors rushed to obey her commands.

"Should we not speak to Kuurus?" I asked as I followed her.

She glanced at me as she buckled on a helm. "Kuurus was never a general," she replied. "I have to talk to the officers in charge. At the barricades. Find out what needs to be done."

I nodded, and quickly we stormed our way from the castle and out to the stables where tasabers had already been saddled for us. The tasaber is a spirited animal, looking like a cross between a horse and a mule deer. But it has the heart of a grizzly. Mine was black, Rannon's white. Beautiful beasts. Sleek and swift.

We mounted and raced across the palace grounds and through the gates into the streets beyond. Gray-Cloaks were strung out behind us on other tasabers. And the sound of our hooves clattered and echoed along the cobblestoned ways.

The city seemed deserted around the palace. I saw no sign of reinforcements hurrying toward the front, and I *should* have seen them for the reserve barracks were located at the four corners of the castle grounds. I frowned. Surely Kuurus had kept a reserve and not garrisoned the barricade wall with his whole strength.

But I had little time to think of it as more explosions rocked the streets in front of us, tearing holes in the nearby buildings. Fires blazed up. Some of our men were thrown from their saddles as tasabers screamed and reared. I fought my beast back under control, glanced up just as a "V" of the enemy's winged reptiles went over with Nyshphalian flyers pursuing them.

We had expected Vohanna's forces to have gunpowder. Luckily, they only seemed to have relatively weak bombs and not cannon or small arms. Although, come to think of it, the Reploids—as Rajan Critus had called them—had shot at Rannon and I with something like a mating between a pistol and a small crossbow. Still, things could have been worse, and at least there were men in our army who had seen gunpowder used and were no longer terrified of it. Some of our naval vessels had even been armed with cannon by Arca Heskern and her scientists, though all of those had accompanied Hurnan Jystral when he'd sailed for the Nysphalian coast to meet the landings by our enemies there.

On the heels of the explosions came the first refugees from the front. Most were injured, often with burns, but some were simply running. Rannon shouted at the latter, ordering them to return to their posts. A few listened, their faces bright with shame, but many were too far committed to flight and not even the word of their princess would put spine back into them.

We pushed ahead on our tasabers, hearing now the shouts of men and the bellows of beasts from before us, hearing the clash of steel and the purr/hiss of arrows sleeting. The very earth seemed to shake. I drew my bow over my shoulder and strung it. The others followed my lead.

A Nyshphalian flyer crashed into a building a block ahead of us. It had been driven from the sky by a brace of winged reptiles with their riders. And now those riders, those

Reploids, turned their attention to our group, sweeping low into the street toward us with the tips of their mounts' wings almost brushing the houses to either side.

"Half and half," I screamed a command, and our bows were lifted, arrows were nocked.

I saw the first winged monster coming in, its bill like a spiked battering ram before it. A name flashed through my brain: *Pterodactyl*. This creature was like those nightmare beasts from Earth's ancient past. Like a flying dinosaur. Though nothing remotely like its riders had ever lived on *my* world. Or so it was said.

"Fire!" Rannon and I shouted at the same instant, and every other man among the Gray-Cloaks loosed their arrows and let them fly. The Pterodactyl screeched as black shafts sprouted from its throat and chest. It twisted in mid-air, its left wing brushing a building. And then it went cartwheeling into the ground, its wings breaking around it like lacerated tents.

But the other Pterodactyl was nearly on top of us now. "Fire!" I shouted again, and the rest of the men loosed, I with them. My arrow struck the underside of the monster's beak and caromed off, but other shafts pierced its hide, wringing from it a scream of pain and rage.

The beast's rider hauled back on his reins and the creature swept over our heads and upward. A small object came hurtling down. I spurred my tasaber forward, Rannon beside me. The other Gray-Cloaks scattered.

The bomblet smashed into the paving stones, exploding to one side of the street. Only a single guard was close enough to take a hit and he and his tasaber were both shredded by the burst. Rannon shouted with rage at the loss of one of her men, then spurred her tasaber angrily on toward the fighting just ahead. I rode beside her, my heart flushed too with the wish for violence.

We rounded a corner and saw down a narrow street ahead of us what was called Markets Avenue, which is where the Road of Wagons begins on its journey to distant Elul on the northeastern coast of Nyshphal. This Avenue is very wide and runs at a right angle to the streets we had been following from the palace.

On the other side of the Avenue from us lay the outskirts of Timmuzz. Most of the buildings there were markets or warehouses, and it was these that had been razed to build a makeshift barricade against our besieging foes. Those foes had already broached the barricade. At least in this place.

Bombs had done *part* of the work of breaking through our defensive wall, but most of the destruction had been wrought by the massive animals that some of the enemy were riding. Those behemoth mounts were dinosaurs. There was no other word to describe them.

I'd heard Rajan Critus speak of "huge beasts that had never been seen before on Talera," but I had not imagined such as these. They were built almost like alligator snapping turtles grown to gargantuan size, as big as two or three elephants put together. But they were clearly land animals, with their sequoia- trunked legs located under their bodies instead of sprawled out to the sides.

Their backs were armored with bony plates and spikes, and there were more spikes on their heads. Their tails were tipped with clubs that were as big as the skulls of oxen, and at first I thought these had been attached to them as weapons until I saw that they were made of bone and had grown there naturally. In half a dozen places our barricade had been battered down by these monsters, and through those defiles had poured the initial waves of enemy troops.

Despite what I expected, I saw none of the Minotaurs among those enemies. I wondered why. But perhaps they were being held in reserve as the Reploids were sent crashing against us first. Finally I was able to glimpse the reptilians clearly, at least the wingless variety of them. They were human-sized but looked almost like ghouls with their underslung jaws, white fanged mouths, and long, thin limbs. Their eyes were small and nearly all pupil; fringes of kelp-like hair festooned their bony scalps.

Our men at the barricade had fought valiantly. I could see piles of dead Reploids who had fallen in the first charges, and the dinosaurs were pincushioned with spears and arrows, though those darts seemed to cause them little discomfort. But courage had not been enough. We had lost many of our own, and the enemy army had broken through.

With the barricade breached, Markets Avenue itself had become a stark battlefield. Men ran here and there, struggled with other beings in black, writhing knots where axes and swords rose and fell, rose and fell. I heard shouts and howls and the pleading of the wounded. Burning buildings lit the scene, like a war in Hell. And amid it all the dinosaurs stomped like bellowing demons through the rubble.

I saw no sign of officers among our troops, no sign of discipline. They were fighting as individuals instead of as an army. And they were being cut down.

"There!" Rannon shouted over the cacophony. My gaze followed her pointing finger down the course of the Avenue and I saw that not *all* discipline had fled.

Just where the dinosaurs and their riders had first broken through our outer barriers, Nyshphalian warriors were gathering to make a stand in the streets. In the center of the Avenue were piled wagons and other materials. I saw tables and chairs of fine wood, tapestries and costly carpets from Birnoir and the Threshian isles. They had all been set afire, and the fires were temporarily holding back the dinosaurs from smashing their way into the main part of the city.

Rannon led the way as our group turned its tasabers and rushed along the outer edge of the Avenue toward this one bastion of defense. No enemy came against us; we were forty strong and well armed, and at the moment the Reploids had easier prey among the scattered Nyshphalian defenders. We dismounted behind the stream of fire that filled the middle of the street.

There were Reploids trying to break through that burning wall, trying to pull away the fuel for the flames. "Kill me those," Rannon ordered her Gray-Cloaks, and the bows of her bodyguards began to sing with deadly effect.

I took the princess's arm and indicated to her a gathering of men who seemed to be directing the defenses here. These milled around an overturned wagon that had been pulled up behind the fiery new barricade. One man stood on the back of the wagon, peering forward from his "high ground." It was he who gave the orders; I could hear his voice cracking loudly, authoritatively, even from where we stood.

With a few Gray-Cloaks to ward our backs, Rannon and

I made our way toward the makeshift command post. The man on the wagon turned as we came up. He was tall, a head taller even than I, and powerfully built beneath the brazen chain mail that he wore. His hair was reddish-blond and hung long and straight over his shoulders, and he wore a bronze helmet with a row of scarlet spikes down the center. I could swear that I'd never seen him before. Yet, there was something faintly familiar about him.

Rannon stopped with a frown. "Who are you?" she demanded of the fellow. He was not wearing a uniform of Nyshphal. Nor was there any sign that he was from the city.

His voice was deceptively mild as he answered. "I'm called Chalathar. Thanks for bringing the archers. And if you're wondering why I'm in command here, it's because no one else was doing a rucking thing."

Rannon bristled but I grasped her shoulder, and as Chalathar turned to give more orders I leaned to whisper to her ear: "It's clear that he knows what he's doing. We'd best let him keep doing it. Make him an officer if you have to. But look how the men are responding."

Rannon's lips thinned and I felt her shoulder muscles bunch under my hand, but she was no fool. One glance around told her the truth of my words. She started to speak, but Chalathar turned again toward us. His eyes were as pale as gin, I noticed.

"If you'd like to take over, you're welcome," he said to Rannon. "But if I were you, the first order I'd give would be to have my flyers use burning oil against those big reptiles."

He leaped down from the wagon with a tiger's grace and started striding away, throwing a last comment over his shoulder to us. "That is, if you want your city to live out the night."

CHAPTER TWENTY-THREE

CHALATHAR

"...if you want your city to live out the night," the man named Chalathar said as he strode away.

Rannon glowered at the fellow's retreating back, then turned and began to give orders. I noted that one of those orders called for flyers. No doubt she planned to take Chalather's suggestion that we use burning oil against the dinosaurs. Actually, this would be a combination of oil and pitch and various resins to make the stuff stick to what it hit. On Earth they sometimes called such compounds "Greek Fire." On Talera it was known as "God's Fire." It was not something I would have thought of using.

Leaving Rannon to command our new defensive line for the moment, I hurried after Chalathar. He heard me coming and turned, his big hand dropping to the hilt of the broadsword that hung at his waist. His whole body seemed to thrum with a barely concealed tension, and I lifted my hands, palms open to show him that I did not wish a fight.

Fifty yards behind us the battle raged. I heard the bellowing of the dinosaurs and the higher pitched howls of men and the non-men with which they struggled. I heard the beat of wings in the sky overhead, and Rannon's voice shouting orders. But I watched only the one called Chalathar.

The enemy had broken through the skin of the city and the fighting would grow harder now. I did not know if we could throw our foes back to the original barricades. But at least the new front that Chalathar had hurled up was holding off the dinosaurs, the city breakers, who could not maneuver easily in the streets. This man in front of me had given us the only chance we would have to contain the breakthrough.

Why? I wondered. But I said: "That wasn't the best way to introduce yourself to the princess of Nyshphal."

Chalathar chuckled and relaxed his grip on his sword. His gin-colored eyes studied me.

"And what about a *prince* of Nyshphal?" he asked. "Or at least a future prince."

A spent arrow clinked on the cobblestones near us. I ignored it. "You seem to know much about our situation here," I said to Chalathar. "Yet, I don't think you are from the city. How is it that you—"

"Are all Nyshphalians as suspicious as you and the princess?" he interrupted.

I nodded. "At the moment we have to be. It isn't a pleasant thing."

"Good," he said. "Against Vohanna you *must* be."

I was startled. "You know of Vohanna?" My voice must have been accusatory for he smiled faintly.

"Do you think you're the only nation she has ever troubled?"

I shook my head. "I never expected that we were."

Another arrow clattered along the street past my boots and I turned to glance toward Rannon where she stood giving orders. The Reploids were massing for an attack to try and overwhelm the resistance at the firewall. If they did so, there would be little to stop them from bringing their dinosaurs into the city and pouring in enough troops to gut our defenses entirely.

"I'd like to talk more—" I started to blurt as I looked back to where Chalathar had been standing. But he was gone, though I had glanced away only a moment. I felt a frown gathering around my eyes, but there was no time to seek explanations. The roar of the coming attack was building beyond the fires, an ululation of rage pouring from the throats of a thousand enemy warriors. I drew my bow back into my hands and scooped up the spent arrows by my feet, knowing that I might need them. Then I turned and sprinted to Rannon's side.

* * * * * * *

I drew and released, and at less than three feet the heavy ironwood shaft punched completely through the attacking Reploid's throat and into the shoulder of the beast behind him. The dead one fell at my feet; the other shrieked and dropped his weapon, which looked like some cross between a billhook and a halberd.

I let go of my bow and drew my sword, the runed blade whispering from the scabbard like some evil-voiced demon. The wounded Reploid grabbed a hatchet from his belt and leaped toward me. I hacked him down, the sword moaning as it whipped through the air. Another Reploid lunged at me, the wooden shaft of his weapon parallel to the earth, the curved steel head gleaming like black chrome. I slashed across with my blade, hacking the head of the weapon free of the shaft and then skewering the beast through the chest.

Flames prowled along the makeshift barrier to my right, the heat baking me through the chainmail that I wore. The ruddy light from those fires shattered off of iron and armor, glistened from the wild yellow eyes of our enemies. I killed another foe, let his blood spill to the street.

Rannon and I stood together, Gray-Cloaks and others of our troops at our back. My love's blade leaped, darted, slashed, the red feathers at the hilt flying about her wrist as the sweat stood out on her face and ran in muddy rivulets down her arms under the net of her mail. I smelled her sweat, and mine. Our enemies I could not smell. But perhaps their scent was too alien for humans to detect.

Less than five dhorrin[4] had passed since the man named Chalathar had disappeared right under my nose and the first enemy attack had come raging in to try and beat down our barricade of fire. We had driven off the initial assault with arrows, but the Reploids had regrouped and charged again. This time we faced them with empty quivers.

Desperately, we fought. But while we battled there was no time to keep fuel on the blaze that offered us protection from the dinosaurs of our foes. The flames were guttering;

---

[4] About twenty minutes.

the dinosaur riders began to push their huge mounts closer and closer to us. We were lucky only in that the pterodactyls of our enemies had been temporarily driven from the sky by our own air squadrons. Else our defensive stand would have been bombed into paste before our fires had a *chance* to die out.

"We have to pull back!" I shouted to Rannon as she cut the throat from an attacker. "They'll overrun us completely."

"One more dhorrin!" Rannon shouted in return. "The flyers need time to load the God's Fire."

I shook my head. Another dhorrin was *all* we had. Our army was dying here. And if it died, the city would not long outlast it. But I fought beside my love as she wanted, fought for the few more minutes that she said we needed.

One of our Gray-Cloaks fell beside me, his belly opened by the wickedly curved beak at the end of his opponent's billhook. I cut the head from that weapon with my sword but the Reploid leaped forward to grapple with me. I caught his wrist, twisted him to one side and rammed my blade into him just where the kidney would lie in a human. He stumbled to his knees, choking on blood, and I kicked him away as I drew the blade from his body with a rasp.

Rannon cried out and I spun toward her. Two attackers pressed her, and the billhook of one had sliced a thin line of red down her cheek. Enraged, I charged with my shoulder down into the nearest of the two beings. He tried to get his weapon between us but I hit him squarely, lifting him from his feet and hurling him a dozen paces into the blazing barricade at his back. His clothes and the thin fringe of hair on his head burst into flames, and then he was running, shrieking, flailing, blundering into his companions as he went.

The second of Rannon's attackers turned to deal with me as I rushed in, and both Rannon and I put our blades into him at the same moment, spitting him like a terval roast. He jerked back a step and collapsed, pulling his body off our blades. We readied ourselves for the next foe, and now I made sure I was as close to Rannon as I could get.

"Are you all right?" I shouted.

"A scratch!" she shouted back. "I'll live!"

But others of our men could not make the same claim.

We were stretched thin and the enemy was still coming. The fires of our barricade were almost out and when the last of them went cold our small band of defenders would be steam-rolled from three sides.

"Rannon!" I grasped her shoulder for a moment. "We *must* pull back. Can't hold here any longer."

My love glanced desperately about. She could see the line of our men wasting away in the inferno of combat. She understood as well as I did what that meant.

"I know," she said. "I—"

Then I heard a sound and looked up. All around me men and not-men paused in the midst of strife. All around me heads begin to turn skyward. I saw our flyers first, maroon hulls catching sunlight, flags and pennons whipping bright and brave. And behind them were the saddle birds of the Nyshphalian navy. Hundreds of them it seemed.

The sky darkened. Flyers and bird riders went over, and as they did small pots of orange clay came spinning downward to rain upon our enemies. The pots were not bombs and did not explode, but they had burning wicks and where they crashed they shattered and flames roared up. God's Fire! A mix of oil and pitch and sulphur that clung to stone and flesh and...consumed.

Fire and smoke roiled upward. The screams began. I saw Reploids running, saw them batting at their own bodies as they tried to beat away the flames, saw them go down in squirming, smoking heaps. And *now* I could smell them! Like an odor wafting out of charnel house.

Under Rannon's orders, nearly all of the God's Fire in the city must have been loaded for use at this place, at this moment. And it worked. The attack broke; the enemy ran. Even those foes who engaged us directly turned and fled, and the monstrous dinosaurs, which were an even worse threat, joined the stampede as their slaty hides erupted in pustules of fire from the clay pots that shattered against them. In running, those beasts trampled their own army underfoot.

It was a rout, and if we'd had the reserves to pour in we could have exploited it. But there were no reserves. At least, Kuurus Jystral had ordered none forward to support us where we fought and died. I cursed him thoroughly for that.

Rannon leaned against the wheel of an overturned wagon, her very stance screaming exhaustion. One of the Gray-Cloaks handed me a clean cloth—where he'd found it I did not know—and I went over to my love with it and began to daub at the cut on her cheek.

She looked at me. Her eyes were bloodshot from smoke and there were dark circles beneath them, and hollows to her cheeks that had not been there a day ago.

"We beat them," I said.

"They won't stay beaten for long," she replied. "Only the flyers saved us this time. If we lose those...." She shrugged.

There was nothing I could say to that shrug. She was right. It was our superior strength in the air that was keeping the city alive. But still, we on the ground had to do our part.

"We better get the men working on a new defensive line," I said. "One we don't have to set fire to."

"Can we make some sort of caltrop big enough to slow those dinosaurs?" Rannon asked. Of course, she didn't use the term "dinosaur," though that was what she meant. And by caltrop she referred to the kind of spikes that are typically either implanted in the earth or strewn on the ground to impede a cavalry advance.

"It would take a hell of a caltrop to stop those beasts," I said. "But it's a good idea. Maybe Arca Heskern and her scientists can come up with something."

"Krutt!" Rannon growled, snapping her fist into the palm of her other hand. "Where are the reserves? What in Sevarian's name is Kuurus doing back at the palace? Sitting on his ass?"

I gaped at her. I don't think I'd ever heard Rannon swear before. It was a new experience. A disturbing one. But she was right. We'd almost lost the war here. Where were the reserves? They should have been posted forward long ago.

"Maybe you better send someone to find out." I said. "Or best, perhaps, to go yourself."

Rannon gazed at me, frowning, and then a smile—fleeting but real—dashed across her lips.

"Trying to get me away from here are you?"

I did not smile back. "You need a *few* minutes rest," I

said. "But besides, Kuurus is not likely to listen to anyone other than you. I can handle things here."

She nodded, almost as if to herself, her white teeth worrying at her full lower lip. "All right," she agreed. "But I'll leave Emren in charge here. I want you with me when I go in to face Kuurus. He's acting most strangely."

"That he is," I said. And I was glad to go with her. I didn't want her out of my sight in the midst of all that was happening. Besides, Emren was a good man, the ranking officer among the Gray-Cloaks who had accompanied us from the palace. He would do as good a job here as I could.

After Rannon had given more orders, the two of us found a pair of tasabers and rode toward the palace and a confrontation with her brother. We passed a few people in the streets as they hurried about mysterious errands. And once I thought I saw Chalathar turn a corner ahead of us. But, if so, he had disappeared again by the time we reached that corner. Finally, we passed through the gates into the castle grounds and dismounted. Kuurus met us there.

"We had a report of your coming," the prince explained as he stood at the top of the steps leading into Jystral Palace.

I wondered how he had received such a report. It would have been hard for someone to have outridden us to get here.

"It was rather clear you were upset," the prince continued.

Taskin Bhent stood at Kuurus's side, but the general looked distinctly uncomfortable. And four of the prince's mercredi guards also loitered nearby in their russet leathers. Their hands hung close beside their belts and *still* seemed out of place to me. Again some faint warning began to buzz in my brain. Again I could not identify the cause.

"Upset?" Rannon said, her voice snapping. "Upset! Why should I be upset? Because my men died in the streets when the reserves didn't come?"

I moved toward Rannon, hoping to soothe her, but she waved me away. By rights, she could probably seize command within the city. She was the eldest, *and* Hurnan Jystral's designated successor. But at the moment we did not need a public confrontation on the matter, and it is not a simple task to replace a military leader in the midst of battle.

That is, even if Kuurus would agree to relinquish command, and in that I had no faith. I knew Rannon understood all these things. Surely, they were the reasons why she hadn't taken control immediately upon her return to the city. But now her anger was boiling and there was no telling what she might do.

"*When* were you going to commit the reserves, Kuurus?" Rannon demanded. "After we were all slaughtered?"

Two of the mercredi moved closer to Kuurus as if to protect him from his sister, and I felt myself bristle as my hand dropped to my sword and I, too, started up the steps. It might have gotten ugly then, but Rannon was not yet so far gone into rage that she wanted to see blood spilled on the threshold of her father's palace.

She halted a few steps below her brother, her blue, blue eyes glaring into his. Kuurus drew himself up, his own blue eyes narrow and cold, and I noticed a thin, dark circle around his irises that marked a difference between the siblings. Strange that I had not seen it before.

"We felt it best not to commit the reserves just yet," Kuurus growled, giving a nod toward General Bhent. "If we had thrown them into the fire at the first breakthrough then we'd have nothing left for the second."

"The first breakthrough would have been enough by itself if we hadn't gotten damn lucky," Rannon replied hotly.

"And yet you held," Kuurus said, his lips curving at the left side into what might almost have been a smirk. "I must admit, the idea of using God's Fire against the attack had not occurred to me."

"It was Cha—" I started to say, and then bit the name off before it could escape my tongue. For some reason that I could not be sure of, I decided not to mention Chalathar to Kuurus at the moment. "It was chance that we did so," I finally said.

Rannon looked at me strangely but made no comment on my reticence. Instead, she turned back to her brother, though the words she spoke seemed to be directed more at Taskin Bhent than at Kuurus.

"Well you better send up some reserves now," she stated flatly. "The lines are far too thin and we need more God's

Fire. And a new barricade built. If the Reploids attack now the whole underbelly of the city will be knifed open."

She didn't wait for a reply from Kuurus or from Bhent, but instead stomped around them into the palace. I followed, offering a bland smile to the prince, and to his guards as they watched me pass by with predatory eyes.

Chapter Twenty-Four

Night Battle

Some sound snapped me into awareness and I sat up on Rannon's couch, my hand reaching for the hilt of the sword that lay on the table next to me. I rose, studying the room, then padded on bare feet over to the glass doors that fronted the balcony. Through the doors I could see the deepening skies of evening, and I could hear the occasional rattle of some Reploid bomb exploding against a Nyshphalian target. But there was nothing that could have made the sound I'd heard. All was silent within this space.

I turned. Across the room stood the fireplace, its hearth half filled with a dark pile of ashes. A stray breeze came whispering down the chimney and stirred those ashes. For a moment amid that swirl of black, two red coals winked. And suddenly my skin crawled and I had the intense feeling of being watched. My hand tightened on my sword hilt, and my mind remembered: no blaze had been lit tonight in that fireplace.

Every hair on my body seemed to curl, and the wind that I knew was not really a wind sucked the ashes up the chimney and was gone. The door to the apartment opened and I jumped wildly, my mouth spilling a gasp that was full of rising fear.

Rannon stepped through the door with a gathering of Gray-Cloaks at her back. She stopped short as she heard my cry, her hand lifting as if to offer comfort.

"Ruenn! What is it?" She moved quickly to my side.

I shook my head, wiped my mouth on the back of my

hand. "Nothing," I said. "Just the remnants of a nightmare. I...I'd fallen asleep. Shouldn't have."

Rannon smiled a little, her fingers brushing along my arm over the cotton sleeve of my gray shirt. "You needed it. It's been days since you've really slept."

I nodded. After the confrontation with Kuurus on the steps of Jystral Palace, Rannon and I had returned to her apartment in the castle and I had fallen asleep almost immediately on the couch, though I had not intended to do so. It *had* been days since I'd gotten much sleep. Exhaustion cannot be fought forever.

Again I wiped my mouth on my hand, and Rannon's gaze caught the motion.

"Are you sure you're all right?" she asked.

I forced a smile. "Fine. Really." I could not say exactly why I did not tell her about the ashes and shadow. Perhaps I was not precisely sure what it was that I had seen.

Now Rannon nodded at me, and smiled again, a bigger smile. "I have some good news," she said. "At least I think it is?"

I made an effort to shake off the last of my fear and raised an eyebrow at her.

"And that would be?"

"I met with Taskin Bhent and Kuurus. They've agreed to a counterattack against the Repolids along Markets Avenue where the breakthrough occurred. Our flyers will lead. Arca Heskern's alchemists have concocted some new type of God's Fire. Apparently stronger than we used before."

"That *is* good news," I said.

"And," Rannon added, "while our sortie distracts the enemy, a squadron of saddle birds have been detailed to break out to the east. They'll try to make contact with my father and the fleet."

This time my smile was genuine. I squeezed Rannon's shoulder. "I'm glad to hear that, Saysa. It's a good plan. It should work."

She nodded. Then her eyes searched mine for a moment. "I took command of the attack. Kuurus didn't want me to have it, but I'm beyond caring what he wants. He didn't push very hard. I think he knows that the majority of the people

171

would support me if I replaced him."

"Of course," I agreed.

"Perhaps I *should* replace him. But if there were trouble.... I couldn't bear what father would say if he found his children fighting among themselves in his absence."

Again, her gaze searched mine. And: "I'll need you at my side tonight," she said.

I think she expected me to try and talk her out of putting herself at risk. But I knew there was no sense in starting an argument I couldn't win."

"I'm there," I said. "Just let me get my boots."

* * * * * * *

It was the twenty-first dhaur, that Taleran hour after midnight which marks the dregs of the day's dark time. The superstitious call it "mordai" and say that it is the hour where the veil between the worlds of the living and the dead is at its thinnest. All I knew was that it was the time when men and their enemies are most likely to be asleep. And thus it was that we chose it for the start of our attack.

The original plan, which Rannon had worked out with Kuurus and Taskin Bhent in the throne room, had called for the attack to be launched a dhaur later. Rannon had changed the time. Rajan Critus, who we were suspicious of, had not been present at the planning, but plenty of others had been and we weren't absolutely sure who the traitor was in our midst.

To light our way we had three moons, blue Nimeru setting into the horizon, and up in the sky turquoise Sieona and gold Tisiminna. Scarlet Rath had not yet risen, but even though the moons are strangely dim at mordai, the three should be enough to guide as. We hoped they'd be dim enough not to alert our enemies to our coming.

I stood with Rannon on the packed earth of one of our airfields. It was cold. Around us rested the bulks of twenty-five of our flyers, each of them loaded with God's Fire and with their crews standing quietly nearby. This small fleet represented over half of our remaining force of flyers, but they would not be alone in the attack. On the roofs of the city's taller buildings, saddle birds would also be preparing to ride. We were going in force and planned to hit each of the three enemy encampments that invested us.

Our main objective, however, was the northern encampment, from which had come the Reploid force that had broken through our barricades. It was there, also, that the dead army of the Minotaurs had been seen marching to join our foe's ranks. For reasons unknown, the enemy armies to the east and west had done little more than probe our defenses while their northern comrades launched a full attack. In return, the first two hosts would get less of our God's Fire payback.

Rannon gave the order and the crews boarded their flyers. She and I and half a dozen Gray-Cloaks found our way onto the deck of one of the larger ships, a craft named the Ghyre after a Taleran predator that looks like a tiger and dog crossbreed. The Ghyre was one of our newest vessels, powered primarily by a pilot who manipulated the toir'in-or power stones, but it also had an advanced rudder and propeller design that eased the pilot's burden.

In moments, our flotilla had climbed into the dark sky and the shadow-black shapes of saddle birds began to join us. Three strike groups formed, the largest of them around the Ghyre, and we each moved off toward our target, flying at rooftop level to avoid silhouetting ourselves against the moonlit night.

The enemy was unprepared for our coming. Completely unprepared. It made me wonder what kind of commanders Vohanna appointed for her armies. Then I remembered what I had once told her, that her warriors were too frightened of her, or too controlled by her, to show initiative. I had used that failing against her before, and it seemed she had learned little as a result. I was glad of that.

We swept over the city outskirts, where our foot soldiers were preparing their own strike to follow ours. We crossed the remnant of our barricade and then passed above the embers of the fires that our Reploid foes had lit earlier in the night against the autumn chill. I thought, perhaps, that it might have been the chill which helped us now. For at least in appearance our enemies were reptiles, and I knew that reptiles have no love for the cold.

All below was deathly stillness. Except! As I stared down toward the earth I glimpsed the Minotaur army standing in serried ranks to one side of the Reploid camp. They swayed together in some soulless semblance of life, like a field of winter killed wheat bending back and forth between gusts of a freezing mistral.

And as I watched, those swaying forms turned their dead faces up, turned their railroad flare eyes toward the sky. They saw us. I do not know how. But I heard a low keening begin, a deep rasping that rose and rose like a wind rushing through channels of stone.

"Let's take them!" I heard Rannon shout. And at her order the first pots of God's Fire were lit and flung over the railing of our ship to fall and strike and burst and burn.

I cast a pot, watched it hit the earth between two Minotaurs. Flames spurted with red life, then leaped from the ground up the legs and chests of the bull-men. I saw them fall and writhe, and one that still had enough of its vocal cords left began to groan, and then to bellow. For a fleeting instant I wondered if their dead nervous systems could feel the pain. For that instant I felt a twinge of regret. Then another pot was thrust into my hands and I hurled that one as well.

I saw one of the giant dinosaurs chained between two massive poles buried deeply into the soil. I hit it in the face with a firepot and it roared as flaming pitch spattered into its eyes. Reploids were rushing everywhere. One tried to throw water on the burning dinosaur but a huge foot lifted, crushed down, pulping its would-be savior to paste. The beast reared back then onto hind limbs that were as big as tree trunks. Its clubbed tail lashed, smashing up tents and running warriors. The poles that restrained it tore free of the ground and the monster was off through the encampment, trampling everything in its path.

Pot after pot was handed to me, their wicks sputtering sulphur in my face, and I threw and threw and threw. Beside me stood Rannon, her mouth set and grim, her eyes alternately gleaming with fire and drowning in shadows as she lifted firepots and hurled them. A cacophony of shouts and screams roared up from below, numbing the ears. And soon the savage-sweet smell of burning flesh reached us even aboard our flyers, the stench of it enough to make men vomit where they stood.

I saw a leathery tent below me that was larger than the rest, and around it stood a dozen Reploids with weapons to hand. They lifted those weapons as we passed over, and fired them at us. I heard the thunk of bolts striking the hull of the flyer, but our course did not falter and I hurled a pot into the middle of the tent. That shelter must have marked a storage place for their bombs. The container of God's Fire struck it and the fabric caught. Then the whole tent exploded, hurling debris and torn bodies away into the darkness.

I shouted in glee, and those around me were shouting too, pumping their fists in the air. I glanced at Rannon, saw her smile as a rictus that scored a darker line against her soot-stained cheeks. And then her face was stricken and her eyes widened in sudden realization of what she cheered—the burning death of other intelligent beings. She shook her head and I grabbed her shoulders, my own vicious smile collapsing as she leaned over and vomited onto the deck. It was evil what we did. Evil! And yet we had to do it. Didn't we?

I drew Rannon up. Her mouth was wet, her raven hair tangled and sweaty across her brow. Her hands found my wrists, squeezed tightly. Then she pulled away, straightening her back. Someone handed her a lit firepot and she held it for just a moment, then chunked it savagely down at the darkness of the enemy encampment. I saw it erupt with flame, heard, perhaps only in my heart, the quiet quiet sob of my love as she saw that she had killed again. I wanted to scream for her, and for myself. But there was more God's Fire to throw, more enemies to slaughter.

A shout of wings to our port side brought my head up. I saw a shadow there, almost hovering. Someone threw a firepot at it. Missed. And then I was yelling at everyone to hold.

"One of ours," I screamed. "A saddle bird." And our enemies had no saddle birds that we knew of, only the pterodactyls that we'd faced before.

The bird rider must have heard my shout and realized that we'd recognized him as a friend. He tugged on his down

and right reins and the wings of his mount dipped slightly,
letting the air curl over its pinions so that it slipped sideways
and came in for a landing on our deck. I could not see the
rider but the bird was a kryll, big as a buffalo but graceful
and savage as any eagle. And behind the kryll came two of
the smaller and swifter sabruns who also dropped down to
settle aboard the ship.

I rushed forward, drawing my sword just in case this
was *not* a friend, and Chalathar dismounted from the kryll
and started toward me. He was yelling, and it took me a
moment to overcome my shock at seeing him here and to
comprehend his words.

"Turn the ship! You've got to turn! Call a retreat!"

I hesitated. "What! We've just beg—"

"Turn it now!"

Rannon came hurrying up. "Who do you think…?" she
started to shout, but just then Ahrethane and Diken Graye
came around the shoulders of the sabruns they had been riding, and while we gaped in astonishment Ahrethane pointed
at something in the distance.

"You've got to do as he wants," she said, her voice
echoing. "Right now!"

We looked where her finger led. Rannon and I. And others. To our north within the night there glittered a spot of silver brightness. It was on the ground but coming swiftly, as if
on a horse at full gallop. My blood congealed. For what reason I could not tell.

"What is it?" Rannon demanded. "What by hell is it?"

"Sorcery," Chalathar replied. "When it gets close
enough it'll destroy this fleet. And everyone with—"

Rannon didn't wait for him to finish. She ran forward,
shouting for her signal men, screaming out commands for
the fleet to abandon the attack and turn back to the city. I
saw the lanthorns flash from our decks, saw answering lights
wink from other vessels. Our pilot brought the nose of the
Ghyre around, the ship's movements seeming ponderous
where before she had epitomized swiftness. I knew it was my
own fear that made it so.

Chalathar stood with his legs wide spread on the deck,
both hands on the hilt of his scabbarded broadsword. He was

staring straight at the advancing spike of silver as if he could peel away the brilliant caul that covered it to pierce to the core of the thing. Ahrethane had grasped my arm; Diken Graye hovered close.

"What is it?" I asked Ahrethane in a bare whisper. "What kind of sorcery?"

She turned and looked at me with her owl-green eyes. Her hand tightened on my biceps, the nails digging against the mail that I wore.

"It's Bryce," she said. "I can feel him there. But he *is* Vohanna's."

My chest seemed to cave in; I gritted my teeth until I could hear them grind together.

"A Bane-thrall," I half snarled. "Vohanna said she would make him a Bane-thrall."

I stared at Ahrethane then, my eyes begging for her to deny my words. But it seemed she could not, and it was Chalathar who spoke instead.

"Well she did it," he said. "He's taken now."

"No!" I protested. But no one would look at me. I smashed a fist into the palm of my other hand, and suddenly my knees grew weak. "No," I said again. And still no one would put their gaze toward me.

Rannon stood a bit forward of my position, still snapping out orders. But now our ship was turned, was accelerating back toward the city. I saw that the other craft were coming about, too. But slowly. Far too slowly. The saddle birds had the advantage on us. Already they had scattered.

I looked off over the railing of the Ghyre and I saw the silver gleam that marked my brother's position glide to a stop. I saw the glow that was his, intensify, and intensify— until it was as if a piece of moon had come down to earth. Then the glow leaped outward, spattering molten silver across the night. It leaped outward, straight toward us, coming for the fleet like a hammer of light, like Satan's comet.

"Get down!" Chalathar screamed.

177

CHAPTER TWENTY-FIVE

HAMMER OF LIGHT

"Get down!" Chalathar screamed, as the massive bolt of silver light fired by Bryce closed on our position, tearing the sky asunder as it came.

Ahrethane and Diken Graye dove for cover. And around them the rest of the crew were shouting, bellowing, throwing themselves behind whatever protection they could find.

I saw Rannon standing, looking back toward the fiery hammer that burned through the air toward us, and I hurled myself forward to grab her shoulders and drag her down beneath me. Even ahead of the bolt there came a wave of energy that made the hair stand up on my body. On Rannon's too. She had lost her helmet and her dark tresses came whipping across my face. I lifted my head.

There were twelve airships in our small fleet. Most had already turned or were turning back toward the city. But the last two in line were still flying straight into the bolt when it hit. I saw them disintegrate as if they had run into a concrete wall of fire. Immediately behind those two was a third ship, half turned so that the bolt broadsided it, ripping it in twain and igniting the barrels of God's Fire that still stacked its decks.

The lightning stroke of magic that Bryce had hurled at us churned on through the resulting explosion, tearing into the aft end of the next airship in line. That ship flipped over into the one in front of it, turning them both into blazing pyres full of shrieking men.

I had looked up, and now I could not look down. Time

had turned to mud and my eyes were locked on the horror as one ship after another exploded. Until only ours was left.

To one side of me I could hear the chanting of Ahrethane as she cast desperately about for some word or phrase to slow the inevitable. And the bolt *had* slowed. As our flyer had accelerated. But we were still losing the race.

The roar of the thing caught us, its voice like rain falling on some monstrous griddle. The light came next, the light of judgment day, its argent tendrils writhing, snapping wild with sparks as it licked toward the stern of the ship. And now I could smell the wind that went before it, like silver and burnt flesh.

I squeezed Rannon harder, my body slung over hers as if I could protect her. Then I saw Chalathar. He was standing, hands on hips as he glared with brutal eyes into the oncoming bolt of fire. The aft rail disintegrated in the wash of the light. I growled low, feeling a snarl carve itself into my face as I watched the inevitable gather to take us.

The ship gave a little jump; a silver aurora whispered against the deck, reaching for us...and falling short. We accelerated away, Bryce's hammer of light breaking apart behind us to dissipate in the air. We were the last of the twelve ships of our fleet, but for the moment we were going to live. I whispered as much to Rannon and I kissed her on top of her head. She twisted about in my arms and curled against my shoulder, silent and agonized in the aftermath of what we had lost.

A few paces away, the man called Chalathar sank slowly down to a seated position on the deck. It seemed after a moment that he felt my gaze upon him and turned to face me. The gin clearness of his eyes seemed clouded with weakness now. He looked away, but not soon enough.

I knew what he had done.

* * * * * * *

Our ship was damaged but we managed to limp our way back to one of the airfields before the pilot had to set us down. All was chaos for a while, with men and messengers running to and fro. There was no word from Kuurus at the palace so Rannon ordered a halt to the ground attack that had been launched as a follow up to our assault with the God's Fire. That attack had gone well, with our troops reaching the outskirts of the enemy encampment before they were pulled back. It was fear of what Bryce would do that made us timid. We couldn't afford to lose an army the way we'd lost eleven ships.

Reports came in from the air raids on the other two enemy camps, and those attacks had gone extremely well. Only one flyer had been brought down between the two Taleran forces, and had it not been for the arrival of my brother, of Vohanna's Bane-thrall, we might have broken the siege. As it was, we were on the defensive again and our foes would have time to repair the damage we'd caused—especially since word came that Bryce had brought an army with him, an army of the Centaurs who had once held me captive on another world.

At least the saddle bird squadron that was supposed to break out and try to contact Hurnan Jystral had apparently made it safely away. We could hope for good things from that.

Throughout the turmoil of orders going out and messages coming in, I kept an eye on the man Chalathar. I didn't want him to disappear on me again as he had before. But I needn't have worried. He seemed content to find a barrel of unused God's Fire to sit upon, and most of the time he spent with shoulders slumped as if in deep contemplation, or exhaustion.

Ahrethane watched Chalathar too, I noted. I wondered if she knew what I knew about him. I went over to her in a free moment and she gave me a tight hug. Diken Graye stood beside her and he grasped my hand very happily. It was the first chance we'd had to talk since they'd come aboard our ship.

"We were afraid you were killed," I said to them. "Rannon and I barely got through ourselves."

"We saw the attack on the two of you," Ahrethane replied. "But we were well back and the reptile ones hadn't yet seen us. We landed in a big gully north of here. Hid out until I sensed you and Rannon aboard the flyer and we came to meet you in the darkness."

"How did you end up with Chalathar?" I asked, gesturing toward the flame-haired warrior where he sat quietly on his barrel.

Ahrethane's eyes narrowed slightly as if in thought. "*He* found us. Just after we'd taken off from the gully. He led us to you."

I frowned. Diken looked between the two of us with confusion in his face.

"Who is this fellow?" he asked.

"I think it's time we found out," I replied, as I turned and led the way across the trampled earth of the landing field. Rannon saw us, and things had quietened enough for her to join us. We stopped before Chalathar and he looked up.

"So will you tell us who you are now?" I asked. "And why you are here?"

"Isn't it enough that I've fought beside you against your enemies?" he asked.

"Not nearly," Rannon said.

He chuckled. "You do know that Vohanna is here in your city, don't you? I mean, physically here? Not outside with her troops?"

"He's right," Ahrethane said. "I can smell her stench."

"We were pretty sure of it," I said. "We've been trying to figure out who she's masquerading as. Who she could have possessed."

"Any ideas?" This from Chalathar.

"Possibly," I said, not elaborating even though he stared intently at me. I noted that he'd not yet answered our question regarding his identity.

"One thing I don't understand," Rannon said. "Surely Vohanna is more powerful than Bry—than her Bane-thrall. Why haven't we seen attacks from her like the one we just saw on our airships? With that kind of power she could have shattered our defenses all by herself."

"Yes, she could," Chalathar said. "But you're not thinking of the price she'd have to pay to do so. That kind of power. To focus a bolt of energy like that. Well, the energy has to come from somewhere. And it comes from the sorcerer's own body. The Bane-thrall will be incapacitated for hours. But he'll recover much faster than Vohanna herself would because it doesn't matter if he uses himself up in the process. That's what Bane-thralls are for. To burn themselves to embers in the service of their master."

I felt my stomach roil and thought I was going to vomit. I swayed in my boots. Rannon grasped one arm, Ahrethane the other.

"I'm sorry," Chalathar said, his eyes upon mine. And I felt in the moment that his words were sincere. I nodded back to him as I managed to regain at least a little bit of control over myself.

Chalathar rose from his barrel. "I will tell you one more thing," he said, looking directly to me. "Go to the dungeons of the palace. Go deep. I think you'll find something of interest there."

He turned then, as if to stride away.

"Wait!" Rannon snapped. Her hand dropped to her sword. "You're not going anywhere."

Chalathar turned, faced Rannon across a distance of a few feet. His gin-colored eyes were deceptively mild, as mild as my love's blue eyes were hot.

"If you try to arrest me now, I will resist," he said. "And that won't be good for either of us. Trust me to be free a little longer and when this is over I'll explain everything."

He didn't wait to see whether she would accept his argument but turned and stalked away into the darkness. I watched Rannon. Her lips were thinned and her hand so tight on her sword that the red feathers around the hilt quivered. But she did not draw that sword, nor call out a command to arrest the pale-eyed warrior.

And then word came of fresh disasters, and once again chaos descended.

CHAPTER TWENTY-SIX

IN DUNGEONS DARK

The smoke from our torches was drawn down the corridor before us, down deeper into the hidden ways beneath the palace of Hurnan Jystral. That meant the air was moving with us instead of against us, and I wondered where it was headed.

"Go to the dungeons," Chalathar had told us. And we had, Ahrethane and Diken Graye and me, to find the "something of interest" that the mysterious warrior had hinted at. Perhaps the moving air would guide us.

It had not been easy to slip into the dungeons. There seemed far more guards around the lower levels of the palace than was warranted considering the siege and the number of prisoners that were usually kept jailed in Hurnan Jystral's cells. But Ahrethane's magic and her druidess senses had helped us find a way. Now we were deeper beneath the city than I'd ever been, deeper than I'd even known it was possible to go.

Rannon had told me once that the oldest part of Timmuzz, including Jystral Castle, had been built on the ruins of a previous settlement along the river Vehr. I suspected that the corridors we now walked, dank with dripping water and mold, dated back to that settlement. Certainly, the sections of the dungeons that were used today were much better kept, and they were clean and decently lighted. We would not even have been able to locate this older section without Ahrethane's magic. She was attuned to the rhythms of the earth and the rivers, and that had guided her.

The cells here had not been used in ages and most of the half-rotted doors stood open on nearly disintegrated hinges. I wondered what mystery could lie so deeply in this place. I wondered how the man who called himself Chalathar had learned of it.

"You think Rannon will end up cutting Kuurus's throat?" Diken Graye asked, breaking the quiet with words that echoed down the long way we followed.

I chuckled, without much humor. "She might. In addition to telling him about Bryce's attack she planned to ream him out about how he's handling this siege. Or *not* handling it."

"Sorry I'm not there to see it," Graye added.

"Me too," I agreed. And I was, though mostly because I worried about Rannon being away from me right now. Certainly, she had her Gray-Cloaks with her, and those warriors would give their lives for her. But that didn't keep my stomach from churning every time my imagination painted my thoughts with more dangers she could run into.

Still, I had learned enough about Chalathar to take seriously what he said. His suggestion for us to search the dungeons had been impossible to ignore. But Rannon was not as free as I was. Just after Chalathar had made his comments and left, Rannon had been forced to deal with reports of new attacks by enemy troops on the outskirts of Timmuzz. Kuurus would have gotten the same reports, and now Rannon would have to find some way of coordinating her efforts with those of her brother and of Taskin Bhent, the ranking officer in the Nyshphalian military. That wasn't a task I envied her, and I wondered if she would finally take the plunge and remove Kuurus from overall command. It all meant that she must stay behind while I traipsed off into the bowels of the castle in search of a mystery.

We came to a place where the corridors branched. I paused. Three tunnels led off from where we stood, each of them slanting downward at a shallow angle, and as I held the torch up to each I saw the smoke pulled into them. The air was still being drawn deeper into the earth. I wasn't sure what that meant.

I glanced at Ahrethane. Since entering the dungeons, it

had been she who had led us. I don't know how, or what trail she had been following. But now, for the first time, she looked confused. She turned her head from side to side, leaning forward at the mouth of each tunnel as if she were trying for a scent. She shook her head.

"Multiple sign," she said. She shook her head again. "I'm not sure." She glanced at me, her eyes full of apology. "I don't know, Ruenn. Not sure which way to go."

I sighed, studied the tunnels. Perhaps I saw something.

"You know," I said, "that Chalathar is a sorcerer? He's the one who stopped Bryce's bolt before it could destroy our flyer."

"What?" Diken Graye asked. But I looked only at Ahrethane.

"No, I didn't," the druidess said. "I knew he had power. But he is a blank to me. I cannot even sense his presence when he's near. How do you know he stopped the bolt? It *was* dissipating already."

"Oh, he stopped it. I know the same way that I know now that we need to go down this middle tunnel." I pointed with my torch.

Ahrethane chuckled. "Better than any guess I could make," she said, and pushed past me and started down. Diken Graye followed, and I close behind. I didn't tell them that I had another reason besides a hunch to choose the middle tunnel. I was pretty sure that the mold on the right side wall wasn't just mold. Some of it looked a lot like dried blood.

Down and down we went, and just when I began to think that my hunch had been wrong, we heard the echo of voices from in front of us and paused. For a long while now we had been passing through tunnels with no cells in the walls. It seemed that we had gone completely through the dungeons and I thought we might even be beneath the river, though my sense of direction was weak this far under ground. But ahead of us now there were people, and if they were not prisoners or jailers, who were they?

We snuffed our torches and Ahrethane conjured a tiny pearl of light that gave us just enough of a glow to see a few feet ahead. Then silently we crept forward, seeking an answer to a question that we weren't sure we knew how to ask.

The voices led us to a small, rounded area, like a hundred other guardrooms within the dungeons. Lanterns burned there and four men sat playing Taleran dice, with empty goblets and food-stained trays shoved to one side of the table where the dice rattled and rolled. Six corridors radiated out from this central circle. In several of them I saw jail cells with doors that were newly rehinged. I glanced at Ahrethane and Diken Graye. Diken drew his sword, quietly so as not to rasp the steel against the scabbard.

I stepped into the open area and was a third of the way across it before my footfalls registered on the players and as one they leaped up and back, venting oaths as they pulled rapiers into their fists. I paused, not yet drawing my own blade. Ahrethane and Diken remained hidden in the corridor behind me.

"Mercenaries," I spat as I studied the four men. And men they were. By that, I mean humans.

Several of the four chuckled. One had buck teeth, I noted. Another was missing an ear. The other two were redheads, much like the ones I'd been forced to kill on the palace roof when they'd come with a Vhichang and an Ss'Korra to assassinate me. None of the four seemed to know who I was, but I doubted that my relationship to Rannon would mean anything to them anyway.

"You got a problem with mercenaries, *boy*?" Buck-teeth asked.

I had to grin at being called, "boy," but I didn't let my amusement show in my words.

"I do if they take Nyshphalian gold and fight for her enemies instead. But we can answer that question soon enough. Just step aside and let me have a look in those cells you've been guarding down here. Maybe we have no need to exchange words in anger."

This time they all laughed.

Buck-Teeth shook his head and gestured for the others to fan out across the small space. "Oh you're gonna get a look at those cells, all right. A close and personal look. At one of them anyway."

I took a few steps to one side of the room, idly plucking

at a fingernail as if scraping dirt from beneath it. This kept their attention from falling on the mouth of the tunnel that I'd just vacated.

"The last four mercenaries who tried something similar are all dead," I said, shrugging. "But if you want to join them, that's fine. I haven't sacrificed to my gods yet today."

Buck-Teeth snarled. He and One-Ear came charging. The redheads followed.

I kicked a chair into the path of One-Ear, met Buck-Teeth's rapier with a parry as my runed blade came smoking from its sheath into the light. From their place in the corridor, Diken Graye and Ahrethane leaped into the room. The redheads turned to deal with them. But they were slow. Diken sworded the first through a shoulder; Ahrethane cast a mist of glittering dust into the eyes of the other. Both of them went down, the wounded one screaming.

I killed Buck-Teeth because he kept charging instead of backing away. One-Ear had fallen over the chair that I'd booted into his path, and in the seconds it took him to rise with curses flaming from his lips, the fight was already ended. He stared at us a moment, then dropped his blade with a clang on the floor.

I pushed him out of the way as I strode toward the first of the corridors in which I'd seen the repaired jail cells. Behind me, I heard Diken ordering One-Ear and the man with the sword wound to lie flat on the floor. There was no need to order the one Ahrethane had ensorcelled. He was snoring cold on the stones.

In the door of the first cell I approached there was a small window paned with heavy glass. No doubt as soundproofing. I glanced in, and what I saw wrung a gasp from my lips.

"The keys!" I called to Diken Graye. "Hurry." He jerked them from the dead Buck-Teeth's belt and tossed them to me. I quickly unlocked the cell and stepped inside.

Kreeg stood over Valyan, who was lying on a pallet of straw on the floor of the cell. The ex-gladiator's huge hands were fisted as he glared toward the door, as if he expected some enemy to be coming through it. His eyes widened when he saw that it was me. His fists unclenched and he rushed across to grab me in a bear hug and lift me nearly out of my boots. I grinned, slapping his shoulders, stiffening my spine against having a rib snapped by his greeting.

He put me down. "Good, Ruenn," he said. "*Good* to see you."

"And you," I said, slapping his shoulders again.

I glanced past the bullet-headed warrior then, toward Valyan, who had somehow managed to struggle into a sitting position with half his body wrapped in bandages. I went over to the Green Llurn and slipped to one knee. Behind me, I heard Ahrethane come through the door, recognizing the sound of her sandals on the stone. But I did not look up.

"I'm glad to see that you live, old friend," I said to Valyan, my voice rattling with emotion.

He nodded slightly, unable to speak from the bindings that swathed most of the lower part of his face. His left shoulder, too, was bandaged and immobilized. Clearly, he could not use that arm. But his yellow eyes expressed much and I knew that he was happy to see me too. I squeezed his right elbow, then rose as Ahrethane bent to examine him.

"I think we better check the rest of these cells," I said to Kreeg, stalking past him and back into the corridor. He followed, stooping to pluck up a sword that one of the mercenaries had dropped.

The next cell was empty, but the one beyond that held another friend.

"Rhandh!" I said, shoving through his door with surprise. The Vlih warrior was seated on the floor with his head down and his back to the wall, and he uncoiled as he heard the brass-bound door open. He leaped up and forward, hands curved like claws to strike, and was nearly to me before he realized who I was. He froze, his arms dropping to his sides. Then he stepped quickly toward me and grabbed my wrists, his face sallow, his black eyes burning feverishly into mine.

"The Jhesana? She is well? Alive?"

"She is," I said. "And safe for the moment. I'll take you to her but first we must open the rest of the boxes here. Find out who else is being held prisoner in these dungeons."

It seemed for an instant that he would deny my words, perhaps because they called for him to be patient. His cheek twitched violently and his strong black fingers vised like gar-rotes around my wrists. But after some inner struggle he nodded, and released me to step past into the corridor. I saw then what had been done to him, and the thought sickened me. His tail, the tail in which the Vlih take such pride and to which they strap blades when they go into combat, had been cut off. No wonder he looked half insane.

I growled as anger built and goaded me, then followed Rhandh into the hall outside the cells. Like Kreeg before him, he picked up a captured mercenary's sword. Then we moved down the corridor, opening each of the jail rooms as we went.

We freed half a dozen men and women, all of them no-bles of Nyshphal whom I had known to be outspoken and free with criticism of the government. Hurnan Jystral had always tolerated such criticism, and it was not the emperor who had ordered these arrests. Before I could ask who *had*, we found a man I'd never expected to see as a prisoner. In the last refurbished cell stood Rajan Critus.

"I'm a little surprised to see you here," I told the guard commander. "Up until now I'd suspected you of trying to have me killed."

Critus arched a dark eyebrow, and I explained to him about the spiked pistol barrel and about meeting the assassins on the roof of the palace when I'd expected to meet *him* in-stead.

"Ah," he replied. "An understandable suspicion on your part. But I'm afraid I was...." He gestured about at the nar-row walls of his cell. "...spirited away before I had a chance to make our rendezvous."

"Spirited away by whom?" I asked.

"I don't know absolutely," he answered. "I doubt any-one here was arrested in the *name* of the someone who or-dered it."

There were nods and murmurs of approval from the no-bles, and even Kreeg and Rhandh offered uncertain shrugs.

"But you have a suspicion," I guessed

Critus nodded. "I'm thinking...Kuurus Jystral."

"*Kuurus*? But surely—"

At that moment, Ahrethane came rushing along the corridor toward us and we all turned.

"We've got to get out of here!" she said. "Immediately!"

Men and women stirred. Some started to push past me.

"Why?" I asked. "What's wrong?"

"There's a gate here," she said. "Down here with us. A sphere gate. And it's operating. I can feel it. Something is coming through. Something bad. A *lot* of somethings."

CHAPTER TWENTY-SEVEN

DOGS OF WAR

A chill raced across my body, leaving fields of goose-bumps behind.

A sphere gate! Down here with us. Operating.

And the somethings coming through had to be an army. Had to be another of *Vohanna's* armies. How many did she have?

A nobleman named Harbis started to push past me in the corridor, his face writ large with fear, and I caught his shoulder and held him back. All of these men and women down here knew what Vohanna was capable of from the last war. Their terror was to be expected. But this was not the time to give in to it.

"No panic," I snapped. "If it's Vohanna's gate. And it almost certainly has to be. We need to get out of the dungeons and get word to someone. Someone besides," I glanced at Rajan Critus, "Prince Kuurus."

I looked around at the others then. "But we have to stay together. And we have to think of some way to block off the dungeons once we escape. *Now* let's go."

Rhandh scouted ahead while I and Ahrethane and Rajan Critus led the rest. Kreeg followed with Valyan, who after a healing spell from Ahrethane was able to limp along under his own power. Then came One-Ear and the other two mercenaries who'd served as jailers for my friends. We'd decided they might be able to answer some questions we wanted to ask, but their arms were bound behind them against any attempt they might make to escape. Bringing up the rear behind the freed nobles came Diken Graye, his sword naked in his fist.

Our passage back up through the dungeons went much quicker than our trip down. We knew where we were going. And we raced to get there. But there was pursuit. Ahrethane sensed it.

"Things coming fast behind us," she whispered to my ear when we paused once to catch our breath. "Not human."

I glanced around at the men and women who accompanied me. I saw them bent over, hands on knees as they grasped after oxygen. We had no greater speed to give. It was not just Valyan. All of those who had been prisoners were weak from days with little food and water. Their reserves were used up.

"Will they catch us?" I asked Ahrethane.

"I think so," she said. And: "They're runners."

Critus had overheard. "What now?" he asked. He didn't look scared.

"I'm going to join Diken as a rear guard," I said quietly to both of them. "When we get a chance we'll drop back, try to slow those who follow. Rajan." I gazed at him, knowing that I really had no choice now but to trust him. "You take the rest of them up. Out of the dungeons. Find Rannon. She'll know what to do."

He nodded. "Be careful," he said.

Ahrethane grasped my elbow as I turned to move away. "You could die," she said simply.

I flashed her a grin. "Vohanna has been trying to kill me for quite a while now. I don't intend for this to be the last time she has to try."

She nodded, without a return smile, then lifted on her tiptoes and kissed my cheek. "Make her pay for the attempts," she whispered quietly, almost fiercely, in my ear. She moved back toward Critus then, and I slipped my way through the crowd to join Diken Graye.

Critus had the group up and moving a moment later, and as we turned a corner into a new and more brightly lit hallway my hand grasped Diken's shoulder and pulled him to a halt beside me. His eyes questioned but I did not explain until the others were out of earshot and had not looked back to notice us missing.

"We're going to have company in a few moments," I told him.

"Ah," he said. "I should have guessed. Ahrethane tell you?"

"Yes."

"Then I believe it. She's quite a lady, that one."

I glanced at him, arching an eyebrow. "Indeed," I agreed. "And rather lovely, too."

He looked at me and blushed. "I didn't mean...." He trailed off.

I chuckled. Of course, that was exactly what he'd meant. But then we heard a sound and there was no more banter between us. The sound came from below, but it was coming closer, coming fast. It was like the baying of hounds. But not quite hounds. It made my skin crawl.

Where we stood, the corridor was only some six feet across, not much of a gap for two of us to protect. This was part of the regular dungeons, and in sconces along the walls were torches that we lit to provide us plenty of light. These torches were made from sawdust packed tightly together with a glue and wax combination and then impregnated with rundal oil. They would burn for a long time. And that was good. I didn't want to fight what was coming for us in the dark.

The baying grew louder, echoing up the hollow tunnels. The sound was vicious, filled with an undercurrent of snarling, snapping rage. I carried my bow everywhere with me these days, and now I drew it over my shoulder and strung it, nocking an arrow. Diken Graye had no bow but his fist tightened on his sword hilt until his knuckles were white. He drew a long, slender dagger into his other hand.

"I'm taking Vohanna off my prayer list," he said.

I chuckled. "I'm sure she'll be hurt," I said, as I drew three more arrows from my quiver and let them dangle between the fingers of my left hand for quick reloading.

Diken watched me. "Shoot well," he said.

And then the first handful of our enemies rounded a corner and surged into the long corridor in which we stood. As Ahrethane had said, they weren't human. Though parts of them were.

I remembered the vat-grown monsters that I'd seen in Vohanna's pyramid during the last war. I remembered the hybrid of woman and insect that we'd fought in the jungle of Vohan during this one. Kurshan, such creatures were called, beings put together out of parts of other beings as if by some insane god. *Or goddess*, the thought struck me. For that was how Vohanna styled herself.

"Dihmus vishka!" Diken cursed.

I drew the bowstring to my cheek. The arrow quivered. I released it. The bolt struck true, into the first creature's throat as it lifted a grotesque head to bay. Down the thing went, tumbling over its six limbs. Two of those limbs were human arms.

The other monsters leaped their dead brother, came rushing. They were like some alloy of hound and hyena and human. I nocked a new arrow, fired, dropped a second of the hybrids. But there were four more of them and they were halfway down the corridor now.

I hurried my third shot. The razored arrowhead sliced only a tuft of hair from one creature's back. And my fourth arrow tore into a shoulder, crippling a limb that hardly mattered on a beast with six of them.

It was past time for bows then. I threw mine down, ripped free my rune blade. Diken hurled his dagger straight into the mouth of an attacking beast, then brought up his own brand, its steel rippling bright in the torchlight.

The beast who had taken Diken's dagger in its mouth gave an aborted howl, then grabbed with human hands to tear the knife free where it spiked a purplish tongue to the jaw beneath. That let the other three monsters reach us first.

I heard Diken shout. In pain or rage, I could not tell. And there was no time to look. One beast sprang at my throat, another behind it. I split one attacker through the breastbone with my sword, but its momentum carried it into me and I was knocked back and down with the thing on top of me.

Hot spittle drizzled on my face; I saw the slavering jaws so close. I let go of my sword and grabbed the muzzle of the thing, wrenched it aside. But the beast was dead, its heart carved in twain by my blade. Blood poured upon me.

I tried to throw the corpse off but a second beast leaped upon the first, its face a mask of rage. This was the one I'd shot in the shoulder. The arrow quivered in its flesh as its hands grabbed for my throat. Its mouth dipped, jaws wide to rend and tear. I got one hand under its muzzle, fought desperately to keep its white fangs at bay. But its brutal hands found my neck and tightened, the fingers gnarled and twisted and stabbed with short, wiry hair. The beast jerked my head up, slammed it back down into the stone flaggings. Black stars burst in my awareness.

Again my head was hammered into stone. I could hear Diken cursing but the words seemed to float in from far away. The arrow bobbed up and down in the beast's arm as it strangled me. But the wound seemed to bother it none at all.

I reached up, wrapped half-numb fingers around the gore-slicked shaft of the dart. The creature paused, turning its head, its eyes like bloodshot copper moons in its narrow face. I yanked the arrow free, its tip clotted with liverish flesh. The beast howled, tried to pull back, but I jammed the tip of the dart straight into the thing's eye socket and through into the brain.

The hound-creature fell away, clawing at its face, and I pushed to a sitting position, my chest raw as I tried to breathe. Diken was locked in a death struggle with the third beast, his leathers ripped to shreds from the thing's claws, the two of them thrashing back and forth with their hands tearing at each others throats.

I saw the last of the monsters then. Its daggered tongue sprayed ichor but one of its hands held the knife that Diken had thrown. It leaped toward us. Toward Diken. And I shoved the dead beast that lay across my legs into the living one. They hit the wall, the knife flying free.

I made it to my knees, grabbing up the first thing that came to hand for a weapon. It was the bow I'd thrown down only moments before.

The beast shrugged out from under the corpse of its companion, spraying blood from its mouth as it roared. It gathered its legs under it, and I swung my makeshift club with all the strength I had left. This bow was made of tlatel wood reinforced with bone, and it cracked wide over the skull of the hyena-beast. The creature went down, stunned, and I threw myself on top of it, my hands finding its jaws, twisting its head around until the neck snapped with a sodden thud.

A near silence fell. I rolled over, glancing toward Diken Graye and the beast he had fought. They both lay still. Far too still.

"Diken!" I cried out, scrabbling on hands and knees toward him.

The beast stirred, its hide rippling, and I grabbed up a broken piece of the bow as a stake for its heart. But then Diken pushed the dead Kurshan off of him and sat up, his chest working for air and with blood and gore coating him. Somehow he'd managed to get his sword up enough to disembowel the creature. Its spilled guts stank like raw sewage.

I felt my nose wrinkle. "You smell like I feel," I told Diken.

Graye laughed. "And you look like I smell."

I grinned, then pushed to my feet with a groan. The Kurshan that I'd stabbed through the eye with the arrow still lived, though it was beyond the urge to fight. It was dragging itself away down the corridor, leaving a snail trail of blood behind it.

I grasped the hilt of my sword and pulled it free from where I'd sheathed it in the chest of another of the creatures. Then I stepped forward to stop beside the crawling beast. I drew the blade up and hacked down so hard through the neck of the thing that the blade rang on stone. The ghastly head rolled free, the severed muscles of the neck twitching.

Diken climbed to his feet as well, reclaiming his own sword. He moved up beside me, then paused. We both heard it at the same time, the tramp of iron shod feet echoing up the corridor from below.

"Krutt!" Diken said.

I glanced at him. "Sounds like the rest of Vohanna's army is marching."

He nodded, wiped his mouth on the back of his hand. "And here I was afraid the fun was over."

"Little chance of that these days," I remarked.

Then our enemies turned the corner and came into the light where we could see them. There were Kurshan with them, more of the man/hound/hyenas straining at leashes, but the soldiers of this army were far worse. They looked as I'd always imagined ogres and trolls to look. And yet they wore the armor of men.

CHAPTER TWENTY-EIGHT

ONE RED FEATHER

They wore the armor and carried the weapons of men, this army of Vohanna's that came now toward us. But their faces and bodies were those of monsters. I should have become inured to such visitations, but to see those bestial forms and the piggish eyes and yellowed tusks upthrust past pendulous lips was still enough to dip my heart in glacier water.

I had met Centaurs and Minotaurs in Vohanna's armies. And now Trolls. In the witch's black pyramid I had seen beings who could have been taken for angels and demons. I wondered if they *had* been.

Had the mythologies of my own world been based in part on ancient sightings of such beings as I had seen, beings who had come through what *I* would call sphere gates? Or perhaps those myths had been based on stories carried through the gates by men who had gone and returned from other worlds. Such explanations seemed likely to me, though mostly what I thought of at the moment was that *these* myths could kill me.

I drew Diken with me as I started to back slowly away down the corridor.

The man/hound/hyenas saw us and came snarling and snapping against their leashes, but their Troll masters held them back. I heard foul laughter bloom from fanged and dripping mouths, and Troll hands reached to draw maces and axes and war-hammers into misshapen fists. A low snarling filled the corridor and the enemy came on, moving steadily on clawed feet, now smashing their weapons on their shields in a cacophony of sound.

"I don't suppose we've delayed them enough?" Diken Graye asked dryly.

I flashed him a grin. "A few more minutes," I said, still backing up. "Then we run."

Ahrethane and the others should be nearly out of the dungeons by now, I knew. If they could get to Rannon and she could get troops to block the portals into the castle from below we might be able to keep this army bottled up. If not, the castle would fall. And with it Timmuzz.

Then the Trolls released their hounds; the beasts leaped forward; the corridor exploded with howls.

"Get ready!" I shouted to my friend.

No chance to run now.

A wild form leaped past Diken and me to face the man-hounds. It was Kreeg, a sword whirling in either fist. He split one Kurshan's ugly head, lopped off an arm of another. Diken and I jumped to the attack beside him. The hounds retreated in shocked surprise, but the Troll warriors saw and up went a roar of rage. They came rushing.

"Back!" I heard a shout from behind me. "All of you. Get back!"

I spared one glance over my shoulder. Ahrethane stood there. Her copper fire hair floated about her face. Her small hands were up, fingers speaking runes that sparked in amethyst and ruby. I saw streaks of light leap from her form to the roof of the corridor over my head, and desperately I grabbed at Diken and Kreeg, yelling at them to fall back.

The Troll army broke into a dead run, shrieking, weapons waving as they charged. A grating sound tore through the dungeon stone. I saw the ceiling ripple. Dust spewed into the air. One of the man-hounds leaped at Kreeg, teeth closing on the front of his leather jerkin. But Diken and I each had one of Kreeg's arms, and we hauled him back just as the roof shuddered and collapsed upon the place where we'd been standing.

The huge blocks of ceiling stone dropped all at once. I heard screams from where the Troll army had been. Inhuman screams. And after came shouts of anger to show that not all of them were dead. For the moment, that didn't matter. Even

199

through a fog of dust I could see that the corridor was completely dammed up. And when I looked down I saw the head and one arm of the Kurshan man-hound sticking out from the rubble pile. The eyes were open and white, but there was no fire of life in them.

Kreeg cursed and I turned to see him plucking a single yellowed fang from the front of his jerkin. He started to throw it down, then thought better of it. He glanced up at me, grinning, then dropped the canine into a pocket.

I shook my head at him but had to smile. Then I was moving past him, my hand dropping to squeeze Ahrethane's shoulder.

"Sort of glad you came back for us," I said.

She smiled too, but it was a fleeting one. "It was dangerous to bring down that roof but it didn't look like there was any choice."

"I don't believe there was," I said. And then: "Rajan and the others?"

"They were nearly out of the tunnels when we turned back."

I nodded, began to jog quickly up the corridor toward the surface. My friends followed.

It was daylight again and the palace grounds were in turmoil when we came up out of the dungeons with our hair and leathers streaked with dust. We had first entered the cell area through a seldom used door on the ground floor between two wings of the castle. We emerged the same way, but the guards, who we'd tricked before with Ahrethane's magic, were no longer standing watch.

There was no sign of Rajan and the others. They must have gone in search of Rannon, though I was surprised that no one had been left behind to let us know. Thoughts of Rannon made me wonder if she'd yet had a chance to confront her brother over the conduct of the war. I hated to think how that had gone. Kuurus was not a reasonable man. And now I had greater reason to be concerned over his possible reaction. If indeed he had ordered the arrests of Kuurus and the others, then the prince was playing with poison. Why? Did he desire power so much that he would jail his own people to keep them from challenging it? What else might he do?

Kreeg interrupted my thoughts. "Why is everyone running?" he asked.

I glanced around. The ex-gladiator was right. Cooks and nobles and warriors and washer women were spilling out of all the doors of the castle, scarcely seeming to notice us as they ran through the grounds toward the front gate of the palace complex.

"They're running toward something rather than away," Diken remarked. And he, too, was right.

"Let's find out," I said.

We started forward after the crowd, but even before we rounded the front of the castle we saw what it was that had attracted the people's attention. Above us in the red autumn sky there sailed a fleet of battleships. And it was the Nysh-phalian fleet, far diminished but still a brave sight, with the maroon sails being furled now as the ships approached their landings.

Hurnan Jystral was home! Surely that meant victory on the coast, and surely it would mean victory here. Men and women and children cried out in exultation. I grinned, slapping Kreeg and Diken Graye on their backs, hugging Ahrethane and pumping my fist in the air as I let my cheers mingle with the raised shouts of the gathered throng.

But Ahrethane had gone still, and her stillness stole my voice. And then a woman in the crowd shouted for us to look as she pointed toward the lead ship, the battleship of Hurnan Jystral. I looked. We all looked. And we saw the flag at the mast of the emperor's war-craft. It flew upside down.

A soldier with the scars of a veteran campaigner cried out in negation and fell to his knees. A merchant wilted where he stood, falling prostrate to the earth. Women, and men, began to wail. Children pulled at their mother's dresses as they begged for comfort and did not find it. I looked at Ahrethane and she would not meet my gaze.

"The emperor is dead," a little girl near me said in a quiet voice.

Others heard, and they took up the words as a refrain. "The emperor is dead. The emperor is dead!"

I wanted to scream at them to stop, scream at them not

to let the knowledge of Hurnan Jystral's loss spread. For with that spread would come the end of hope for the people of Timmuzz. But I knew already that it was too late. The panic was rippling outward; the people were beginning to run. There was only one thing I could do now.

"Rannon," I said to those who stood with me, to Kreeg and Ahrethane and Diken Graye. "I have to get to her."

Yes, I had to reach my beloved's side. To stand and die with her. For I knew that even if the whole world ran, she would not.

"Where?" Diken Graye asked.

I turned, looked up at the palace, ignoring the surge of the fleeing throngs around us.

"There," I said, pointing up at the balcony behind which stood her father's suite within the castle. "If she saw. If she knows. She'll be there. Not in her own apartment but in the rooms of her father."

I started to run, hearing the pounding feet of the others behind me. Into the palace and up the long marble stairs I went, into the corridor leading to the dead emperor's state-rooms. At first we found no guards, for all the emperor's own had gone with him to war. But when I saw the door to Hurnan Jystral's apartments I saw a group of Rannon's Gray-Cloaks standing there in sadness and martial splendor. They did not stop me as I pushed past them.

"She bade us leave her alone," one said in an anguished voice.

I nodded, hoping that Rannon did not wish, as well, to be left alone by me. And I opened the door and stepped within. Immediately I smelled it, an odor like flesh burned in a silver fire. It was the same odor that I'd detected when Bryce had struck at us with a hammer of light, when he'd used magic against our raiding fleet that only the man named Chalathar had been able to stop. I felt panic crawl up in my throat.

"Rannon! *Rannon!*"

There came no answer. I rushed across the apartment, thinking, hoping to find her in her father's night-room. But something glimpsed from the corner of my eye dragged me to a halt. I turned, moved over to the fireplace. The silver scent was more powerful here, like acid in my nostrils. And within the hearth, where a fire might have been built on a quiet winter's day, there lay a single red feather, a crimson feather like those that always dangled around the hilt of Rannon's sword.

CHAPTER TWENTY-NINE

FRIEND AND FOE

One red feather lying on the hearth. One feather from the hilt of Rannon's sword. It meant that my Saysa was gone. That she'd been taken. And by the smell of silver and meat I knew who had come for her. *Bryce!* My brother. Vohanna's Bane-thrall.

I picked up the crimson telltale. Ahrethane and Diken Graye and Kreeg had entered Hurnan Jystral's quarters with me. They stood silent, watching. I think they expected me to scream, to rage. But all of that, I let happen only inside. I tucked the feather beneath my mail, beneath my shirt, next to my skin. Then I walked past the others to the wall of the apartment where hung a display of weapons. My hands took down a crossbow of black steel and polished Samphur wood. I loaded it with dark bolts.

Sensing that something was wrong, Rannon's gray-cloaked guards had also entered the room. Faintly, I heard Diken explaining to them what had happened. But now I spoke, and they all gave me their attention.

"Prince Kuurus knows something. And I intend to find out what. It seems likely that he had Commander Critus arrested. And I'm sure he lied to me about Kreeg and Valyan, and he lied to Rannon and I both about Rhandh the Vlih. All of them were imprisoned, and I believe it was a word from the prince that sent them to those cells. Now the princess is missing. *After* she was to confront Kuurus.

"I don't know where Critus and Rhandh are now. I don't know if Kuurus had anything to do with Rannon's disappearance. But I know the emperor is dead and the city is near to falling. And Kuurus has done nothing. Anyone who goes with me to face him may become subject to his wrath. I'll not hold any man's choice against him."

I glanced over my shoulder, out over Hurnan Jystral's balcony. Most of the fleet's remaining ships had landed. And beyond, at the outskirts of Timmuzz, clouds of fresh smoke rose to show that our enemies had renewed their attacks. Here and there, the smoke was cut by the shadows of the Reploid pterodactyls and by the Nyshphalian flyers that fought them, but it seemed to me that the lizard birds outnumbered the flyers. And I thought, also, of the Troll army bottled up temporarily in the dungeons below me. *Only* temporarily.

There was nothing I could do about any of those things. And there was nothing else I had to say to those who stood in this room with me. I smiled grimly and passed among them on my way out the door. Ahrethane and Diken Graye and Kreeg followed me. As I knew they would. Nor was I surprised when every one of the Gray-Cloaks followed as well. They knew that Rannon had put her trust in me. And in Rannon they had put *their* trust.

The seat of power for Nyshphal, the throne of Hurnan Jystral, lay close to the heart of Jystral Castle. But before we reached it we heard ahead of us the shouts and clangor of battle. I rushed forward through the remaining corridors, the crossbow swinging in my right hand.

The throne room's entrance was on the third floor of the five-level palace, though you had to get through a waiting room and a guardroom to reach the throne itself. A massive staircase, of black marble veined with fool's silver, rose to the third floor and ended before a set of intricately carved gold and white doors through which petitioners to the emperor first had to pass. There was an open area around the mouth of the stairwell that was perhaps sixteen tahng (fifty feet) across.

Three corridors emptied into this open area, and when we came out of the middle hall we saw that two barricades had been thrown up across from each other in that space. One barricade stood nearly at the mouth of the stairs, right in front of the doors that guarded the way to the throne. The other was just in front of our own position, and I saw Rajan Critus there giving orders to men who fired arrows and crossbow bolts at enemies across the way. That fire was returned.

I ordered the others back and dropped to my belly to crawl my way forward, calling for Critus's attention so he wouldn't mistake me for an enemy sneaking up behind him. He heard, turned and saw me, then shouted for his men to give me covering fire. I slipped up beside him, noting and nodding to Valyan who squatted to one side with a crossbow in his right hand, his one *good* hand. How the Llurn could even move, much less fight, I did not know. But there were few in this world with more spirit than my green friend.

"What happened here?" I asked Critus.

The guard commander's long black hair, normally well combed and sleek, hung in sweat-soaked tendrils across his face and he flung it back with impatience.

"We couldn't find Rannon," he said, his jet-eyed gaze constantly roaming, glancing across mine, then looking up and down the line of his defenses.

"She's been kidnapped," I said. "It was Bryce."

He looked at me. "Your brother?"

"He's Vohanna's servant now," I said, tasting those words like bitter drink in my mouth. "But," I added, "after what you told me in the dungeons, I'm suspicious of Kuurus as well. He's playing his own game of power."

"That's why *we* came here," Critus said. "To face him. But the guards wouldn't let us pass. Even me by myself."

"You didn't really expect them to, did you?" I asked.

He shrugged. "One of the prince's pet mercenaries was around. He ordered us all arrested."

Critus chuckled as he remembered the scene, and as he remembered so did I. I remembered the six mercenary guardsmen, the mecredi whose presence around Kuurus had bothered me so much. I remembered how they had held their hands, not like swordsmen but like...someone else with whom I was familiar, someone I could not place at the moment.

"Arrogant, the fellow was," Critus continued. "He didn't like it when we refused to put down our weapons."

"And?"

"It was a standoff until Rhandh broke it."

"Rhandh?" I knew I hadn't seen the big Vlih warrior when I'd crawled up.

"Yes. Between not knowing where Rannon is and the loss of his tail, I think the Vlih has been driven half insane. He charged them." Critus looked at me straight on then. "But the mercredi had a gun. Like the one you had."

My chest seized. "He shot Rhandh?"

"He shot him," Critus agreed. "But not to kill. Got him in the shoulder. They dragged him off."

Thoughts roiled through my brain. *A gun?* It couldn't have been the spiked one that *I'd* had. But there had been another one, given to Arca Heskern for study. And I'd seen Heskern in the throne room with Kuurus. *Maybe it was—*

A crossbow bolt went singing over our heads. Valyan answered by zipping a couple of return bolts toward the enemy positions. I heard a shout but it sounded more like startlement than pain.

Under cover of Valyan's fire, Ahrethane and Diken Graye had crawled up beside us. I looked at Ahrethane, thinking to ask whether her magic could help us get past the guards, but she seemed to read my question before I spoke it.

"Vohanna's close," she said. "I don't think I better try any spells here. We might not like what we'd get."

I nodded, feeling frustration take root inside me.

"We have to do something," Critus said.

I took a quick glance over our barricade. Kuurus's guards had thrown up *their* line of chairs and tables almost right in front of the main staircase rising from below. An idea occurred to me.

I ducked back down next to Critus as more enemy fire whispered my way. I think the commander saw by my face that I'd come up with something.

"What?" he demanded.

"We can't cross the open space here," I said. "Not in the teeth of those crossbows. But what if we came at them from below?"

He rose up to take his own look, then dove back beside me.

"The stairway," he said. "Doesn't look like they're watching it that closely."

I nodded, glanced at Ahrethane. "You should stay here," I said. "Listen for Vohanna. Try to warn us if she's coming."

"If you hear a whisper in your ear it'll mean she is," she said.

I nodded, squeezed her slim hand and offered her my crossbow. I couldn't use it for the close work to come. To Rajan Critus, I added: "Keep the bastards under fire. Don't let them even think about the rest of us." Finally, I turned to Diken Graye. "You with me?" I asked him.

The brown-haired warrior's lips curled. "Been waiting long enough to take a cut in the Witch's direction," he said.

"Me too," I replied. We dropped down and crawled our way back to Kreeg and the Gray-Cloaks.

In addition to the primary one, there were four other sets of stairs at outside corners of the castle. We took one of those sets to the first floor, then doubled back to the foot of the main staircase. Chalathar was waiting for us there, leaning on a marble balustrade. Behind him loafed three rough looking characters.

"Been expecting you," Chalathar said.

I arched an eyebrow.

"You *are* going up to see Kuurus, aren't you?"

"We have to get through his guards first," I said.

He nodded. "I know. I've brought some friends along for the fun."

For a moment I studied his companions, hard-cases all. Two were men, the third a big Nokarran whose light gray fur was mottled with dark rosettes so that he resembled a snow leopard walking.

"Looks like you need a leash for 'em," I said to Chalathar.

The Nokarran smirked. Chalathar chuckled. "Then they couldn't kill," he replied.

Now it was my turn to nod. "Let's make that happen, then," I said, stalking past him and starting up the steps.

The main staircase of Jystral Castle was wide enough for six men to walk abreast. And so, six of us led. There was myself and Diken Graye and Kreeg, who had replaced his sword with a bold black axe that he'd taken from the wea-pon-wall in Hurnan Jystral's day room. Next to us strode Chalathar and two of his cronies, the Nokarran and a tall, almost gaunt human who carried twin kahnnas, which are sharp-curved blades about halfway in length between knives and sabers.

I was not particularly surprised that Chalathar had joined us. Somewhere in the hinterland of my thoughts, I'd ex-pected to see him again when it came time for sword strokes. This was such a time.

We went up two stories and began to hear the shouts and the zip of arrows whizzing back and forth between the two barricades. There we paused. Critus's men were firing at will, trying to keep the enemy occupied so they wouldn't ex-pect an attack from beneath them. I glanced at Chalathar. He flashed a huge grin, his white teeth feral behind the reddish-blond stubble of a burgeoning beard.

"You can have Kuurus," he said. "I'll take the rest of these krutt-lovers."

I said nothing. And for his smile there was no answer in me. Too much had happened. But I tightened my grip on my sword and nodded to him and the others—to Kreeg, who also smiled, and to Diken Graye, who licked nervous lips but did not waver. Then we went on the run up the last dozen steps, shouting battle cries to warn Critus we were coming so his men wouldn't shoot us by mistake.

The barricade in front of the throne room doors reared suddenly before us.I saw overturned tables with the stains of rich foods upon them, and shattered vases and piled chairs of samphur and mahogany. I saw the guards who crouched there. They'd heard us coming; their eyes were wild. They were Nyshphalians, men of Rannon's city. But their hands were filled with bows and crossbows and they were prepared to kill us for Kuurus.

I leaped the barricade. Came down. A crossbow bolt tugged at my left side, scraping the mail there. I kicked the weapon from the soldier's hands, hacked a second man's long bow in half with my sword. The bowman leaped up. I smashed an elbow into his face just under his helmet, pulp-ing his nose in a red spray. The other tried to dagger me and

I caught his thrusting arm under mine and broke his jaw with a fist that was filled with the pommel of a sword.

Diken leaped with me. He cut down one man, blocked another who stabbed at me with a spear. Chalathar and Kreeg and the Nokarran came *through* the barricade rather than over. They kicked aside tables and wine-filled amphora, splintered chairs and stools, and then they were in among Kuurus's guards with their swords and axes harvesting in a field of foes.

An arrow feathered past my ear. A crossbow bolt cracked on the marble floor between my boots and skittered off. I killed both the men who'd shot at me, my rune-blade splitting helms and heads alike. Kreeg was grinning savagely as he fought beside me. His axe hacked through a table, lopping off the arm of the man who cowered behind it.

The gaunt warrior with the kahnnas wielded his curved blades with lethal passion as he and Chalathar cut their way forward on the other side of me. I saw the Nokarran pick up a man and hurl him over the balustrade into the stairwell. Then he leaped forward to grasp one side of the gold and white doors as guards tried desperately to slam them shut.

I raced ahead, shouting for the big cat-man to hold the doors. From nowhere loomed the arrogant mercenary who Rajan Critus had mentioned earlier, one of the mercredi who had become Kuurus's personal bodyguard. The man's right hand was clawed near his right hip and in that instant I realized what had bothered me about he and his companions so much. They held their hands like my Uncle Quint had held *his* hands. And Quint Maclang had been a gunfighter! The mercredi were from Earth! The fact that he cursed suddenly in English only confirmed it. And he would have a gun, I knew.

I shouted a warning to the Nokarran but it came too late. The mercredi's fist snaked beneath the long leather duster that he wore and came out snarled around a bright revolver, a nickel-plated weapon that I'd never seen before. He shot the Nokarran with it, sent him staggering back.

With the clearness of a blue mountain morning I saw the man's thumb cock the pistol's hammer a second time, saw the barrel swing in my direction with a coil of smoke smearing in the air behind it. But my own hand was already moving—my left hand—dipping to my side, pulling a dagger free, side-arming it with every bit of power behind it that I could muster.

My aim was off. It was the dagger's hilt and not the blade that smashed the gunman's hand. But the blow startled him, threw off his practiced motions. His finger spasmed on the trigger and the shell went whining over my head.

By that time I was too close for the man to duck as I brought my rune-sword crashing over my head and down. The gleaming edge thunked into the juncture of his shoulder and chest, hacked almost through his neck in a spitting shower of red. He looked surprised as he died. I don't think he'd expected blades to beat bullets.

Chalathar and Kreeg seized the entry and I rushed through, stooping as I went to grab up the fallen gunman's pistol. A sumptuous waiting area greeted my eyes, followed by a short hallway leading to a final guard cubicle before the throne room itself. I shot two men in the hall, hearing the rush of feet behind me as Chalathar and the others came storming.

There were no other guards but there was a smaller set of gold and white doors that opened into the throne room. These were not barricaded and I did not stop to wonder why. Instead, I leaped against them, slamming them back so that I and those who followed me could pour into the chamber beyond where Hurnan Jystral had once sat in ruler-ship over the empire of Nyshphal.

I heard the snick of gun hammers being cocked. The five remaining mercredi guards, including the two blacks and the one with the bulging biceps who had stared at me so intently when I'd first seen him, had formed a line before Kuurus. They each carried a pistol, though they held their fire.

But that wasn't what stopped me cold in my boots. Nor what stopped those who accompanied me. Kuurus stood behind his mercenaries, next to a table upon which some shrouded form writhed. There was no sign of Taskin Bhent, who *should* have been there, but ranked behind Kuurus were beings I'd not expected to see. These were Reploids and Centaurs and half a dozen of the Minotaur dead. All were soldiers of the armies that besieged Timmuzz. All were armed to the teeth. Kuurus, it seemed, consorted with our enemies. And of all the things I had thought, I had not thought that. Even though it seemed obvious now.

My sword was in my right hand, the confiscated pistol in my left. I felt the bite of them in my palms as my hands clenched tightly. Rajan Critus pushed up beside me, and Ahrethane was with him. I heard them both gasp. I could not see Chalathar, though Kreeg and Diken stood nearby in confusion. Then the sheet covering the figure on the table slipped. It was Rhandh who twisted beneath it. Things had been...done to him.

I looked from the big Vlih to Kuurus, and to the foes of Nyshphal who stood at the prince's shoulder.

"You son of a bitch!" I snarled. "What betrayal is this?"

"I have betrayed no one," Kuurus said, his voice pitched oddly.

I sputtered. "And what of your father? Your sister? Your *people* for Sevarian's sake?"

Kuurus laughed. "You mistake me," he said. He lifted a pale hand and I saw the fingertips glittering as if painted with light.

I frowned, and from beside me Ahrethane whimpered a single word, "No!"

Kuurus's gleaming fingers brushed across his face, and when they had passed on I saw that the blue irises of Rannon's brother had turned as black and hard as the wings of ravens.

It was Vohanna who now looked out of Kuurus's eyes.

CHAPTER THIRTY

WITCH! WITCH!

My legs turned to sticks, and then to water as Ahrethane whispered savagely from beside me: "That's no sign of possession. That *is* Vohanna."

Vohanna! Witch!

Her gaze weighed upon us like lead strapped to the limbs of a man trying to swim. And so again I faced her. Last time I'd surprised her. I'd had milkstones to battle her with. I'd had a fleet at my back. I'd had...Rannon.

Not this time.

"What is going on here?" Critus demanded.

"That's not Kuurus," I answered quietly. "You're looking at the Witch herself."

"But...." He glanced around as if wanting someone to explain to him why the world didn't work the way he'd thought it worked.

I tried to clarify things for him. I asked Vohanna a question.

"What have you done with the *real* Kuurus, Vohanna? Is he dead or just locked away somewhere?"

She smirked with lips that belonged on another. "See for yourself, sweet Ruenn," she said, pointing behind me.

I turned at the sound of a commotion from the hall that led into the throne room. For a moment I glimpsed Chalathar standing behind his men—as if hiding. But then my attention was riveted by a party of soldiers who pushed through the gold and white doors and came among us. They were scarred and ragged, some of them bandaged and all of them wearing the blue and gray uniforms of the navy of Nyshphal. Kuurus Jystral led them!

The prince, Rannon's brother, passed among us with scarcely a glance. His focus was on Vohanna, though his gaze could not miss the warriors of the enemy who stood behind the Witch. He stopped.

"I believe, Vohanna," he said, "that you are between me and my throne."

I heard the men behind me draw themselves up as they readied to fight for Kuurus. They thought he was threatening Vohanna, and though few Nyshphalians particularly liked the prince he still carried the royal blood, the blood of Hurnan Jystral and of Rannon, who they *did* love.

I knew that Kuurus's words were no threat. I knew Kuurus and I knew Vohanna. And suddenly many things fell into place for me, the prince's sudden comings and goings in the city before the start of the war, the ease with which Vohanna had almost perfectly aped his mannerisms, the fact that he'd once called me names in English. I expected what happened next. Vohanna smiled and offered the prince a mocking bow that ushered him past her and up the five scarlet steps to a seat on the snow-wood throne.

The Nyshphalian marines who had accompanied Kuurus milled for a bit, but then took up positions before the great chair. By the glances that passed back and forth between them I could see their confusion. But they were good soldiers, trained to obey their commanders, and Kuurus *was* their commander, had been since the death of the emperor. They did not know what I knew, what Rajan Critus and the others among us had to learn.

Kuurus looked out from his tall seat across those of us standing before him. His gaze found mine and quickly moved on, falling now on one man and then another, on Rannon's Gray-Cloaks and upon rank-and-file guards who'd joined us in the fight outside the throne room.

"Lay down your arms," he told us. "I have negotiated a peace with Vohanna. Lay down your arms and her troops will be withdrawn."

A murmur of anger stirred in the throats of the men around me. And here and there, yells punctuated the grumbles.

Rajan Critus shouted louder than anyone.

"No! There is no accord with such as this Witch." His lips were flecked with spittle as he raged. "In the last war she destroyed half our fleet! In this one, half our nation! Her plans led to your father's death, Kuurus! She has even taken your sister. If you try to make such a peace you will only make rebels."

I saw Kuurus bristle as Critus stormed. I saw him push himself half out of his seat to make reply. And I saw the glance that Vohanna exchanged with him, saw him sink back in his chair with only the faintest of nods.

"I understand your fears, Commander Cri—" the prince started to say. And I cut him off.

"He knows all that, Rajan." I looked from the guard commander to Vohanna, and then to Kuurus on the throne. And though I stared into the prince's eyes my words were meant for Critus and the others. "You think that Kuurus speaks true. That he wants, even if misguided, to find a way to save Nyshphal. But the prince lies."

A babble of voices erupted. Kuurus did stand now, leaping up with his hand on his sword. But I shouted everyone down.

"It was planned from the start! It was what Kuurus wanted. The only way he could get the throne. I suspect Vohanna even sent him to Earth." I pointed to the mercredi. "Those men with the guns are from *my* world. Not Talera. The only thing that makes sense is that it was Kuurus who recruited them."

Silence slammed down. And the look that passed between Kuurus and the mercredi was proof to me of my suppositions.

But now I added the final word.

"And look at his irises," I said. "The Witch didn't control Kuurus. She didn't possess him. He chose!"

By now, everyone in Timmuzz knew of Vohanna's black orbs and of how those she owned revealed their allegiance with crimson eyes. It was why Vohanna had been forced to hide her own eyes in order to portray Kuurus. But Kuurus was no sorcerer. He did not have such power of disguise. His bright blue gaze was his own.

For a moment, no one spoke. And then Vohanna laughed.

"Nothing anyone can say changes the fact that the war is lost for Nyshphal," the Witch said. "Prince...or rather *Emperor* Kuurus has offered the only choice there is for this city and this nation to survive."

My left hand still held the pistol that I'd taken from the mercredi outside the throne room. There could be only two bullets left at most. I doubted lead would kill Vohanna. But Kuurus it would. Maybe I could stop this ruinous alliance before it took full form. My wrist tensed; my finger tightened slightly on the trigger.

"And there is another reason why you must submit," Vohanna was saying, not even trying to conceal the gloat within her voice. "If you love your princess, you must submit."

I froze, but with my thoughts flailing.

The Witch gestured with a hand and a tiny spot of whirling gray formed in the center of the room and began to grow. I watched a sphere gate form there, and out of it stepped my brother Bryce, all silver with light even down to the molten madness of his eyes. Behind him on a cart he pulled a wheel that was big enough for a giant's wagon, and upon the wheel was strung Rannon.

My Saysa was unconscious, and I thanked the gods for that—thanked the gods that she could not see or know what had been done to her. Like Bryce, she had been tattooed all over. And in each cheek a milkstone had been implanted that bled with light and energy.

The sphere gate whispered shut; I started forward; from all around there was shouting that suddenly went silent. I paused.

"Wake her up," Vohanna said to Bryce in the quiet. And my brother, or the thing that had once been my brother, stroked Rannon's wrist with fingers from which motes of silver shimmer swirled.

Rannon opened her eyes and they were as crimson as the hearts of rubies.

I cried out, bit my tongue, tasted blood. The pistol

slipped from my hand to the floor with a clatter. My legs couldn't hold me and I collapsed to my knees.

All hope was gone.

CHAPTER THIRTY-ONE

AND IF THERE BE GODS

It was over. All over. With Rannon in thrall to Vohanna there was nothing I could do. From my knees, I glanced at the face of my love and from there to the face of the Witch.

She smirked. "Fight me and she dies. A word from me and the stones she wears will implode. She'll not be so pretty then."

For a moment the rage came surging up in me. Then it flickered, and failed. I lowered my head. Even my sword slid from my grip.

It was all over.

But Chalathar laughed. I recognized his voice and glanced up, more from reflex than from any possible hope.

Kreeg and Diken Graye took my arms, helped me to stand. Ahrethane and Valyan joined us. And though I felt empty, I watched with the others as Chalathar walked out from the back of the crowd, his weapons sheathed. Vohanna frowned. Her hands lifted and the air seemed to crystallize in indigo blue at the tips of her fingers.

"Do not exert me, fool," she said to Chalathar.

"Oh I believe I *will* exert you, Vohanna," the huge warrior replied. "As I have in times before."

"Vohanna's frown deepened. Her black eyes swirled and leaped with light.

"I do not know you."

"Under another form you do. In years past you called me Amenophor."

I gasped out loud. *Amenophor!*

In olden days the people of Talera had worshipped as gods a group of beings known as the Asadhie. Gods they were not, though they *were* the beings who formed Talera and brought the various races and the plants and animals here. There had been twelve Asadhie. Or so the story went. Vohanna had been one of them, and still she wanted to be worshipped as a god. Amenophor had been another. An enemy of Vohanna. And that might mean—

In that instant while my thoughts churned, Vohanna's face and form—or rather the face and form of Kuurus that she wore—flickered and changed. Pale skin turned olive; the hair lengthened, silkened, darkened. And now the Witch stood before us in her true form, gesturing toward Chalathar as she shouted:

"Kill him for me, Bryce!"

Bryce jerked like an automaton, his eyes glittering like a candlelit pool of silver. A snarl curled his black lips as his hands lifted and the lines of the tattoos on his body burst into bright relief.

Chalathar dropped into a crouch, a matching snarl on *his* face, his own hands rising. I recalled what the strange warrior had told me about Bryce—that as a Bane-thrall he could drain himself to launch a sorcerous attack because his life didn't matter to Vohanna. Could even the being known as Amenophor stand against such?

Chalathar's revelation had given me sudden hope. But if Bryce killed him....

I shook off Kreeg and Diken's hands, leaped forward. But Ahrethane was quicker. Her slender form hurled itself upon Bryce, and he was too focused on Chalathar to see her coming. She didn't try a spell; she linked her body with his, her arms going around him.

Vohanna and I cried out, "No!" at the same moment, but that didn't matter. In the jungle of Vohan, the fiery-haired druidess had told me that *her* magic and the magic of Vohanna were alien to each other. To bring them together would be unfortunate she'd said, and now I saw what "unfortunate" meant.

Bryce was *of* Vohanna; Ahrethane was of sky and earth and water. Their two powers could not coexist in the same

219

place. A concussive wave of sound erupted from between Ahrethane and Bryce, a sound like a thousand bells being crushed at once. Beings were thrown from their feet, blood spraying from noses and ears and mouths. I felt myself lifted and hurled down again like a toy, my hands grabbing for my ears as an electric surge of agony lanced along my nerves.

Heat followed the sound, blistering past and over me, scorching the soles of my feet even through my boots. I rolled over in pain, pushed myself to hands and knees. Only Vohanna and Chalathar were standing, and even they swayed. Where Ahrethane and Bryce had touched there stood a smoking hole burned clean through the marble of the floor. And Bryce and Ahrethane themselves were face down and still. I could not tell if they lived.

Vohanna was hurling curses at Ahrethane's prostrate form: "Hedge witch, harpy, worthless harridan." I thought she was going to attack the druidess's body whether it was alive or not.

My runed blade lay only a few feet away and I picked it up as I staggered to my feet and started on a stumble toward Vohanna. All around were the cries and screams of the wounded, and men and not-men were scattered across the floor like cordwood tossed about in a tornado.

Chalathar hit Vohanna first. He didn't touch her with his hands or his sword, but a weave of amethyst and golden light spurted from his fingers and slammed into her like a rail. She was knocked backward. Three steps. Then another. The glow pulsed against her. She screamed, but it sounded more like rage than pain.

Black flames spidered suddenly around her. A coruscation of sparks fountained high, then coalesced and whipped toward Chalathar. I heard the Warlock grunt as he was hit, but just as quickly he struck back. More flashes of light went pinwheeling across the room, like a firework display without the sound.

Ahrethane and Bryce remained still but others were rising to their feet now, on our side and on the enemies'. Blades and other weapons were being scooped up in half-numbed hands. Bloody faces snarled. Some of them were between me and the Witch.

I saw the pistol that I'd dropped moments before and dove for it, grabbing it up and rolling to my knees. One of Vohanna's mercredi guards had found his own pistol. It was he of the bulging muscles, he with the yellow-brown eyes. Our stares met; our hands lifted. But I was faster and I shot him once through the forehead so that he went flopping backward to the ground.

Then a figure loomed over me with the gleam of an axe held high. It was a Minotaur, seemingly unfazed by the explosion of magics. Perhaps it was because he was dead already. His flesh hung like ribbons on his bones.

I cocked the hammer on my pistol but he kicked it from my hand. I rolled away just as his axe came down to smash marble chips from the floor. Then I climbed to my feet, my sword ready.

Kreeg rushed past me; I saw Rajan Critus stab a second mercredi through the chest. Only Kuurus fled as all around me individual battles erupted, men and Kaldi and Llurns on our side, Reploids and Centaurs and Minotaurs and more men on the other. And through the middle of it dueled Vohanna and Chalathar, their hands slashing fire at each other. I couldn't worry about any of those things.

The bull-man charged me, his head lowered, horns glinting. I slashed upward with my blade, hacked one of those horns completely away. The shock jarred the creature, knocked his head up. I saw the empty sockets twisting with crimson embers of light. His hooves click, click, clicked on the floor as he came again. He swung his axe, a brutal blow. I blocked with my rune-blade, steel ringing.

He was too close to avoid and we clinched. I smelled him, not so much like rot but like the dust of a tomb left long unopened. I punched him in the face, and it wasn't like hitting bone. It *was* hitting bone. It hurt. And the fire-glitter of the thing's eyes only sparked higher.

I hit him again, with the hilt of my sword instead of my hand, and the last cartilage in his nose crackled and flaked away. He shook his head, then hooked at me with his remaining horn. I dodged, grabbed that horn, twisted his head down. I brought my knee up, slammed it under his chin, and as the blow stunned him I brought my sword around and sliced cleanly through the decayed tendons of his neck, sending his head rolling.

Gunshots cracked through the throne room and I glanced up through a haze of smoke and sparks in time to see the last of the mercredi swarmed under by a rush of Gray-Cloaks. A costly rush it had been. A dozen of Rannon's men lay stretched and emptied on the floor.

Rannon's men. Rannon!

I looked for my love. I saw her. Her body writhed on the giant wheel on which she was hung. And Vohanna stood next to her, between Rannon and the gore-stained table upon which lay Rhandh the Vlih.

The Witch was feeding off of them.

Feeding. There could be no other word for it. One of the Witch's hands clamped on Rhandh's forehead; the other gripped Rannon's wrist. Tendrils of wet flesh had sprouted from Vohanna's fingers and inserted themselves under the skins of the two. I could see their forms jolting, *see* the veins swell in Vohanna's arms as she sucked energy from their bodies into hers.

That tithe of stolen energy had turned the battle against Chalathar. The big warrior was backed against the wall, fending himself with blasts of amethyst light that were instantly beaten down by the swirling black-flame-whips that poured out of Vohanna.

I hurled myself forward, killing another Minotaur who dared step in my path. But Vohanna saw me coming. She flicked a glance my way and I was slammed to the floor, my sword and my breath both flying from me.

I tried to get up, gasping as jagged firefly glints burst in my eyes. I'd fallen across Bryce. With horror, I saw his artificial hand move, felt it as it grabbed like a vice across my ankle. I jerked back, jerked free, got to my knees.

Bile burst ripe into my mouth as the hand's fingers scrabbled at the floor, the nails scritching. Then the obscene thing...released itself from Bryce's wrist, sliding free with a low sucking sound. Something very much like a tail tore its way out of my brother's arm and whipped back and forth across the flaggings.

I kicked at the scuttling terror and it dodged, turned and

started to crawl toward Vohanna. The skin of it was almost translucent and through that skin I could see a pulse and flow of colors, all the colors of flesh and blood.

Milkstones, I thought. *There* had *to be milkstones in it.*

I threw myself forward on my belly and grabbed the thing behind the knuckles, squeezing it tight as it squirmed like a roach. It was hot. Savagely hot.

One glance showed me that the battle between Vohanna and Chalathar was nearly over. The strange, red-haired warrior had been beaten to his knees. Blow after blow of dark light hammered into him. Smoke rose from his mail. Soot blackened his rough-whiskered face.

I cast about desperately for something to strike at Vohanna with. I couldn't get close to her, would have to hit her from a distance. Then I saw the nickel-plated revolver that the bull-man had kicked from my hand. It lay half beneath a fallen body. I scrambled for it, scooped it up, rose.

"Vohanna!" I shouted.

She glanced my way, and I threw Bryce's hand to her. She released her grip on Rannon's wrist and caught the squirming thing close to her chest. A smile shrieked into her face. She thought I'd just given her the last weapon she needed to kill us all.

The Witch cried out as more power surged into her from the toir'in-or stones in the artificial hand. Her body gleamed as jet black winds and obsidian smoke danced wildly around her. And I brought up my arm with one swift movement and pulled the trigger on the pistol.

There was only one bullet in the gun and I aimed it, not at Vohanna but at the ghastly, handed thing that she clutched between her breasts. The bullet struck true and shrapneled. A fragment must have nicked one of the milkstones, and in an instant a column of lightning smashed upward from the point of impact.

Vohanna was thrown like a corn husk into the air, came crashing down again across the snow-wood throne of Nysh-phal. Her chin and lower lip were gone, her face half burned away. Her chest was a gaping raw wound that spilled cinders across the polished white wood of the great chair.

But she wasn't dead.

I threw the emptied revolver away, drew my dagger. But I didn't get a chance to use the steel. Chalathar had gained the moment he needed to recover. Vohanna's body flopped, began to quiver madly. Suddenly she sat up, but Chalathar had reached her and his hands locked down on her head, his fingers tightening, tightening.

The Witch cried out in a rasped and broken voice. Her own hands started to lift before falling back limply onto the chair. Her eyes opened and they had turned a boiled-egg white. Then she slumped, collapsed in on herself. Her eyes began to rot in front of my gaze. She closed them.

In the next moment, Chalathar turned away and in his palms he held two solid black milkstones that he'd drawn from the Witch's body. And Vohanna was dead there upon the throne of Nyshphal.

I went straight to Rannon and cut her down from her wheel, catching her in my arms and lowering her gently to the floor. I chaffed her wrists, called her name. Behind me, I heard others stirring, heard the sound of fighting die away as Vohanna's servants lost their will to battle and surrendered. But truly I could not care. I cared only that the woman I loved should live.

And then Rannon opened her eyes, and her gaze was clear...and blue. And the toir'in-or stones that Vohanna had implanted in her cheeks fell out to tinkle like children's marbles on the castle floor.

EPILOGUE

PERHAPS

Standing in a throne room that was burned and blackened and still bloody from the fight against the Witch of Talera, Rannon Jystral and I were married. Rajan Critus performed the ceremony and there was little formality about it. But there were many who witnessed for us as we exchanged our vows, as we stood before Rajan in stained and torn leathers with weapons close at hand that still bore the clotted gore of combat.

It was neither the time nor the place that Rannon and I would have chosen for our wedding. But we loved each other now more than ever. And Rannon had just become empress of a realm that was still at war. Word had come from outside that the armies of Reploids and Centaurs had fled immediately after Vohanna's death, and that the Minotaurs were wandering like mindless zombies. But the soldiers of Revenor and Ubai whose fleets had attacked our coast had not been controlled directly by Vohanna. I doubted that *they* would run.

We would have to make them.

The fighting that lay ahead of us might well be as hard as that left behind us. Rannon needed me now, at least in part because there were fools even on this world who did not consider a woman fit to rule without a man by her side. It was not something I understood, but it was something I knew had to be considered.

And so my princess and I were wed. And after, my wife went among the others who had fought in this room and thanked them. She did not go to Kuurus, who had been arrested by Rajan. She did not go to Ahrethane or Bryce because neither of them had regained consciousness—though Chalathar told us they were not quite dead. She *could* not go to Rhandh, except in spirit, for the courageous Vlih had died on Vohanna's table with his life's energy leached away.

Last of all, Rannon went to the man named Chalathar—or Amenophore if you prefer. I did not hear what she said but I saw him nod and bow. And after she turned away to begin giving the commands that would set things in her country aright, I went to Chalathar myself.

"Greetings, Ruenn," he said.

I nodded.

Here was a man who'd once been thought a god on Talera, but he did not seem in that moment any more than a simple warrior who I'd come to like. Beside him stood the last of his men, the tall fellow with the kahnnas. Both of them were wounded and bandaged, with Chalathar as gaunt-eyed as any starving wolf.

"We owe you," I said to them.

Chalathar smiled, and there seemed nothing in the curve of his mouth that was not genuine.

"As we owe you and Rannon and the others here," he said

"For what?" I asked.

"I could not have defeated Vohanna alone."

Again I nodded. "Yes, I see what you mean."

He looked at me, strangely it seemed, then leaned forward slightly. "There are others out there like Vohanna," he said. "Some are Asadhie. Others are beings created *by* the Asadhie. They, too, would like to rule at the cost of human lives."

I knew that by "human" he did not mean only men, but included the many races who shared this world with us.

"And do you also fight such other foes?" I asked.

"*We* fight them," he said, motioning to include his companion.

I nodded, my thoughts having already started to turn elsewhere.

"Perhaps…," Chalathar said, drawing my attention back

to him.

"Perhaps what?"

"There are others besides my friend here who aid me. Warriors. Men and women from all over Talera. They work to bring peace to this angry world. From time to time I call upon them. Sometimes when I cannot go myself I open sphere gates and send them through, often into dangers that threaten their lives. But I believe it is necessary. As do they. And so, perhaps...."

"Perhaps what?" I asked again, though I thought I understood.

"Perhaps one day I might call upon you?" he finished.

I stared at him for a long moment, then glanced across the room to Rannon. Even though she readily gave strength to those of her people who came to speak with her, I could see in her face and body the lines of exhaustion. Vohanna had drained *her* of much energy, as well. And though the milkstones had fallen from her, and the tattoos had faded to nothing with the Witch's death, I did not yet know what hidden damage might have been done within her.

I glanced back at Chalathar. "There is much for me to do here," I said.

He nodded. "Of course," he said. And he turned with his fellow warrior, and they picked up the bodies of their dead companions, and they made move to leave. I knew they were going out from Nyshphal, to other places and other fights. Theirs was a worthy cause, to bring peace to a planet that hardly seemed to know the word. I wished them success so that others would not have to suffer as Nyshphal had suffered, as we continued to suffer.

After a moment, I called to Chalathar and he turned. I looked at him.

"One day," I said.